Mascara

Mark Wagstaff

Published by Cinnamon Press,
Office 49019, PO Box 15113, Birmingham, B2 2NJ
www.cinnamonpress.com

The right of Mark Wagstaff to be identified as author of this work has been asserted by him in accordance with the Copyright, Designs and Patent Act, 1988.
© 2025, Mark Wagstaff.
Print Edition ISBN 978-1-78864-174-6
British Library Cataloguing in Publication Data. A CIP record for this book can be obtained from the British Library.
All rights reserved. No part of this publication may be reproduced, stored in a retrieval system, or in any form or by any means, electronic, mechanical, photocopying, recording or otherwise without the prior written permission of the publishers. This book may not be lent, hired out, resold or otherwise disposed of by way of trade in any form of binding or cover other than that in which it is published, without the prior consent of the publishers.

Designed and typeset in Adobe Caslon Pro by Cinnamon Press.
Cover design by Adam Craig © Adam Craig. Figure image based on an image by ChrisGorgio / iStock

Cinnamon Press is represented by Inpress

Mascara

Convenience

This is London. Filthy. Astounding. This is Elie Saab. Black. Tight. Sweet with my old Chanel jacket. A moment hung in the mirror. Right pocket. XD 9 millimetre. Clean. Persuasive. I draw and fire in point one of a second. London is all opportunity.

Brush my hair. Centre parting. Good hair. Strong, no splits. So black, Miquel says, I must have Catalan in me.

Taste the breeze whipping off the river. These sailors see a slim, styled woman on a penthouse balcony. They might wonder who I am. I'm not your business. Till I make you my business.

No spikes today. Vagabonds. Neat and practical. Saint Laurent bag, of course. 24 Faubourg, my signature scent. Shut windows and doors. Prudent precautions. Lot of bad types about. Lot of nutters.

Check my eyes. Eyes are key. Blue eyes. Tall black lashes. Quality makeup discreetly deployed. Imperfections tidied. Still a few years before I go under the knife.

The building is secure. The neighbours have too much to lose. Never know what happens when a door opens. Nemesis comes strange ways.

Chrome lights charm reflections from Italian marble. Figures cross smoky glass. The concierge, Ralph he calls himself, bustles into my eyeline.

"Can I get you a cab, Ms. Delamarre?"

Flash him the bleach. "That's fine, thank you Ralph. I'm being met."

Elegant fingers caress the view like he owns it. "Have a good day."

Chelsea Embankment is busy and drab. A damp colourless April. Old wounds ache on days like these. Holed by the indifferent bullets of men I should have watched.

Of course they send a nice motor. A bloke with skin like cheese lets down the window. "Welcome to London."

I practice getting in and out of cars. I'm fluid. His manner is gaudy as the zircons on his cuffs. An errand boy, playing king.

We drive to Earl's Court. No doubt they feel this is manly work. I cross my legs for this elegant thug to enjoy unblemished skin. My legs turn heads.

"I trust your accommodation is satisfactory."

I enjoy this demure voice. "I've a brilliant view of the river."

"I'm sorry we couldn't consult you on check-in arrangements."

He means this 'Delamarre' crap. "I'm responsive to clients' needs. You can call me Ms. Hepburn."

Choice real estate rolls by. Mansion blocks full of gold and paintings not seen since World War Two. Must-go restaurants, where no one gets a table. Appointment-only boutiques—I love that word—where skinny personal shoppers run themselves rank for me. Because I talk the language in an accent that scares them.

"All this used to be Russians." He gives the glass a knock. "We adapt with new interests."

I play the girl. "It's really complex."

Though the car's wide as a bus, I feel his tension. "Mr. Miller looks forward to see you."

"Everyone looks forward to see me." Like Marcel's sponge cake, these streets have indelible flavour. I jack forward. Punch the sliding screen. "Stop here will you."

Rattled, the driver cranes around. "It's the Old Brompton Road."

"I fucking know where it is. Stop a minute. Mr. Miller," I tell the jelly boy, "will understand." Open the door into traffic, tinkling my fingers at drivers who grip the wheel as they cream their pants. Scamper up to the old pub. It's pleasant. Sedate. I'm sure the food's lovely. But once, this was The Coleherne. As a very young girl I met an older guy here who told me how, one night in the eighties, he got cruised by Dennis Nilsen. Taken to Cranley Gardens and soaked with booze. Then Nilsen said, "It's this again," and pinned him in a choke hold. My bloke was wily. Turned Nilsen over. Legged it into the Muswell Hill dawn. He said the drains at Nilsen's place stank.

He told me this while he caressed my body. This man who chose and enjoyed me. Who would have been boiled, but for one lucky punch. When Nilsen confessed, he said, "I have no tears." That's when I felt sorry for him.

This was The Coleherne. Now it's not.

We head north by secluded Kensington villas and down a ramp near Holland Park. I had a phenomenal fuck in the Japanese garden there one night. The rippling water and sense of balance made for an almighty thrash.

As the car rolls into this concrete cavern, blokes in suits fluff about.

I exit with my usual grace, to soak in their admiration. Some large piece of linen is waiting. "Welcome, Ms. Hepburn. I'm Tony."

Tony is what I call well-travelled. Handsome, in a robust way. Square face, placid brown eyes. Carefully scruffed hair. Six vertical creases across his brow, like he had a good time staring at things he didn't understand. No tie. If he gets away with no tie Mr. Miller must value his work. His suit's American cut. Brooks Brothers maybe. Late forties, early fifties. Well-kept. But too old for me. I'm totally shallow with men.

We walk along a corridor the late Queen might have enjoyed. Quiet, plush, full of unholy tat. I have no taste for antiques. These photophobic Persian rugs and velvet chairs you can't sit on. Japanned dressers with the keys lost and paintings of dismal Surrey. What's beautiful is what's useful.

Tony smalltalks wearily about Russians and Chinese.

"You have spoons on your wall," I tell him.

He glances at these fussy masterpieces. "They're old Dutch. There's a windmill on that one."

"I wouldn't."

"What décor do you prefer, Ms. Hepburn?"

If I give him a serious answer, it would be the apartment in Barcelona I share with Miquel. White walls. That tall, moulded ceiling, its centre rose sprouting a fan with sycamore propellers. Those modernista cement tiles that remind me of a mosque. Everything stone and beech and solid and useful. A strategic half-dozen of Miquel's mother's paintings. The tortoiseshell peineta she gave me to dress my hair. Miquel cried when we got home, because giving me that made me official in his mother's eyes. It laid her gentle, generous approval on our arrangements. I wear the peineta on high days, done proper with a mantilla. And a heavy dress because formal headwear doesn't work with a slip.

That's what I could tell Tony. But this is smalltalk. "I'm happy with flatpack."

Down the hall, a young bloke on guard—tie knotted and jacket buttoned. An entry level suit. When he sees Tony he flinches, like a whole-body salute. When he sees me, his eyes are on strings.

"Visitor for Mr. Miller."

Primark lad knocks the door then fans it open. I sashay into the presence.

Mr. Miller's queer-boys line the walls. He likes a certain type. Young but not callow. Languid manners. Lads that kiss the finger without irony, insouciant. All can handle a gun in domestic settings. Six of these decorations frame a space big as a ballroom. There's stuff going on in the wallpaper: some classical hunters and prey. But I watch the man in the middle.

Mr. Miller is eighty and then some. Got his first taste in the high days of orderly crime. He knew the families. He saw them banged up. Every racket became his racket. His hair thinned so it fits his scalp exactly. He's precise, fair, admirable, well-cut. These gorgeous, ludicrous boys aren't playthings. They're what money and taste can procure. He has lovely eyes and a mouth whose rage or amusement is a bare twitch. He moves to me, arms wide.

"Felicity." He speaks soft, as befits a man of great power. Wraps me in the most genteel embrace. "You're more ravishing than ever. Gentlemen." That smile because they're not gentlemen. "I'm sure you know the achievements of our guest, Miss Felicity Hepburn."

Some wonder why I'm this. I bear no malice. It's been that way since I turned thirteen and pinched my first dress from New Look. The moment I put on that dress, I was home.

A lad unfolds from the wall, elegant and smug. Takes my gun hand to his lips. "Enchantée." His accent up-country. "I hear this," he rubs my fingers, "has been super-busy."

So I know why I won't fuck him. "It's best to be busy."

Mr. Miller beams. With nothing to prove, we're here at his convenience. "You'll excuse me, Felicity, if we come straight to business. Robert."

A young charmer assembles himself to a state of tender attention.

"Sherry, there's a good boy. What would you recommend?"

Mr. Miller's courteous. Chivalrous, even. Still, it's a test. The lads expect some contribution. "Something dry perhaps, Mr. Miller? A Manzanilla."

"Robert. As the lady says." Mr. Miller offers his arm, and we pace to a door at the corner. It's an insight, walking with someone old. There's nothing feeble about him. Unhindered by silted bones. Yet his arm against mine has peculiar lightness. An appreciation that strength and suppleness shape a life.

Mr. Miller's den is a cupboard with Tiffany lamps. No doubt an escape hatch lurks in its cunning panels. He points me to a button leather armchair in a butterscotch shade I thought extinct. I wait till he sits, before crossing my legs.

"Did you have a good journey?"

For all that 'straight to business' stuff, he wants us making smalltalk when his boy knocks with the drinks. "First class ain't what it was. I had to show them how to make a Distrito Federal."

He smiles obligingly. "And Heathrow?"

"Pleasant as ever on a fake passport. Carolina Delamarre? It's not like they don't know me."

A three-note fist hits the door.

"Enter." Mr. Miller gives it clout and I stop myself giggling when the boy Robert slides in, hoisting a bottle of gypsy and two big glasses.

"Miss Hepburn was saying," that tone of airy menace, "the drudges at Heathrow were tedious with her paperwork. Can we try a bit harder in future?"

Robert aims to smoulder. But he's a February bonfire. "I should think Miss Hepburn can manage all situations."

I'm inside his eyes and begin devastation. My gaze forces doubts he's barely known since, I'm guessing, he first sold his teenage arse to bookies. I'm royalty, my eyes tell him. I'm a Hepburn.

"Will that be all, Mr. Miller?"

"Ask Mr. Dexter to step in."

"Sir." He backs to the door. "Miss."

"How much use is he?" Don't care I sound harsh.

"To start, we need shared understanding." He pours a generous glass. "These boys are not employed to get things wrong. They don't understand why someone who hasn't worked in London for years gets VIP treatment. They've heard of you. Who hasn't? But they haven't seen what you do."

Zesty chamomile pricks my tongue. "You don't need the soft soap."

"Of course I do. You have an ego the size of an airship. It's unbecoming a legend to complain about a duff alias."

I can only smile. "I shall consider my bottom spanked."

"Which reminds me: how is that husband of yours?"

"Not quite my husband yet."

"If he doesn't marry you soon, he's a fool." Mr. Miller draws down his cuffs. "I'm sure you keep up with the news. We face challenges. The

Russians are sliding back. The ambitious Chinese. Nigerian entrepreneurs. Mexican pharmacists. It's disorganized." He stares at the boxy room. "The old firms weren't always tidy. Their methods could be crude. But family meant competence."

"Mine were highly competent."

"Your Father had an honourable career." He leaves a reverent pause. "The issue is with the phones."

With scent and taste taking me home, perhaps I look startled. "Your phones?"

"Felicity, do engage that magnificent brain. Secure, timely, accurate communications are an asset class. Speed and precision dictates my balance sheet. But lately and persistently we've suffered interference."

"You been hacked by the filth?"

"Would that it were. If this was the filth we could have a word. But I suspect a freeze-out. Russians, or their friends from the Dark Web. Dark Web." Some quality of his smile near-serene. "Am I wrong to pine for the days one could just take a gun to the fuckers?"

"I'm a great believer in guns."

"You keep in practice, I take it? Between tennis and sangria."

"Last week I split an orange at fifteen hundred metres."

"That's ridiculous."

"There's a lot of space in the Collserola."

A fist at the door, rapid and severe.

Mr. Miller's strong fingers clench my knee. "I trust you, Flick. I need your help."

"With what?"

"I don't know. That's why I need you."

We compose ourselves, two innocents.

He shouts, "Enter."

Handsome Robert barely draws breath before getting boshed aside by middle-aged blue button-down and tan chinos. Tidy grey hair side parted. Plump face set off by square glasses. His head hangs forward and he's already talking, the type who starts before he begins. "Mr. Miller, you want to see me? Have there been more intrusions?" His voice is up north. Posh north. York or Harrogate or something.

"Freddie. This is Miss Hepburn. She'll deliver the fieldwork."

I tweak my hem and look fascinating.

He stares. "Pleased to meet you, Miss Hepburn." A thorough,

military handshake. His eyes linger on the untroubled swoop of my Elie Saab.

"Freddie is ex-GCHQ."

"Intelligence, Miss."

"Yes." Wonder what took him this side of the curtain.

Mr. Miller gestures Dexter to sit, which he manages, breathlessly. "We must be quick and robust. That's why Miss Hepburn is here to strengthen the team. Several times each week." He turns to me. "Communications are compromised. Messages erased. Data sabotaged. Calls wiped by white noise. These are not system problems. The system is sound. Something is circumventing our encryption in highly targeted ways. These incursions occur to maximise disruption. Freddie is examining patterns. Sticky fingerprints, if you will."

Freddie manspreads lavishly. "The spotty Herbert in his bedroom. Curiosity. Challenge. Too much time on their hands. And Mr. Miller's work is lucrative—I may say glamorous." He fixes a misplaced look on me. "That makes persistence worthwhile. You can only break into the Pentagon so many times."

"And if it's not some spotty oik?" Mr. Miller was always strong, dangerous. I'm not used to him sounding tired.

"Then it's business. Russians have the tech, the contacts. They need hard cash. Could be Chinese. More discreet than spreading deepfakes. The African boys want to move beyond boiler rooms."

I taste dry hints of salt and sand. In the glass, I see the waterfront at Sanlúcar de Barrameda. Columbus sailed from Sanlúcar on his third voyage. And that psycho Magellan. We went for the sunset races at the mouth of the Guadalquivir. Full of wine and bravado I bluffed my way onto a horse. Just managed to stay in the saddle, as the crowd clapped and cheered. I feel how Miquel lifted me down. How he held me like a new bride. I need to know what these men are saying. I need to solve their problems. Till I'm rich enough to spend each day with the man I love. "What about locals? Someone new and wily?"

Freddie Dexter sees an attractive woman in a black dress. Legs crossed and a good run of muscles. Poised with a tulip of sherry. No doubt he makes assumptions about me. That I am a woman is as much fact as my beating heart. "You mean, a superior sort of oik? More nimble and serious?"

"A disruptor." I like how that tastes. "In other sectors we see incumbents struggle to adapt. When new players move in, without sunk costs." I want to giggle and flick my hair because I love how that makes me feel. But I'm serious and they're serious, and we're in a room without windows. I earn the money. Miquel plays guitar and piano. Dabbles in films. Curates campaigns. Takes stray dogs to the vet. I want to make enough so I can be a wife for him. With my hair swagged in a scarf and flour on my cheeks.

"I don't dismiss it." Freddie Dexter huffs about, not fitting well in the chair. "We should explore all avenues."

"A bloody takedown." Mr. Miller's more grim than I ever seen. I take his hand. Feel for his strength among the doubts of age. "A regular pattern of undivided intrigue."

Dexter, watching through bushy brows, coughs too loud. "Once we pinpoint the source, fieldwork should be effective."

"I must understand," says Mr. Miller, "the access point for these intrusions. If we're slack, I want a fix on where and how. The method matters as much as the perpetrator." He stands and so do I, now he's my master. "We reconvene tomorrow. 9 a.m."

Sometimes, in the Collserola, I feel a viper watch from the scrub. I caress my gun and think, Could I get it? Could I get that snake before it gets me? Intense stillness leaves a bruise. These men are astounding. Their appearance. Their years, that I'll never have. Because, one day, that snake strikes first.

Dexter opens the door, flooding the room with shiny, business light. I sway through, my fingers with their little, tinkling wave. So much of being a woman is performance.

Tony and the rest are gone. Two lads guard the entrance. Muscle Marys in linen.

"We won't solve this tomorrow." Though Mr. Miller would love that. "But I want progress towards deliverables."

"You know what I can do."

He pinches my chin. "Sweet Felicity."

I kiss him and ignore Dexter, who tries words too fat for his mouth. I walk to the lofty doors, between the disco bunnies. This one's side-eye bothers me. No doubt he's big in the weight room. As I saunter by, I slam my elbow across his windpipe. Pin him to the wall, an ungainly butterfly. Choking and dripping spit. "You're surprised how strong I am, aren't you?"

His bald head pisses sweat. His eyes boil.

"If you weren't suffocating, you'd be impressed how much I can pile on your neck. Those 'roids have made you slow, love." I release and he stumbles. Pull his head level with mine. "You never disrespect me."

Daisies

The cab drops me at Sidney Bechet's old place. Dad was a fan. He said anyone could jazz a horn but the liquorice stick was for maestros. Artie Shaw, Buster Bailey, Dink Johnson. Dad said Johnson's Krooked Blues was his theme tune. That juicy, dirty sound. He knew Acker Bilk when Mr. Bilk lived in Plaistow. Not exactly New Orleans.

Once, I'd think, if I ever came back to London, I'd live here. These stuccoed streets round Fitzroy Square. Relish a grand and horny middle age. But I won't come back. It's an ungrateful town. When I was little, the Telecom Tower was a magic wand. I saw a tall, lithe fairy princess raise it across the city, showering wishes. I wished that princess to make me a girl. And she did. That vestige of wonder, that was the London I knew.

Grafton Way is placid townhouses. Plaster and brick, solid wood doors, arched fanlights. That communal basement runs the length of the block. I unhitch the gate and go down. The window blinds shut. White plastic venetians. The window's grimy and the blinds are stained. Makes the place unremarkable. Two cameras beneath the pavement. I'm already a star in their pictures.

The intercom buzzes like wind through wire. The voice in the speaker is heavy. "What you want, love?"

"Come to see Roc."

"She didn't say."

Un-fucking-believable. What happened to: 'Roc who?' or 'There's no one of that name here'. What happened to healthy suspicion? "Maybe it slipped her mind. Can I come in?"

"I'm not sure she's free."

"I look a right fucking pudding stood here. Is that good for business?"

Then the dog barks and there's clumsy noise. The door pulls back on an old blonde in faux leopard, Ralph Lauren sweatpants and Turkish slippers. A moody Alsatian sticks its big head through her legs.

She's puffy, I guess from vodka, but no doubt shrewd. "We got no vacancies."

Deep in the building a door slams. The maid steps back, pushing the dog to the wall with both hands. Two blokes so irresponsibly dressed they can only be tourists clip through the hall, buffeted on that voice.

And there's Roc in a basque, tits like medicine balls, yelling in backyard German. "You want a go? You want to?" She makes the finger in the hole. "That what you want? You shit."

Her pro name is Roccola. Guess no one calls her Rachel. She's drenched in ink. Roses with eyes. Medusa heads. Dragons. Skeleton angels. Crying girls and a snake nosing up her bum. The fractals on her vagina are the greatest art ever made. Her hair's beautiful lilac. Her face shines like new.

The two pissy tourists bomb through the door. The maid slams it, the dog barks and I'm in the low-voltage shadows.

Roc squeals. "Big sis."

"Little sis."

We embrace. Her warmth eats me up. "Elie Saab? Gorgeous." Roc fusses my hair. "What's this? Hershesons?"

"A little salon in Barcelona. What's these?" I pat her tits.

"Clever wiring, darling."

The maid chews her cheeks. "It's a knocking shop not a social."

"Sandra." Roc beams. "This is my sister Felicity. All the way from Barcelona. I haven't seen her in three years. So give it a rest, eh, love?"

"Might as well pack it in." The maid stumbles to answer the door. "It's just giving work away. Tell Anita she's wanted." The dog starts again. "Shut it."

"Come on, sweetheart." Roc grabs my hand. "I can spare twenty minutes." She leads me down the hallway, slamming her palm on a door. "Anita. Knickers off, there's a treasure." A tired shout inside the room.

Back of the basement is Roc's place of business. A windowless, chipboard space. The bed's firm and she tidied the sheets, like a bed she might sleep in. Nudes from the net spread on the walls. None beautiful like my sister.

She gets a litre of Gordon's from the cupboard. "No tonic, sorry. Or ice. Or glasses." She grins and I grin, and we stand, admiring each other. "It's lovely to see you," she says in her posh voice.

"Lovely to see you." I'm glad and wish I could sound it. "How do you keep getting younger?"

"Exercise and avoiding daylight." She swigs the gin, to show it's not spiked, and hands me the bottle.

Through the booze, I taste her lipstick. "I can't stop long." That's me: clumsy with what matters most. "I'm working for Mr. Miller."

"How is he?" she asks with a hooker's pleasant manners.

"Not tiptop." With gin on the shoulder of sherry my blood takes a curve. "You had a lot done since last time."

She models her skin. The Medusas glow with sullen vengeance. "I'm a canvas for my dreams." She takes her weight on one leg. "Notice anything?"

A flush of skin on her right calf. "Estelada Blava."

"Free Catalunya." She raises a small, tight fist. "It's to honour you. What's this with Mr. Miller?"

"Interference of the unwelcome sort. You like it here?"

"Steady business. Routine, low-key orgasms." Through red light, her intelligent eyes engage me. "Who's the naughty party?"

"Knee-jerk, it's Russians. Or West Africans. Or Indian hotshots."

"But you don't believe it's any of them. What you looking at?"

"How you move. Always tits-first."

"They're a reliable compass." She folds herself onto the bed, a painted cat. "Who is it, if not the usual?" She pats the sheet and I sit next to her.

"Modern rivalries. Mr. Miller, though. Why him?"

"It's a risk, you coming to London."

"I'm getting paid an obscene amount."

She grips my arm. She's strong.

"I can't stop." I take off my jacket and lay next to her. Her basque has a slippy, polyamide feel, its balconette severely wired. "46H?"

"You're too kind." She drinks attention like poppies in sunlight. "So you've come back to dive in?"

"It'll pay for the wedding."

"How is Miquel?" It's a real ask. Kind and involved.

Roc's never met Miquel. I feel bad about that. These two who mean the most. "He's great. More than. Getting gigs. Even over in France. He's working on a movie about the Cause. Jazz and video, that's the way. Better than killing people."

Under red light, her blue eyes are frank simplicity. I'm never without mascara. An old woman in Besalú told me I got the eyes of the dead. I pretended my Català wasn't good enough to understand what she meant.

"About the wedding." Roc speaks at my chest.

"You're maid of honour. It will be a Catholic do." I'd settle for civil, but he's got a mother.

"My present. I'll carry a baby for you."

Fine silence ropes us from the world.

"What a kid, eh? Made from you, me and Miquel." She grins, but the power's down. "Won't be no stopping 'em."

"Thank you sweetheart." When we kiss, I'm reminded of hot, breezy days at the beach. Splashing about. Laughing at boys. Ice cream on our noses and hands sticky with honeycomb. "You sure it's alright, with the business?"

"I can charge more when I'm pregnant. Blokes love it."

I've not much cause to be delicate. When I try, it doesn't suit me. "You not seeing anyone?"

With subtle precision, because she understands how flimsy life is, Roc shapes her fingers around my neck. "Yeah. See my profile. 'Roc. Thirty-six. Likes: tattoos and fucking for money. Dislikes: dating. Assets: vast knockers, tiny flat, skin-tight bond to sister.'"

"Always, babe." Miquel won't get between us. But I'm too tough to say it.

"These vertebrae. Rotten with tension. Little sis knows a cure for that."

As I leave, right up the road, I still hear the maid's bloody dog barking.

An ugly mews off Tottenham Street. A barred metal door. A sign: By Appointment Only. I don't believe that sign's talking to me.

Take a few toots of the buzzer to rouse the receptionist. She's not keen. "You have an appointment?"

"This door seems to be locked."

"There is no admission without an appointment."

"I got an XD 9 mil in my pocket. That's my appointment."

"I must consult my senior."

"Do that, treacle."

By the time I have a quick flirt with a lad up the street, the door pops open. The reception suite is velvety walls, studded with grey-tone prints. There's nothing to say what this place does. Or the cost.

A frost-haired, lark-eyed Pole, the receptionist sulks in flat-fronted Jaegers. Presumably she's here because Daddy's in the business. With a tongue of Katowice steel, she says, "My senior will see you this once."

"I'll fuck a pig with a stick." The mouth from which this worthy ambition springs is cut in a face of assuring blandness. The stubble it's wearing looks drawn-on. He's let his hair grow, which I suppose fits whatever image he's got of himself. It licks the collar of a jacket that might be Brunello Cucinelli. The trousers are nice, but the shirt is creased. And he's not wearing a tie. That disgusts me. "It is you, isn't it?"

"Of course it's me, you liquid shit."

Too flash to conceal what he's thinking, he says, "Agnieszka. Trot up the road and get us a smoothie, will you. Kale and apple. And for you?"

"Black coffee."

Agnieszka clenches. She can probably handle a gun. "You want I leave you with this person?"

"Oh," he says, with airy mendacity. "I won't come to harm with this pussycat."

She shoulders a sweet little Michael Kors bag and heads out without a jacket.

He gives me a look of pure dirt and punches the keypad to a door behind the desk. Follow him into the most neutral corridor. Walls, ceiling, carpet, all the same grey. There's mystic pictures. Monochrome lines could be blood diffusing through water. Slick spindles might be bones. Try to focus beyond his huffy breath—no sound of people or machinery. When I knock my Saint Laurent oh-so-clumsily on the wall, it rings hollow. These miasmic pictures have uses. That Mandelbrot surely has a camera at its dark core. No wonder Mr. Miller is despondent. Soon, we'll all be packaged in a protective atmosphere.

This set-up runs the length of the mews. The other premises are shallow shop fronts. We arrive in a curved chamber. Four doors off, all the same grey metal. He unlocks the third, counting from left. An office. A ludicrous digital wall runs a panorama of stinking jungle. He's got a vulgar glass desk and trophies for ball games. Cameras presumably everywhere.

He gestures me to sit. "I caught interesting footage from Heathrow."

The speed with which he throws the video to the big screen suggests he had it ready, which is interesting. It's me, swishing through the Green Lane. A robot voice repeats: 'Stop. Security area.' The doors swing shut but I shoulder by. The Customs lovies don't stir. I'm a tad hot around the mouth, after an unstimulating wait at Passport Control. "Tasty."

"You're in good nick." He scrolls back to where I barge the doors. "What interests me, as a security professional, is something triggered that unit to isolate. Yet you walk through and get nothing but lustful looks."

"I wouldn't call that nothing." Time to own this conversation. "I'm here for a favour."

He reins his bulk to a semblance of seriousness. "Mr. Miller has competition."

"You've done your homework."

"You should remember who we deal with."

For the cameras, I give a shimmying laugh. "You're a shopkeeper, love."

This risible man is too quickly offended. "Ms. Hepburn, it seems to me you're here as an errand… girl. Perhaps we should discuss your master's spot of bother."

I've had sticky fingers from all parts. But the stickiest is distrust. Distrust glues everything. No doubt this room is equipped to kill, and I should be demure and grateful. But humility is such a contrivance. "Mr. Miller's business is compromised by malicious activity. Telecoms disrupted. Transactions exposed. Best case: some prick, pissing about. Worst case: it's nasty."

He stretches in his big leather chair. So obnoxious, it's a struggle not to shoot him. "When a client engages my company to guard against commercial espionage, the information we provide is pursuant to a contract. A contract for which money has changed hands. Yet your errand implies I should disclose this information as a matter of fucking charity. Is that a fair reading, Ms. Hepburn?"

With exquisite slowness I scratch my leg, nudging my hem further north. "Mr. Archer. The name you use, I think? Toby Archer? I'm not unfamiliar with greed. Nor am I unfamiliar with delight at the death of my rivals. Your shirt says you don't have a wife. But there must be some bit of fluff you're attached to. How would she like your body parts, gift-wrapped?"

"You flatter yourself, Ms. Hepburn."

"I have men to do that for me."

Agnieszka's in the room with a cardboard tray. There's a nifty kink to her Jaegers around the right pocket. "Kale and apple smoothie." She sets it on his desk. "Cinnamon dolce latte. Black coffee."

She holds the cup towards me. No cardboard sleeve. I take care with my hands. I need them supple. Push it back at her. "Taste it."

"I have no hangover."

A rumbling guffaw from Archer. "Ms. Hepburn makes art of paranoia."

Agnieszka sips and shoves the cup back. "Disgusting." With blatant tactics, she parks on the couch behind me.

Archer drains his autumn puddle. Pats his gut. "Antioxidants and iron. Your Mr. Miller, he's an old-fashioned type. He thinks enemies should talk boundaries. You'd be better employed telling him the world has moved on."

A farty squeak as Agnieszka shifts at the edge of the couch.

I turn to her restless breath. "Agnieszka, you're a bright sort. What makes for success in business?"

She primes herself and it dawns on me Archer can't be doing her. That hardness would crack him like chalk. "In business you must have a strong offer and make it with a strong hand. You should not let your customer think they are smarter than you."

"Precisely." I squint at Archer. "I've got the strong hand."

"And what, Ms. Hepburn, is your strong offer?"

"Your scrubber makes a good point about keeping face with clients. I know your clients. They'd be delighted to know each other." With exemplary speed and grace, the XD 9 mil flies from my pocket to aim at Archer's head. "Tell her I see her reflection on the big screen. Tell her to bag that piece. Because I'll have your head before she finds the trigger."

It's gratifying, his shiny fear.

Agnieszka's by the door, a Ruger LC9 in her fist.

"Put it back in your trousers, love."

She burns with embarrassment.

Archer tries it stern. "This is why people hate you."

"Don't flirt, it's not in your skillset." To get purchase, I stand, smoothing my dress. "I have a list of equipment and services for you to provide to Mr. Miller." I'm making this up, hoping I don't trip myself. "His people can give you delivery details. I'm talking stealth camera lens finders, in case any cameras at his place are harder to find than what I see here with my eyes. Wireless signal detectors, LTE, Bluetooth, wifi, VHF, UHF, all that, emissions from GSM jammers, recorder suppressors, antennae detectors, bug killers of all sorts. 50 mhz to 60 Ghz. Signal detector wands his boys can fit in their Armanis. Matching and contrasting colours, he'll like that. Countersurveillance transducer system, with capability for speech protection and environmental noise. GSM protectors, pocket-size, obviously. Drone detection and jamming: don't want anyone's shopping getting too close. Regular system sweeps with decent spectrum analysis. And on-site assistance. That's sugar drawers here."

Agnieszka makes a vivid, insulting gesture. "I do not work for you."

"Don't overprice yourself, dolly. You're here for experience. With you onboard, Toby here can focus on growing his beard. I assume you recorded all that. Since you wrote none of it down."

We walk to the street, my gun in her neck. I'm not bothered Archer's behind me. I've pissed better men than him. Agnieszka's surprisingly cordial. She even says, "I'm sure Mr. Miller will value my contribution."

I run two fingers across her cheek, noting old acne trenches filled with powder. "If you ever pull a gun on me again, your face will be Jackson Pollock."

"Next time, you will not know."

"That's the spirit." I walk off laughing.

Camouflage

The cab driver licks his top lip when he speaks, so a clump of wet 'tache hangs off his nose. He watches me more than the road.

"You party round Shoreditch?"

Within my life this happened: 'party' became a verb. What he means, though, is not: 'Do I stand in wallpapered rooms with prog and warm lager'. He means: 'Do I fuck in this neck of the woods'. So I tell him, "Drop me at The Old Black Dog."

"Shithole, that pub. I'd take you somewhere better."

"Lucky me."

We're askance from the Shoreditch of influencers. A street off the Cranston, where unboxing is chicken and chips from Chinese Jimmy. The driver turns around as I hand him the money. This dress hugs like clingfilm. My legs are superb on account of my sporty lifestyle.

"Just do you a receipt."

He gives me a business card with 'Call after twelve' on the back. Guess he feeds the missus a triazolam and goes hunting.

Before the grand vista of the Cranston Estate—nice flats inside, but the walkways are moody—I reach for a smoke. Miquel's a jazz musician who hates smoking. Rightly so—it fucks your hair and skin. See the old men who fill every shady corner in Catalunya with ash and tales of unlikely heroics. Worse, I smoke Ducados Negro, which are sour and harsh but, smoke them enough, they're not. My empty stomach gets it fast. My head buzzes. My legs want to move so I swish down Ivy Street, the image, I'm sure, of a hooker. This kid bouncing his ball off the fence tries not to stare. Already tall, he'll be handsome soon. Up in those flats there's a boy or girl watching and longing as he does that little dance with the ball to get my attention.

Swilling my cloud of black tobacco, I check the pub. A squat, unattractive structure. Doors and frames peeling. The blinds ragged. Adjust my bag on my shoulder. The chain gives a sensual clink.

Bare boards and burn lines. Couches spit stuffing. Chairs are splintered. Tables scratched apart by kids on jellies. A bloke stares at the dartboard like he doesn't know what it's about. Women in skintights shout, "What's that?" From the men I get, "Flat chested bitch." These are rough sorts with rough ways.

Old age has diminished Gerry. His once-magnificent bugger straps are light cotton wool. His eyes are gone in those tinted shades. I'm sorry to see his shirt is frayed and stale.

"Fucking hell." His teeth a ferocious yellow.

"Hello Gerry."

He wipes the spit off a barstool and helps me up. His bony old hand gets cheeky with my waist. "Flick Hepburn. Look at you."

His voice has a tone of wonder that, fleetingly, makes me thirteen again, in a stolen dress from New Look, a man's hand telling me I'm a beautiful woman. "Can a girl get a sandwich?" I glare at the punters. I could shoot them all and, after local tears, nothing would happen. "Hummus salad sandwich. And a G&T."

"Salad? Where d'you think you are?" He pours the gin freehand. "On the house, gorgeous."

I lick my lips like a proper tart. Because it's rare, these human moments.

"What brings you back?"

"A mutual acquaintance." I can't ask what he's heard. I don't know who holds his debts.

This stringy bitch erupts from the kitchen. Worn skin. Grubby jeans. Most likely only mid-forties. But it's all gone, shot to fuck. Those nubby hands made my sandwich.

"You the hummus salad?" She stares. I know what she's thinking.

"What's the damage?"

She makes up some ridiculous price, which I pay without question.

"Keep the change."

"I want nothing from your sort."

She strops off and I pinch my leg, to give the blood somewhere to go.

Gerry eases over. "What's all that?"

"What sewer you get her from?"

"Have a word, she's the guvnor's."

"Not his wife."

"Course not. She's, you know." He nods like a maniac.

"Here's to old England." This sandwich is a squalid mess. I'm remarkably tolerant with it. "Does Nolan still drink here?"

"Nolan?"

"The big Irish fecker."

Gerry recoils. "Things have changed since your last royal tour."

"Yeah. I got more gorgeous. Where's Nolan?"

"Since Belfast went to shit, he made with the Boston boys. They wanted a genuine Paddy."

Some people are strangers to subtlety. "So he's in Boston?"

"Not now. The Feds tried to flip him."

"Feds? What you talking about?" My brief visits to the United States have been much inconvenienced by delusional men.

"And he's got heat back home. That thing with the money. I can get him a message."

"I'd rather surprise him."

That whole-body spasm jangles his bones. "Behave, he'll string me up."

Grab his head to stop this needless movement. "Gerry. He will not kill you. Because I will tell him not. Whisper his address in my shell-like."

Mr. Nolan, it seems, has a penthouse in Hoxton.

"You won't tell him." Gerry's white as his sideburns.

"I grass no one. So long as they're polite." Give him a friendly slap on the chops. Now my hand stinks of Old Spice. The smell of lesbians worldwide.

As I swish out, the grimy piece from the kitchen is talking to one of the mouth-breathers wrapped round an empty glass. Big shaggy mess of a man. An undercard slugger. This article steps in my way.

"Here," he says, with his fat top lip. "You a bloke in a dress?"

Well of course that gets attention. The wasters smirk. Bits of language clog their throats. The kitchen tart puts up her chin, like this could go well. I give the big bollocks a look. "What did you say?"

His barbecue-beef breath swarms me. "Tranny cunt."

I give him one in the liver. Grab his head as he falls and both elbows, clean on his neck. And again, to hear the snap. He crumbles, whining and retching. I boot his gut and he's jelly.

"Anyone else?" And I'm away, swinging my hips for the boys.

Walk to Hoxton, to burn the adrenaline. Purcell Street. Flats and leaky cars. Brick walls and empty grass. Miquel doesn't get what I love about streets like this. Not that Barça doesn't have frayed seams. But London is London. Across from this moody shopping parade with its

Fort Knox pharmacy for the blue bag crowd, there's a community garden. Nothing says London like a community garden. Mature trees, bit of grass, a plaque to honour the quiet souls that made this. I should give to these places. A little something to care for the roses.

When I was a very small girl I saw my grandad in prison. In the Scrubs, so we had to go right across London. Big adventure. Grandad was a specialist, robbing bullion vans, right back to the 1950s. An apostle of the sawn-off shotgun. He'd tell me about London when he was a kid. The cobble streets and trams. How the filth would give you an open-hand slap in broad daylight. He'd tell me about the gangs his grandad told him about. Diamond Annie, Maggie Hill and the Forty Elephants. I always liked the sound of Maggie Hill. My grandad died in prison because the bastards wouldn't fetch a doctor. My dad was not the same man after that.

Falkirk Street. Kids tipping out from college. School had nothing to teach me. I got out quick as I could. But I'm no role model, nor should I be. These kids can do proper things. Cheffing, construction, programming—especially that. Follow your dreams, these signs say. Whatever a dream is like.

Kingsland Road, all shiny new flats. Costs a bit, living here. Like Stepney, that's desirable now. Full of people who call it 'Limehouse'. The fact I could buy any one of these gaffs doesn't make me want to. It's rich fuckers, all for the drugs. Score off the local jellyhead and choff it in the wine bar. Not that I think poor people are saints, any more than I think they're scum. Having a gun and using it skilfully brings perspective.

This is it, this delightful real estate. If leaky old Gerry knows he's here, could be Nolan thinks he's safe. Pride was always a thing with the Provos. As I check the door, there's a neatly stacked frame at the desk. She sees me, so I have to walk in.

This concierge models an interesting grey-blue jacket, cinched at the waist, big shoulders, flared cuffs. One bright yellow button, fastened. Teamed with a grey wrap-over scarf and straight trousers. Topshop or something. Sits nice with her skin tone. She has that professional smile. "Welcome to Kingsland Heights. How can I help you today?"

"That's kind, the welcome. I'm after one of your inmates."

Her hand floats under the desk where, no doubt, there's a button. "I'll try to assist."

"Declan Nolan. Big lad. Likely has weight on him."

Artful, that smile freezes. "I'm sorry, there's no one of that name here."

Gerry wouldn't lie to me. Unless he developed a death wish. "He may use a different handle. He's Irish and big. You can't miss him."

"Actually, do you mind telling me who you are?"

My options are: walk, or irresistible force. It's all on camera. And lodging heat in her spine might not be straightforward. There's a third option. It's messy. "I've not been entirely straight with you."

"I did think."

I'd like to shoot her. But the moment's gone. "There is a reason for my deception." I use a Coach ice-purple wallet because, as a career woman, a purse ain't the right look. Mum had a snakeskin purse with the gold thumb-clip. She had it her whole life. Women took pride in making things last. They weren't label bunnies like me. In my wallet, with the cloned credit cards, I keep IDs for various occasions. I don't flash them around because that shows a failure of cunning. Which is this situation. "That's me."

She nods, far too amused.

This is my Scotland Yard ID. I'm Detective Inspector Lynda Temple. "Specialist Operations. I stick tight with persons of interest. So tell me, Chloe," I point at her badge, "where's the sack of shite that is Declan Nolan?"

But she's a stone-cold wonder. "We have no one of that name."

"Still?"

"We have a Mr. McGuire. He is quite large. Flat Six-Twelve. I can give him a buzz."

"I'd rather surprise him."

"I thought you might."

I don't like lifts. Too easy to stop. To shoot what's inside. Like I have. But me walking six flights gives her a good three minutes to juice this McGuire. If she does, I'll kill her. Provided he doesn't kill me.

Unlike our Victorian ancestors, we're obsessed with private space. Which means these hallways are shatteringly dull. Where the Victorians would have nice plaster, dadoes, harem tiles, mirrors in moody gilt frames, there's white walls, pine floors and shit modern art. It's architectural mac and cheese. People pay millions for these apartments. They see this every day and don't care it's just a paint ad. Our place in Barcelona is minimal but exquisite. And the building: the stairs are marble, the oak bannisters glisten, the plaster's ruched like curtains and painted Sacramento green. That's me, these days. Homesick for décor.

He's watching sport, by the sound. Crowd noise and the rising inflection of someone calling the game. We don't have a TV. We go to jazz bars and theatre. We have four-hour dinners and fuck intensely. Homesick for décor.

This door has two locks, both look easy. If missy downstairs has warned him, he'll be primed. TV noise continues. Touch my gun for luck. These cameras. Chloe's watching. So I give the door a strict wallop and movement becomes apparent. The heavy tread of a ton of shit. The door shudders. Something clatters behind it. This imbecile was a paramilitary once.

He opens the door on the chain like a little old lady. A pizza slice of red sweating face. A flabby, bloodshot eye. Spit-licking lips. The smell of whiskey and ranch dressing and too long indoors. "Why aren't you dead?"

"Declan. Always a pain."

"What d'you want you nonce?"

Let that slide. It seems Chloe didn't grass me. Which is also interesting. "I'm on a tour of local disasters. You asking me in?"

"Fuck off."

"Declan, we're on camera. That tart downstairs thinks I'm filth. If you don't let me in, she might suspect bad blood between us. Maybe you don't want that."

He kicks the door and fumbles the chain. He's probably armed but I need to stay breezy.

This room must have been nice before the bomb. There's takeaway cartons split on the neutral shag. Four whiskey bottles. Two dozen cans crushed and hurled about. The TV has tomato sauce dripping down it. The walls are greasy. Smoke drifts on the scent of sweet and sour piss. "I love what you done with this room."

Standing is a challenge, so he hobbles to the stained couch, falling so hard it groans like a dying rhino. He roots in the debris for beer. I'm starting to think I might leave disappointed. But psychosis is a posh word for enthusiasm.

"Declan, old son. You're wondering why I'm here."

His face is slack. His jaw hangs the most horrible way. As though reeling from altitude, he grabs at asthmatic breath. "Why aren't you dead?"

"Because I met no one yet of sufficient distinction."

"Bullshit." His bleary gaze finds the TV. Rugby: an inexplicable pastime of beefy thighs and odd shaped balls. I'm all for men in good physical nick. Gymnastics is more my game.

So I plant these creamy pins in front of the screen.

He waves his hands in a feeble, traffic-directing manner. "Gerroutofit yabastard,"

So I give it some boot and that's the end of the telly.

He glares in baleful impotence.

"How was Boston?"

"Fucking Yanks. Doing the Brits' dirty washing."

"No rows over money, then?"

A greasy finger dangles towards me. "What cunt was it grassed I'm here?"

"I kicked a few dustbins and out you fell. I'm surprised you're let loose, to be honest. MI5 give you immunity?"

"I don't cut deals. Not like some."

This fool spits more than he should. "Alright. Let's talk about me. I bring you the opportunity of a good deed."

With a huge churn of redundant flesh, he lurches at me. A big, stupid animal intrigued by the hand that kills. "You still keep a little cock under that skirt?"

Reflex is break the wall with his head. But I pay for good skin. "This is a dress, not a skirt. It's worth more than you spent on clothes your whole life. And after being in this shithole I've got to burn it. Now pay attention, there's a good boy."

Green gunk drips from his nose.

"My client is facing issues beyond your comprehension. My role is robust response. The more robust the challenge, the more I respond. The good you can do me is a nice Kalashnikov. Not crap. Nice army job. And enough Russian shorts to kill everyone. All in a handy carrying case that does not, I say not, have trackers. And you give it me free. Or I mention your whereabouts to the balaclavas."

"Are you mental, nonce?"

"Declan, don't let yourself down."

He makes a palaver, punching cushions. "What in fuck makes you think I can get one?"

"Because you know nasty people. If I shop for hardware, it rouses the interest of some massive fuckwits. But with you, it's just bingo night."

"What's this crap about not paying?"

"I'm an influencer. You're doing this for exposure."

His horrible eyes on strings. "So how am I meant to get it?"

"Declan, if I cared about that, I'd answer you, wouldn't I?"

The intercom buzzes.

I clamp his shoulder. "Did you press some little button to call your leprechauns?"

"I'm expecting someone."

"Who, the undertaker?" Hand in my pocket, I go to the door.

This is a beautiful woman. A curly brunette, navy mini dress, white collar and trim. Could be Forever 21, Urban Outfitters—generic, but suits her. A dress that's easily up and off. She hugs a neat burgundy clutch. Knock-off Celine, I reckon. She looks at me with surprise, I might say malice.

"I thought I was first."

"First at what?"

"Mr. McGuire."

The notion of Declan Nolan as competitive sport derails me.

She's itchy. "Let us in."

Her voice brings a mighty effort as the great man gets to his feet. He hangs on the couch, an ugly dog cocked on a fence. "You Cherise?"

Hand to my gun. "What you here for?"

Her eyes expect trouble. "Same as you. Thought I was first."

Then the penny drops. "You an escort?"

"Jesus, does it show?"

The full horror sinks in. "You going to do him?"

We both look at Nolan, humping the back of the couch.

"I'm paid," she says.

"I'll pay you not to."

"Who are you?"

"Get your phone, I'll ping you the money."

Then Nolan blows up. "What's this fucking caper? I bought that, front and back. It's not your fucking business you ugly tranny."

His eyes bulge and he swims for breath, as my slim and sensual hand puts a choke on his pipes. "Whatever nasty stump is lurking in your smalls gets none of her. You owe me a present, remember?"

By now he's busting capillaries. His stench would stun a horse.

"You probably don't want to kill him." Cherise seems concerned at our banter. "I couldn't give a statement or nothing. I'm out on licence."

"Were you actually looking forward to having him up your starfish?"

She shrugs. "It's the job, innit."

Whip my palm across Nolan's face. "You don't deserve nice things. Have your weasels deliver my present to Sally Rainbow's. Tomorrow's good."

"How do I get it for tomorrow?"

"By looking for it today."

He lumps around, checking his grotesque components remain intact. Cherise, now she's paid, stands awkward, remaindered. I could put her down easy. An escort visit gone wrong. The police would give that a bare half hour. Wonder what she went inside for. "I'm sure you got calls to make."

"Yeah," she says, not looking hopeful.

Nolan glares me out. Old terrorists never forget.

Jog downstairs, eye on the cameras. Daylight fades. It's the cruellest month.

There's screens under Chloe's desk. I exist in captive moments all over the world. "Did you find who you were looking for, Detective Inspector?"

"Your co-operation is much appreciated."

That smile is habit become intent. "Your impersonation of a police officer needs a little polish."

My flat stomach clenches. "I'm not aware I impersonate anyone."

"I'll see your card. And raise you mine."

The plastic likeness of Detective Sergeant Chloe Bell. "Fraud specialist," she says, with needless good humour. "I'm sure you know impersonating a police officer carries serious penalties."

How much happier I'd be if I popped one in her brain. How that would end—at least for now—this trading. "I'm sure you know obstructing inquiries also has repercussions." Lay my card beside hers. Both have the shield, the unflattering picture—though hers is worse—the hologram, the Commissioner's autograph. My police ID is not fake, exactly. It's a product of realistic decisions. "What you doing here?"

"Interesting people buy London property."

That I've tumbled in covert ops is scarcely jolly, with my client, the ticking clock and increasing potential for drama. "Looks like we have an operational overlap."

I'm somewhat surprised when she says, "We could discuss it over a drink."

Fancies herself as Mata Hari, dancing with strangers across the lines. It's a stupid suggestion and I react sloppily. "Friday, maybe."

I walk, prickling with arrangements. Checking she really is filth is essential. Confirming her interest in Nolan would be wise. Not today. I'm done with today.

Recreation

Cab it to Ladbroke Grove. The body's weary. The spirit needs restitution. Tell the driver, "Take me somewhere gay". He drops me at this pub by Oxford Gardens. Trees blossom under the streetlamps, as men hurry by in that self-absorbed way of the young and beautiful.

There's couples and crews. Lads shoot pool. The women are plain and cheerful. Swing up to the bar where a nice young man with blond bed hair waits my pleasure. "Large gin. What tonic you got?" He's got classic, aromatic, elderflower. He's got tonic with cucumber essence, which must be like drinking moss. He shows me the bottles. "Classic."

Take the corner of a long table. Get checked by the neighbours. Message Sally Rainbow, to say I've a delivery coming. So now someone else knows I'm in town.

The young man to my right is a looker, and not flash with it, which I like. A young black man. Smooth, short hair. Pleasant round face. Shaved goatee. Light green shirt. Dark green cardigan, two buttons done, sleeves rolled to the elbow. The shirt's Van Heusen, no mistake. Cardigan's maybe Weiland or a good knockoff. He fills it splendidly well. Those grey strides are smooth. Can't see his shoes but I'm guessing brown with laces. He nurses a bottle of Karakter, which I believe is some Belgian wallop.

Our eyes meet and the devilment rises. This is a moment of delicacy. Slowly, I fold my hair behind my left ear, to give him movement to follow. He's uncertain but this is on him. He's the man.

"Hi," he says, to my great relief.

"Hi."

He glances to the door and back at me. "Don't think I've seen you before."

My fingers tingle. "I've been out of town."

He knuckles the phone lying next to his beer. "I thought I was waiting for someone."

"I don't use apps. Old school works for me."

Sweet, he shakes hands. "I'm Curtis."

"Your mum like Curtis Mayfield?"

"Curtis, Isaac, she loved those guys."

Swing around, so I'm his point of attention. "I'm Felicity. Flick."

"Pleased to meet you."

He goes to the bar. Men stare at me. Gay men are gorgeous. Their curiosity is my spotlight. I love my Miquel. I'm fiercely loyal. But I'm not ready for the convent.

Wonderfully, Curtis is an accountant with Westminster council. My profession relies on geometry, on hair's breadth differentials. A man talks numbers to me, I'm rubbing my knees. So I tell him accountants are hot and he smiles sweetly and asks what I do. "I'm a picture researcher. Art history books." I name some European publisher of illustrated doorstops. "I negotiate rights and permissions. I find the best pictures to illustrate the text and sort the licensing. Some pictures cost a fortune." It sounds a job I wouldn't mind doing. "I been in Barcelona," I say. "Researching at the Museu Picasso. Blue Period. Around the death of Casagemas."

"Sounds more exciting than running spreadsheets."

"Spreadsheets are phenomenal."

Then he laughs. "Do you go dancing?"

Tipping closer, my knee abrades his. "I'm murder on the dancefloor."

Before I can whistle a cab, he says let's get the bus. I can't remember getting a bus in London or anywhere. I used to. A heartbroken teen, in love with Dean Marks. That boy would drag me everywhere. I'd trail longingly after, living for when he pushed me down or had me against a wall. He wasn't my boyfriend. He just liked to fuck me. It mattered so much, to belong to somebody. Now I'm grown, and in charge of myself, and desirable it seems. Curtis looks at me with baffled wonder. We'll have a good time.

The bus is a box of framed light. Follow Curtis upstairs. My dress hugs my bum. Every man looks and I look back. Today hasn't been hard but I miss my siesta. Catalunya went nine-to-five years ago. But me and Miquel keep the old ways. Slow lunch. Few hours in cotton sheets. When I was a girl, I'd go twenty-four seven. A little puritan, I thought it was wrong to waste time. But I got older and less patient of good advice.

Curtis points to this and this. Where he goes shopping. Where his friends live. I make caring noise. Giggle at his jokes. Eventually it occurs to him he's a man and I'm a woman and there's nothing remarkable about slipping an arm round my shoulder. Feels good to be held. I snuggle in and he explains London to me like I been asleep a hundred years.

It's a local club behind a parade of shops. A frisson of glamour on an empty street. Of course the bouncers look. I don't relish hiding my gun out here. But Curtis is regular. He fist bumps the lads. I wiggle and act charming. Curtis pays for us both, so I'll buy the drinks. I can afford this better than he can.

Through tinfoil curtains, the dancefloor seeps dry ice. The DJ spins euro-filler. Men move through low-hanging fog. Two hundred men, maybe. Everyone looks. I expect this. The only woman in the place, their confusion is wholly proper. A pair of drag queens stare. One makes a big "Ooohhh" with her lippy. I must be good-humoured. The life of a drag queen is fragile.

Curtis, total sweetheart, scouts for a table. Beneath the lights, his shirt and cardigan stand off from his skin. Dark eyes all mischief. Plant my lips on his ear to ask what he's drinking.

At the bar, the drag queen moves to me, staring down her long nose. "What's this?" she says. "The intern look?"

Gracious, because Curtis treated me here, I plane my hands down my hips. "This jacket's Chanel. You know that. The dress is Elie Saab. I'm not sure what interns wear."

She's modelling a splendid concoction: black pencil with sequin fripperies. Fine mesh across her fake boobs. Stretch polyester is so forgiving. Her barnet is twenty-six inches of blood red weave that, I guess, looks shocking in daylight. The prosthetics are gruesomely interesting: a pair of big fillets that bubble around when she stands still. "Oh yes, it's nice packaging. Just not much to show, is there, love?"

Careful, because I don't want to spoil my new friend's night, I run my hand up the drag queen's neck and take a small twist of skin. She jolts forward. Her fake tits rub my shoulder. Keeping pleasant, I say, "Bitch me again and I'll pop you like a cork. And FYI, love, it's not me with fake hair."

The DJ funks it up. We're dancing. An older crowd—late twenties, thirties—frugging to disco. Old-school shapes I remember the first time. He lays down Village People 'Macho Man' and I'm strutting and mouthing the words. This song makes me so fucking gay.

A pretty bitch locks eyes with me. I know his story. The shape of his lips when he spits a kiss. Silk panties, trapped in chinos. He wants real clothes. A blouse, tight skirt, heels. Spit a kiss back and he turns away. What matters is this. Someone looks at him wrong, he'll wet his lashes. Someone looks at me wrong, they're dead. I was always a woman and always a killer. I help people die correctly. I dance. The queers stare. We're tribal, we like labels. We like to be subsets of subsets. But I'm me.

Speak to the DJ. He's battered and friendly in a Turkish leather jacket. Sovereign rings so old they're iconic. Both my numbers are in his case. "Funny," he says. "Don't get many girls in here." I giggle and kiss his cheek and get a big lick of Blue Stratos. Like Proust and his crumpet, everything takes me back.

Get Curtis on his feet for my tune: Sly Fox 'Let's Go All The Way'. That bassline wastes my gut. He spins me like some rock 'n' roller. I throw down flamenco stomps, mixing male and female hand shapes, which Miquel would find horrifying. My flamenco education has far to go, but lace and boots beguile me.

The DJ gets to my slowie. Gwen Guthrie 'Ain't Nothing Going On But The Rent'. It gets squeals from boys who maybe heard it from older lovers. No romance without finance. Miquel pushes himself to get gigs, to be Man Playing Guitar in every movie. He doesn't like that I earn more than him. I don't want him feeling bad. He's who I miss, while I dirty dance this lovely accountant.

We smooch and sway off-time. A slow, confident kiss. He squeezes my back and we're locked. His hard-on, keen and tight. We bundle outside. If it's cold I don't feel it. There's couples and hook-ups. A crowd, then it's gone. Men melt away, their buoyancy hushed by the night. The bus comes and we rattle upstairs. Three young men at the back take notice. Different energy lights my spine.

They start the hate. Grunts as Curtis cuddles me. Catcalls as we kiss. Then one of these kids, his voice not even settled from when it broke, says, "Fucking niggers taking our women." Curtis freezes. There's decency in how he tries to ignore it. That decides me.

"A nigger and a slut. Black man's tart."

"His monkey dick in her piss hole."

The monkey noises start. There's other people here. They do nothing. I wouldn't expect it. It's late and they have families to get to. Curtis grips me tight, and I know he's suffering. He's a good man, clever, not impetuous. He's heard this shit his whole life and grown a skin of self-preservation. He's embarrassed because he thinks he can't protect me. I feel that in his loving arms.

These lads start spitting. "She needs a real man. Then she wouldn't crawl to the jungle."

One throws a can. Maybe aiming for Curtis, it clips the back of my head. What happens next has become inevitable. Tell Curtis, quietly, "Go downstairs, love. Ask the driver to call an ambulance."

He's terrified. "I'll stop them."

"No, darling." I squeeze his hand. "Please go downstairs and tell the driver to radio an ambulance." I kiss his lips and foul, provocative language stains the air.

I'm sure he feels weak. I don't want him upset. But there isn't time to explain he's in my world. Shaking as he stands, he walks to the stairs, absorbing shit from these dumb boys. He looks at me and I smile and wave—he must know to trust me. Once Curtis goes downstairs, I'm on my feet.

The lads quieten a bit, unsure what's happening.

"Alright darling." One gives a lippy smile. "You come to the real men."

"I think your attitudes are somewhat out of date."

"Nah," says one, "we're the future. Tomorrow belongs to us."

"Thing is," I tell him, "you won't see tomorrow."

Then it comes down. Grab two and smack their heads together. They're dazed and the other one's on his feet, puzzled I don't run. He grabs. I catch his hand and twist it over. Drive my thumb to mangle his wrist. He screeches and punches. I soak it up. The other two lunge and I jab their chests, tumbling them in a heap. Then the ratty one pulls a knife.

Go for his blade hand, ignoring fists on my head. My hair's messed up. Bad move with an angry woman. Chain him forward so his knife touches my dress. My fingers are wire. Choke his wrist till he hollers. His hand pops and I've got the knife. They freeze like the music stopped.

There's red on the air, on clothes and skin. Shove his face in his mate's gaping neck.

The bus stops. There's sirens behind. The civilians have legged it downstairs. The mouthy one watches his mates shamble in blood. The bloke with the split neck turns white. I open more flesh, for distraction.

"You fucking cunt." He clatters their wreckage aside to get me. He's got a blade and it's old-school. Scorched with adrenaline I unzip his skin. I don't want to wreck this dress, so I push forward, stab his chest. He cups his spilling body like a prayer. "You cunt."

"Yes," I say. "Yes I am." Drag him to the stairs and kick him down, flailing and frothing. As he lands, good folk scream. Jam the knife in my pocket. Try not to think how his blood stains my lining. Grab Curtis and cannon him off the bus. "Run." Haul him till his feet get the idea. Don't stop till we hit quiet streets.

"Did you kill them?" My man's breathless. His eyes curious, scared.

"They lost blood but, youngsters—they should pull through."

"Why did you?" It's like this enormous idea can exist only as a pointless question.

Being nice, because I want to be nice with Curtis, I say, "You can't ignore that and sleep easy."

"I didn't fight." It may be how the light falls. A touch of mist to the air. It's like his eyes are wet.

Push both arms around him. "You didn't need to."

"They could have killed you."

He clutches my neck. I don't say he's pulling my hair. "No they couldn't. They're nothing but impulse. I'm serious-minded. So I win."

We walk to his flat, propping each other like old drunks. He's jumpy, reacts on nothing. I wonder a man can be so removed from physical things. Those scumbags and me, we're weapons. We throw our bodies into the fight. Curtis, most people, follow process. That's the core of a civilised society. You can't settle everything in blood because who'd empty the bins? The Catalan, he's imbued with the ways of blood. With matters of honour. It's funny, but not funny, to think in England—of all places—a fight should seem grotesque.

Cutely, Curtis asks me to go quiet on the stairs, so we don't trouble his neighbours. An old house, cut into flats. Doors everywhere, skewed corners, a walled-up arch. And to make it nice, someone left a half-moon table and silk flowers in the hall. Trusting future residents would take care. The table is chipped and the blooms are dust.

Curtis lives at the top, which I like. It's good not to have people above you. His place is neat. Books and tech. Muted colours. Framed art with queer connections. No feeling that anyone else is here. "It's lovely. How long you been single?"

"Couple of years. I'm taking things casual."

There's space on a shelf where he packed away pictures. I don't like to deny I'm in a serious relationship. Engaged, though I don't wear the ring. It's best to avoid explanations.

I perch on his pretty couch while he pours brandy. No music because that would trouble the neighbours. I'd find it hard to live this way, but for now it's sweet and flattering that he wants to keep me secret.

"Those kids can describe you. You could get arrested."

"Why I sent you downstairs. You did nothing wrong." The notion of getting arrested is interesting. Though I was provoked, I showed intent beyond self-defence. But bang up in the dreary Midlands isn't on my Gantt chart.

Like Cleopatra I nip to the bathroom to freshen my look. Few dabs of scent. Layer mascara. Pile up foundation. I've looked young since I was young. I'm more terrified of losing that than anything. Blokes who drew first blood same time as me are grey now. And hitched to Miquel I'll have to stay young forever.

Curtis's bedroom is what estate agents call compact. A bed and a wardrobe, nothing more. We lay in the hesitant moment, feeling for where to begin.

"What do you like?" He's so serious. So kind and serious.

"Don't ask preferences. Don't ask how it feels."

We're naked. He's a beautiful body. Firm skin, musty with dancing. There's an ease to him, it makes being here no hassle. I lay with my rump in the air and he kisses his way up my legs. He kisses my buttocks, which makes me shiver like a dog. He's concerned at my wounds. Five puckered scars, they surprise me yet with their shine. "What happened?" His voice, the softness of a properly powerful man.

"I got shot on several occasions." Look at him. His face is heartbreaking. "They're lessons."

"Do they hurt?"

"They burn sometimes. I hear them creak, or think I do. I was offered surgery but they'd take the skin off my arse."

"How did you get shot five times?"

"Art history's full of people who can't take a joke."

A condom box stares me in the face.

Pleasantly I say, "I test regularly. But of course do that, if you want."

He looks at me. He looks at the box.

I'm glad because I want his spunk inside me.

Now he searches for lube.

"No need. I'll open for you." The technicalities of sex with cautious men.

Curtis has a nice cock: mid-length and thick. Still a taste of the soap he used hours ago. I make a proper slow meal of getting him hard. All the while he strokes my hair, he can't stop touching me. With Miquel he slaps my arse and makes it an order, 'Obre ara,' open now. But Curtis eases and squeezes, till I say, "Fuck me." I'm for men's delight. That's what I like.

He moves inside, bites my shoulders, pinches my nipples. "Please," I whisper, "please." His fingers choke my cock. That little throwback, stiff and slick in his grip.

A strong arm curls under my chest, to force me onto his cock while he scrubs mine. I bounce against his body, his sweat on my spine, his breath in my hair, every sinew controlled by this beautiful man. "I'm cumming," I whine, "I'm cumming." His balls and stomach smack my arse. His convulsion. We're there together. Deep in his chest Curtis growls and a bolt of spunk fills me up. He thumbs my cock. I shoot over his bed. He owns my trembling body. "I love you, I love you, I love you."

"You," he says gravely, "are a special woman."

We wrap around, our cocks kissing, our bodies slick with sperm. These moments, nothing matters.

Give it half hour, then poke his ribs. "More fuck."

His eyes like owls in the Collserola. With lovely, natural springiness he bounces me onto my back, hoists my legs and he's in. My knees to my chest, I watch his cock in and out. He pins me with commanding force. The sublime beyond calculation. How can a man, who does this, worry he didn't jump into some stupid fight. He works my dick. Brings its modest length to life. "Are you cumming?" he says. With wicked mischief he lets go.

"You bastard." I wank till I spunk my stomach.

He laughs as he delivers another load. When he pulls out, I'm gaping. Sly breeze creeps through my gut.

Later—it feels much later—I wake to the shocking quiet of early day. I feel streets layered with stillness. Nothing happens for miles. At home, I'd slip on a dressing gown and smoke in the tiled yard. I wash before getting back to bed—Miquel hates the stink of smoke. He says it's risking my life for something empty. As if other things fill me up.

This density of silence frames my ceaseless thoughts. In Mr. Miller's salad days your enemy got tooled up, nicked a motor, scorched your turf. Then you did the same, tit for tat. A contact sport, Dad called it. To Mr. Miller, it's bewildering his hard work can be compromised from far away. So to soothe his anxiety I'm lumbered with a shitload of kit and moody Agnieszka. An AK to pick up tomorrow. That weird concierge who reckons she's filth. And it all makes noise because this beautiful man lives in the quietest street.

With a charm I've come to expect of him, Curtis booked the next morning off work. So if his date came good, they could linger. And if not, he'd have time to rebuild. I can't imagine thinking that way.

He's up for breakfast, which is awkward. Once I'm done, I don't hang around. "Sorry." Try to look winsome. "Early meeting."

Take a quick scrub in his tiny, spotless shower. Can't wash my hair: no hairdryer. Walking round with wet hair looks careless. Redo my face. Give my eyes plenty. The power of heavy eye makeup is compulsion. Mascara makes the most lethal part of me the focal point of the room. With powder-smooth cheeks and bloody lips, a little shadow in the cleft of my chin, I'm a luscious nightmare. This is no accident. It's my life's work.

Lovely Curtis has a look I know well. A man who thinks he might see me again. Who thinks this might be some prelude to a soaking-together of bodies that could endure. It's crucial to accept disappointment. So much for me has gone too soon or never begun. So many shots wide. So much careless catching of bullets. I'm disappointed Curtis would lay hopes on me. As he'll be disappointed, when the sound of my boots is gone from the stairs.

He gets his phone. "I'd love to do this again, Flick. Let's meet soon."

For one second, I think to give a number that finds me. But where would that get us? Most often, I toss a few scrambled digits, kiss and run. But he's nice. So I tell him, "It's awkward. I'm getting married."

He's crushed. He'll never know how kind I been. "So this was just a thing?"

"I don't want to hurt you." But I am. "This was fantastic. You're fantastic. But I got someone. And it's difficult, being with me. I'd make you unhappy."

"But you don't make him unhappy?"

"I'm so sorry."

We kiss and cuddle, for old times. We say we'll bump into each other again. When I get outside, I feel like trash. Which is a pity, because it's a nice day.

Sincerity

This café's a time warp. The clock—stopped—a tropical scene of palms at sunset. An old juice machine slaughters a dozen oranges for half a cupful. I loved watching them as a kid, seeing the oranges mangled and torn. A framed print of a girl in hot pants straddling a Ducati. A Four-Fifty Desmo I think, though I'm no expert on bikes. One time, I guess her shirt was blue, the hot pants red, silver boots. But years of grubby London sun faded her to the ghost I suppose she now is.

Above the counter, the nazar turns its gaze on me. Below the amulet, a thin, exhausted woman, fine black hair scraped in a tail, a face too sharp for lines. Even with southern skin, the discolouration beneath her eyes is immense. Like she hasn't slept since childhood. I hope a young man bathes her feet after each hard day; knuckles the knots from her shoulders; maintains her as the icon of his love.

Bone sacks hunch over mugs of tea, while lads who drive vans shovel fry-ups and arrange the day's business in cocky, musical voices.

A pretty, downy-faced type who seems German takes my order. Before he starts with the menu, I say, "Jacket potato, cheese and beans, salad and a tea."

He looks helpless. "We have hash browns," he says mystically.

"I said what I want."

Check my phone. The Old Bill sniffing a serious assault in West London. Three bright hopes for the future with 'life-changing injuries' whatever that means. No word on the suspect. That's a signal. I was all over the cameras. Them little mongs will be doing e-fits soon as the gas wears off. It would have been less hassle to kill them. In my pocket there's this knife, which I rinsed in Curtis's shower. The blood gone to the sewers, and I cleaned the drain. Those kids, the driver, lumpen civilians all saw me. Which means, at some level of authority, a decision got taken. I get tetchy, owing favours.

Blond boy parks a mug of tea. The mug has a rainbow glaze. The tea is boot leather. "Your food is coming," he says, his Rhineland accent apologetic. He's likely a tidy sub on his day off. Licking the riding boots. Where I live, there's people hate Germans. They hate Spanish, so of course they hate Germans. I'm more tolerant. Let people prove they're crap.

Read a blog on certificate fraud. Certificate fraud is an investible market. Like any security, there's incentives to game. Certificates work because browsers believe whoever owns the certificate manages the site. The browser and the certificate swap numbers, as it were. For a spicy fraud you don't want a fake certificate. You want a real one. The trick is to blindside the audit. That's where I'd invest. Mug punter thinks he's logging into his bank. And he is, the certificate's real. But the website is my back pocket. And this interests me, because I wonder if Mr. Miller is the mark in a sandbox fraud. It's not that someone steals his business. They test their business on him.

The lady herself brings breakfast. I'd say forty-six, forty-eight. Fine bones. Worn skin. Sad eyes, from expecting the worst. Sleeplessness pervades her every gesture. Fretful watching for ghosts. These types—Turks, Cypriots—they know the past won't let go. Even me, with a few years in Catalunya, I see the land alive with ghosts.

She sets down the plate precisely, tweaking it with cracked fingers. I'm ready with some pleasantry, but she stares with captive fury. Like a wasp in a bottle, how it jumps and roars, so angry and small. "What do you want with us?"

I realise this is serious. "I come to eat. Just that."

"We do not want your trouble."

Her intensity disrupts me. The nazar glints on the wall. Without anger, I ask, "Who do you think I am?"

She makes a gesture, a pushing-away. "Enjoy, please, and leave us."

Russians, who relish everything that makes them miserable, call them babushkas: curdled, over-involved women who lay the bad eye at each turn. L'àvia in Català. I see them, in headscarves and housecoats. They say nothing to me. Miquel's connected and I'm dangerous, so they say nothing. But these same superstitions drive their cursing and crossing themselves. And this one: she's no age for that. She still bleeds and leaks out her love. But the same fear. When a songbird sees a hawk's shadow and sets loose its cry through the woods, other birds take flight, squirrels and mice run screeching. Panic becomes its own purpose. The precision of threat, lost in a mire of commotion. Fear is a dirty thing.

The German lad settles up. I'm generous to the tip plate so they understand how deep my ownership runs. I catch her eye. I smile. She gives a sharp, downward nod. I wonder what she said 'Yes' to.

At the street corner, a rare sight: a walk-down toilet. I thought these got swapped to hip little bars. But here it is, pissy tiles and all. There's heritage to these places. Brave girls, years before I was born, knelt here for a taste of cock. Risking thugs and rozzers and tricks gone bad, so they could be warm a while. I don't take for granted I have it easy.

This cubicle's rank. That smell of ingrained piss. Slicks of mould glisten yellow. The brown-spotted floor where girls had to fix up as blood deserts them. Water sighs from the cistern. And another sound. Flat shoes on the stairs. A woman would make patterns: repacking her bag, adjusting her straps, taking a call. This is a man. He's impatient. It's intensely interesting, hearing those shoes. Getting their build and texture. Trying to gauge when he's furthest, when he's paying least attention. The fundamental of every situation is to own it. He thinks I'm trapped. But he can't leave without me.

Drop the flush, unlock the door and step out.

"Hello love." An amateur. Regular ugly. Short matted hair and furry jowls. Field top and baggy jeans. I bet no one since Mummy has dressed him. He gawks at my extraordinary looks. "Had a piss, then? Wet your flaps?"

This vulgarity suits his filmy rind of sweat. I stare at him.

"Big mistake, darling, coming here. This is mine. You're mine." His knife is kitchen equipment. Dull with filthy light. "Want it easy, darling? Or hard?"

I stare at him.

He scoops the knife like a spoon. "Cosy. Just you and me."

"I can describe you to the police."

He laughs. I smell his tooth decay. "None of the others got out. You're no different."

I have a sister I love very much. She risks her life, every day, on inadequate men like this. "I'm different." He flinches when I show the knife. A coward who kills unarmed women. His blade is cumbersome against this bastard tool.

"Don't be silly." He chokes. "I know how to use this."

"Mine makes corpses, not sandwiches."

"I'll carve you slow. You'll wish you were dead."

"It ends here."

Fear takes hold. He swings his blade, pushing his scent of piss and desperation. I don't look at the bloated face, the churning mouth. With each swing of his knife, my eyes catch the sweet spot. Dance back and he steps on, toiling for it.

"How many?"

"Three." His breath's shot. "You're number four." He goes, blade full out—a blunt force manoeuvre. I parry and steel collides, an otherworldly cry.

"What you do with the bodies?"

"I got my van."

"Fuck 'em, do you?" Course he does. "Only way you get any."

That works like a slap. "Why ain't you got tits?"

This knife I took off a bad man knows its trade. It's in his clothes and his chest before he understands the lethal swing to my arm. It's in his heart because I know the path through ribs and sternum. No final push. No rowdy eclipse. He's bewildered because, unlike me, he never envisaged defeat.

A knife to the heart penetrates chambers and arteries. Profuse haemorrhage follows. Release the blade, drawing a channel for blood. Now he falls, breathing but dead.

Speak softly as brain death occurs. "No more tears."

When he's gone, I wad toilet paper for a glove, get his knife and stab him again. Stir his kitchen blade to destroy the original wound. It makes a sucking, aching sound. It smells like a butcher's shop. Someone'll find him. Then there'll be hoo-ha. An ageing mother might cop the heartbreaking chore of burying a child.

Clean my knife. Take a moment to breathe. Pressure builds, it needs release. Now I'm assuaged. Not for long. Never for long.

I go out and steal his van.

Animals

The van smells of death. Dirty blankets in back. It's junk, it drives like crap. And my prints on the door, the wheel, the wires where I sparked the engine. It smells of death.

Drive to Sally Rainbow's, in old Camden. Couples moved here when they were fresh. Stayed to have kids. Became grudging of anything with a pulse. Actors from popular dramas, gallery vultures, sold-out politicians, writers who kept at it too long and went crap like they all do. Folks who fret for the homeless and get bashes cleared from their street. And their kids go to Sally Rainbow's. A high-octane nursery.

Like any posh school the place is a fortress. The wall has those loopy spikes that spin your feet. Cameras pry from all angles. It irks me, how much face I've given away. The playground's got an activity island, a slab of wooden bars like a giant xylophone, and a pirate ship playhouse with blood red sails. Among vicious maniacs, pirates get the most love.

Press the button and feed my pearlies to the camera. What sounds like a young girl answers, rounding her vowels for the clientele. "Hello, this is the office. Can I help you?"

"I'm Felicity," I say, all treacle. "I messaged Ms. Rainbow about prioritising my child." Telling that lie stops me up. Roc, Miquel and me will have a baby. I'll be mum and stuff will matter. Toilet training, timestables and tests will matter. I'll cry on their first day of school. I'll buy them the best and fret their missing out on the hardships that made me.

It's colourful and encouraging. Kids' paintings cover the walls. Strident posters tell them: 'Don't Stop Till You're Proud', 'Be Amazing', 'It's Okay Not To Know, But It's Not Okay Not To Try'. That could be said so much better.

As I head to the office a small girl trots through, in what Mum must think is a sweet blouse and flappy skirt combo. "Hello," she says, all confidence.

"Alright."

Without preamble, she points to a hectic painting. A mess of black and orange and baleful eyes. "Tiger," she says.

I study the work. "It's a cat with bulgy mincers."

"It," says the girl, with indelible scorn, "is a tiger." She flounces off, flicking hair over her shoulders.

Sally Rainbow never ages. She has smooth chubby cheeks, a big, cute nose, eyes sunk by laughter, hair that's blonde regardless. She's dressed for an event in some previous decade. What Mum would call a cucumber salad frock. Sally's hands are freezing. "Flick. Too divine. What brings you?"

For all her exquisite lip gloss, Sally is a single point of failure. An undesirable amount of business touches her hands. "Spring cleaning," I say, thinking that sounds clever.

She holds me arm's length, like something on sale. "Elie Saab and Chanel? Simply wonderful."

"Just old things I flung on."

"You have such éclat." She grips my elbow that confidential way of posh birds. "Some of the mothers here… My darling, they have squillions in the bank and turn up in a smock with socks. Or those oversized puffy coats. Or a bloody McCartney." She shudders. "It would be so much better to have you at the gate."

"I'm settled in Barcelona."

"And contemplating a baby." With abrupt affection she pats my stomach. "I can tell when a girl gets broody. We'd be delighted to have your child here. They would get the very best start. And make lifelong connections." Her full-cheek grin suggests all kinds of things I know nothing about.

"Sally, did a package arrive?"

If looking nonplussed is a thing, at least she's well-mannered. "A heavy item. It seems to contain components."

Bright commotion fills the corridor. Tidy kids going for exercise. Their high, self-assured voices tumble over each other. What they got, what they want, what Mummy said they must do to succeed.

"I don't pry," Sally says. "But might this be to do with Declan Nolan?"

The thing with Sally is not knowing what she knows. She's the poste restante. It all swills through here. "So interesting you mention him, Sally. I was wondering if that great hero was still on the radar."

"Oh, darling." That shrewd look. "I don't know Mr. Nolan. I did hear he'd gone to seed since his last exploit in the States. You know what happens when men don't have a woman to hand."

I'm not sure I do but I make encouraging noise.

"Men," she says, "with their pride and whatnot. It must burn him, that shift from command to commerce."

But, of course, she doesn't know Mr. Nolan.

Outside, kids run around. Boys shout, girls screech, one of the helpers settles some dispute. They pick a child off the floor and he clings like a shipwrecked sailor. Somewhere there's singing. "How much you screwing these parents?"

She laughs too brightly. "You won't pay anything like it. Mates' rates."

Sally's hands are remarkably cold. The fingers that catch my shoulder are dreams of dead men.

Beneath the school there's a basement, with boilers and storage and switchgear. Yellow signs promise high voltage and danger of death. One cupboard has a false back. Stairs behind lead to the second basement. It's cumbersome, but Sally has more to lose.

She wipes her fingers over a keypad and we're in a room of bags and crates. Her stockkeeping could destroy us all.

Sally points to a bag and I dig it out. She's concerned for her manicure. This, in easy pieces, is an AK-47, the simplest, most reliable assault weapon in the world. In every tight spot, this is the workhorse of vengeance.

"Just bang it together," I say. "Make sure it's operational."

She makes a face. "I'd rather you didn't, darling. With the children."

As we're in a room of incendiary matter, that seems somewhat precious. "I won't fire it."

"You think Mr. Nolan would deceive you?"

"Did I say that?"

"Excuse me, Felicity, so much to do. Running a school is such paperwork." She shushes me to the door. "We were rated outstanding at our last inspection. An extremely rich learning environment, they said, where children delight in each new discovery. Isn't that marvellous?" Her hands describe the marvellousness. "They noted our children are confident to take risks in the outdoor area."

"Well that's something."

"This is the environment your daughter or son will benefit from." She beams. "We'll bring out the very best in them. I'm sure you would love to make a donation."

Check messages. Agnieszka has the 'shopping'. I haven't explained to

Mr. Miller what I plan to do or that he must accommodate Archer's bit of fluff. A note from Roc. No words: kissy noises. She'll be at work. I think of her every day in the warmth of bearable distance. But in the same city, it's constantly urgent to see her. But we're businesswomen, we have reputations. Mum and Dad would be proud. If they were still here.

Noise is an invitation. An Audi A5 with the lid down. I'm fonder of Italian jobs, but it's candy apple metallic. Makes a nice boom as it gathers speed. It's so me. Fast as Elie Saab allows, I swish to the lights. The driver's a nonce—cropped brown hair with spits of grey; a balding, boutique combover; balbo beard and fleece like Madchester. He swills about in the most grotesque baggies.

Drape myself over the door. "I like your car."

He gives a look of disposable scorn. "Nice face. But I don't rate flat birds."

I shoot him. I'm not sure how it happens. I must have had hold of my gun. He didn't rate me.

Adrenaline kicks me forward. "C'mon," I squeal. "Give us a go." Get the door open and bounce him into the passenger seat. Fuss and stroke his face, in the desperation of what I've done. My bag lands in the squat back seat. Its contents rattle. The lights change and traffic gets impatient. Slam the gears and eight long seconds from nought to sixty. Pull a left, no clue where I'm going. The engine roars. He jolts around. His seatbelt should be on.

Change down into the next quiet street. Keep up the girlfriend act. He's warm but waxing over. Struggle to clip the belt. He flops about. Can't think it looks natural. Got to lose him before he goes stiff. I make noise, chatting and joking. When you draw attention, you decide what people see. They look at the handsome car, at the pretty girl. He's a muted shape.

Blood leaks, just a little. The rest drains into his arse. When the heart stops, blood sinks low. Gravity conquers all.

It's late in the morning. I'm hauling a corpse. That perv in the bogs had too much invested. But this was impulse. That's not how things get done.

Head to Park Royal. Warehouses and trading estates. Sawn-off roads end in heaps of gravel. This was industrial once. Cars, engineering, Guinness. Thousands of blokes doing work to be proud of. Now it's all opportunity. Here's a nice view of the graves. This was farms when

Acton Cemetery opened. George Lee Temple is buried here, the first British bloke to fly upside down. He died upside down, crashed at Hendon. It's what he would have wanted. When I visited Grandad in the Scrubs he used to tell me this stuff. He knew every tale of old London. Though he liked the touch of a shotgun, him and Dad were reticent on the trigger. They believed you carry a gun to deter curiosity. Shooting was madness to them. It got you the rope or a needless ten on the tariff. My dad would be disappointed in this. A daughter never wants to disappoint her dad.

Consider this landscape. The blank walls of factories. Rough ground with trial pits, dug and flooded. Blocks of student rooms. The Tube and the cemetery. This man beside me attests my presence and, though it seems ridiculous, I wipe his face and hands and search his clothes for hair. Traffic rolls by and the hum of trains and drilling from tower blocks. Coarse suburban wind scrapes my skin.

Drive around, conspicuous in this delightful car. It makes hellish noise between these sheds where they mould shop fittings. Display stands, shelves, mannequins and, delightfully, severed hands, for gloves and rings. I learn this from a shabby display front, like the closed-up shops of the old East End, frozen when elderly owners snuffed it. Old Jewish guys, who beat the fucking Nazis but left some vital part of themselves behind. Those derelict shops no one took over, dusty and peaceful and sad.

Phone to my ear, so it looks like I parked for a call, I nudge him, keep him involved. His phone's blowing up with missed calls. Popular stiff. Mould his waxy hands around the phone and tip him forward. At distance, he might look lost in a game. It's thin subterfuge, but I need to scope my exit.

This loading bay, stacked with shelves. These cameras, wonder who's watching. Get out the car. Walk on this call, swing my hips, pacing and talking. These shelving stacks, a forklift, pallets, chemicals. Any second, someone will tell me: piss off. Every second, it's obvious he's not moving.

The engine makes bastard noise. Let traffic pass. Don't force the manoeuvre. Don't be a distraction. Finally, I'm across the road and reverse into the yard. The car hates reversing. It's heavy and sullen. The man is hardening. Death is orderly change. First the pallor. Then cooling to air temperature. The body goes limp, but then comes rigour. With no energy to grip or release, muscles freeze at the last thing they did. These predictable signs let pathologists make their deductions.

His face is a mask. The rest will follow. I hate him. Hate makes me reckless. Wrap a tissue around my fingers, extract his wallet and prise the phone from his hands. His fingers are baked. Check wrists and neck for medical bracelets. Kiss his neck, to make the move natural. Dead flesh is an ungenerous taste.

He got guts ache. He's groggy. We stopped for him to be sick. You wouldn't spew in a car like this. As I haul his weight, I continue the show: stroke his back, nuzzle his cheek. I can't walk his feet. It's drag and sweat and the hideous scratch of trainers on concrete. I hate him.

Here's a tool vault. A shipping container with a jailhouse door. Can't set him down, can't leave him. He hangs in my arms. Kick his feet apart, lean his head on the wall. I'm seeing tears with the hate and frustration I feel. The tool vault has a pair of locks. I've no time to be clever. Shoot the fuckers. The noise is immense, but the car's running and the factory lads might think it's industrial clatter. Heave open the door on all sorts of delights: rolls of flex, bolt cutters, drills. With a stab that splits my shoulders, I shove him inside. He brings down a rain of spanners.

Two blokes on the ramp, fucking filming the car. Ignore their invitations. Lunge in and gun the engine. It's miles till I breathe.

Stash the motor in an underground lot near Sloane Avenue, bankrolled on charm and a hooky licence. But they're used to rich birds with dud paper.

Walk back to the apartments, swinging a bagful of rifle. I'm behind on work. I wasted bullets. I'll have to show contrition. I'm not built for that.

At the corner of Flood Street a young girl in hi-viz asks do I care about animals. She has grey hair—I presume dyed—a pierced septum and lively eyes, and I think: she'd do for Roc.

"Do you care about animals?"

"What animals?"

She's taken aback. "Animals. Non-human species with rights to their own existence. We're morally obligated to consider their needs."

"I'm vegetarian."

She glares at my Vagabonds.

"Plastic shoes fuck my feet."

"It's so important to live mindfully in the world." Her eyes are extraordinarily clear, enlarged with vast distance. "Animals are not our property to eat, wear or abuse. Their voices go unheard. Don't settle for a world where cruelty is the norm."

"Cruelty," I say, but can't think what to tell her.

"For just a few pounds a month you can change the world."

I make a generous donation with a dead man's credit card.

Filth

Ever the gent, Ralph offers to carry my bag. Give him a girly brush-off. "It's really not heavy."

"We're here to help, Ms. Delamarre."

The proper routine. Gun ready. Search the place in silence. Always a little kick of the heart when I slam back the bathroom door. Only an idiot would hide in the shower. But idiots are lethal. Search under the bed, my dress tight across my back. Check nothing lurks among my pretty things. Scan for bugs. Pay attention to any strong wifi. Check wires, see nothing's added or changed. This is left-brain Flick, painstaking, forensic. It's that other bitch starts trouble.

Shower and fresh clothes. Joseph cashair knit and belted A-line Prada. Redo my eyes. Eyes are key. There is no such thing as too much mascara.

Agnieszka picks up. "This connection is secure?"

"I scrubbed for bugs. I'm on the balcony."

"The signal though."

"The roses grow thick in the Urals comrade."

She lets that by. "I have fulfilment on your request."

Wonder if she says that in bed. Far below, the busy river brings a blue barge, striving against the swell. A toy, beside wide-hulled catamarans gorging the tide. Blue above, black beneath. Two port holes and three wide windows.

"What are your plans for my contribution?"

Get some firmness in my voice. "My client needs ownership of the process." The boat slews, nudged on the wash.

"You will advise your client where I am useful."

"We'll agree your brief."

She laughs. A scant, repulsive sound. "The great Felicity Hepburn is a project manager."

"We're dealing with technical things, love. Malicious intangibles."

"It is not me with the reputation. I must go."

The blue boat turns full about. One oblong window propped open. Press into shadow as a rifle shot hoys over the building. And there was me thinking nobody cared.

The landline rings. Those handsets, so easy to mod as a bomb. Ridiculous, I use my hairbrush to flip the cradle. The ringing stops and I'm alive.

This place sells discretion, so naturally the concierge is apologetic. "Ms. Delamarre. Is everything alright up there? The security team are investigating an external incident."

Down on Chelsea Embankment three bald men in suits point at the river. From this height, they're flummoxed mimes. The boat is at Battersea Bridge. It'll be trash by midnight. "Thank you, Ralph. I was taking my nap. You woke me."

Cab to Westminster Pier and walk the rest. That punt could have put me over. A matter I'll raise with the bloke I'm here to see. Wherever the Met plant themselves, they call New Scotland Yard. This is the new New Scotland Yard. Gives the plods a nice view of the water. I'm glad they kept the sign, though it's repro. Whenever I see that sign, I think of 'The Sweeney'. I would have loved it back then, when coppers were coppers. My dad got scars from the Sweeney. Few nights away. Few slaps. They got their cut. He took me, when I was little, to meet a boozed-up Detective Inspector, had his eye on a bar in Málaga. To hear my dad and this bloke talk business was music. A simpler, more violent time.

The lads with their Heckler & Koch look me over. MP5s. Lightweight, air-cooled—not bad, but old-fashioned. Surprisingly hard to reload in a rush. To avoid tiresome questions, I'm Detective Inspector Lynda Temple. They greet me with a worrying lack of argy-bargy.

I'm too common to get architecture, but this lobby is extraordinarily tacky. I glide to where dollies in blazers gape like I'm cabaret. "Detective Inspector Lynda Temple. To see Superintendent Terence Rotheray. If he's conscious."

She looks just slightly disgusted. "You have an appointment?"

"No, love, but he'll see me." If he doesn't, I'm in shit.

"I'll call his office."

"No, love. Call him."

Of course she's pissed. I'd be pissed if someone told me my job. But I matter more than she does. She makes the call, staring at me. She says to wait on the couch.

The old New Scotland Yard was scuzzy and tired. It suited the people who worked there. This new gaff has a ceiling like mushroom gills, shiny wood floor, leather benches. Late afternoon, it's busy with blokes in cheap suits and women in structured jackets. Coppers, civil servants, spooks. Her, in the button-down and Ralph Lauren trousers, she's a spook. Bet money on it. They asked me, long ago. But I didn't fancy the terms and conditions.

An angry-seeming woman chews her way to the desk, has a word, then power-walks towards me. Black blazer and slims: old school Topshop. Stack heels to give her a lift.

"Detective Inspector Temple?" Her voice a steak knife.

I stand, to be taller than her. "You are?"

"Detective Inspector Mahvash Mirza."

"Moon-like beauty. Mahvash. Urdu, I think."

"You'll excuse me," she says, with bracing coldness. "I do not know the meaning of yours."

"Lynda? It's German for snake."

My XD sets off the machine and a rather concerned young constable asks me into his backroom. D.I. Mirza says, "You are armed response? I didn't know you are armed response," like that makes sense.

"I'm a specialist."

"This isn't a Glock," the young man observes, accurately.

"It's an old issue Springfield. I like to stick with what I know."

This perturbs them. "May I see your warrant card?" Mirza studies the unflattering picture, the hologram, the Commissioner's autograph. "Are you based here?" she asks, obtusely.

"No. I'm a specialist."

"What's your speciality?" asks the young man.

"'Specialism', love. I'm not a circus act." A reckless passion to empty clip after clip into their useless bodies expresses through how my fingers tighten.

"I'm Superintendent Rotheray's assistant." Her voice a tight, sharp pain. "You will understand he has much to deal with."

Ignoring the irony—she can't see it, so it's futile to point it out—I'm keen to stay sunny, to get what I want. "Does Terry know I'm here?"

She seems frustrated. "I triage such requests."

The gun is heavy in my pocket. My hands are hot. "Really, I'm here to see Terry."

"For what reason?"

"Operational. Like your moon-like beauty."

The misnamed 'scenic lifts' travel through a glass void, to give snippets of coppers doing their mystic best. Police have a natural way of arranging themselves. Detectives sit in raucous teams. Uniforms perch around open space. The big dogs get an office. Changing the building won't change nature.

Mirza says to wait while she updates Rotheray. This meaningless language gets on my tits. I fume in a scrappy playpen with only a secretary to scowl at. She has earbuds and ignores me, clearly not thinking I might ventilate her brain. This lack of respect for unseen risk irks me. In the jungle there's snakes, even when you can't see them.

Check my phone. No bodies found. Of course they've been found, with steps taken to manage the noise. So Mirza must know who I am. She's prepping Rotheray while I sit here, hating some girl in earbuds. So I crash Rotheray's office.

Superintendent Terence Rotheray is a large, uncoordinated man. Bits of his body react to my arrival in different ways. His big head with its random coat of hair jerks up while his chin vibrates. His hands make a brief surrender, then curl like dead flowers. Some impulse propels him to stand, but he can't make it.

Mirza, hands clasped on his desk, swivels round, angry and pleased. My impatience proves whatever she said about me. Outside, spring light is failing.

"Detective Inspector Temple." He chews each word like a nettle. "I'm not sure I said 'come in'. Did I say 'come in'?" he asks the moon beauty.

"I would have noticed if you said that. In a private conversation."

Any woman who thinks she can out-bitch me gets ruined. "You discuss fellow officers, ahead of a private meeting you're not involved in?"

"I'm Superintendent Rotheray's assistant."

"Tea, love. Splash of milk. No sugar."

Rotheray gets diplomatic. "Thank you, Mahvash. Perhaps Sienna could get us tea?"

"We need to review budget forecasts…"

"Ask Sienna for time tomorrow. Many thanks, Mahvash."

I watch the door close behind her. "Sienna? That mitten out there?"

He raises his meaty hands. "It's what parents do." Among loose skin around his eyes, shrewdness coalesces. "You're not supposed to use that card to get in here. It was issued for a purpose. Which expired."

I don't want him pissed, so I warm up the smile. "I've had a teensy bit of a trying day. I'm here for reassurance."

"Your ego gone fragile in the Spanish sun?"

"Catalunya, Terrance. It's another country."

"Of course, you're political now."

"I was taking the air this afternoon…"

"At that Chelsea gaff with the global trash?"

"It has gone down a bit. Anyhow, Terrance. I'm on the balcony and someone picks me up with a high velocity rifle. On the Thames. On a bloody barge. Did that cross your radar?"

For him, shrugging is all upper body. His shoulders vibrate for some time. "A loud bang on a busy day. Local police may have had reports. I'm sure they were diligent."

"It's personal."

"You know your friends. And what's this about Declan Nolan?" He scowls at the door. "Yeah?"

The girl from the outer office slops in mugs of tea. The one she gives Rotheray has the old gag: 'Sometimes there's justice. Sometimes there's just us.' Mine says 'Stolen from Scotland Yard'.

"Sienna's such a pretty name," I say, and she gives me a foul look. "There's something else, Terrance…"

"Declan Nolan."

I tweak my skirt.

"I don't think we were aware you planned to visit Declan Nolan. Just like we weren't aware you were coming to England. You remember, Felicity, there are terms and conditions."

Of course he knows: the boys on the bus, the perv in the bog, the stiff in the shed. I scramble after confidence that, once, was automatic. "I'm sure you've had a full report from Detective Sergeant Chloe Bell. When I see her on Friday, I'll tell her she did a good job."

For a second, he's baffled. "See her on Friday?"

"I think she's planning sapphic manoeuvres."

"She'll get a treat then." He scowls at his tea. "It's not all forgive and forget. Paddies, American Paddies, you know how serious they take things. What's your business with Nolan?"

"Nostalgia, Terrance."

But I underestimate his frustration. "You are supposed to tell us when you visit the United Kingdom. We need to know because you cause problems. You been here three days and it's carnage."

"I was provoked."

He sucks a breath. "I had to call favours. Not once. Not twice. I could have a judge remand you within the hour. And you won't get the easy ride to Broadmoor. So what's your offer, Felicity?"

My arse will be stone cold before I go inside. "I come here, Terrance, because someone took a shot at me in a civilian setting. I'm sure the Commissioner won't enjoy having to answer why nothing was done about that."

"Of course. You're the victim. If only people would let you get on with your mayhem." When he leans across the desk, the weather changes. "Why are you here?"

I don't feel so bright. "My client expects discretion."

"You silly tart."

"Since you put me under duress. I'm contracted to one of London's most respected businessmen. His communications are compromised. I've put in place human and autonomous mechanisms to flush the bastards."

"This gentleman has a name?"

It's not grassing. It's not like Rotheray will kick doors in. "Mr. Miller, if you must know."

Even without conscious movement, bits of Rotheray twitch and shimmer. "The old darling. Industrial espionage? He needs a killer to sort that?"

I'm offended. "I solve problems, Terrance. I have a diverse skillset."

"What's Nolan? Your consultant?"

"We had dealings, the Croydon business, you know this. He's sound on covert."

Rotheray's laugh is seal clubbing. "You met him? He couldn't do covert with zombies. CIA couldn't sober him up for interrogation. You know what prudes they are. The mystery of the Provos' money is his legacy to us. D.S. Bell is all over his financials. She's a handy piece. She got your number. So, really, why see him?"

"I network."

"With people you hate?"

"Especially."

"And you saw Sally Rainbow."

"I was checking her curriculum. I'm hoping for a happy event."

He squints at me. "Where will you get time?"

"I'm settled."

"Except, Felicity, right now, you're on my manor. Causing upset."

"Someone tried to kill me on your manor."

"I'll tell you who's going to kill you. You. Your vanity and temper will kill you. How long is this do with dear Mr. Miller?"

"I can't say. I need to nail what's happening." He thinks he's smart. He's all warrant card. "Believe I want to get back to Barcelona. People there don't take pot shots."

"Safe place to raise your kids."

"Fuck off."

He shakes his head, an elaborate collision of muscles. "Felicity. You were born in the wrong body."

My fingers itch.

"You're an intellectual in the skin of a thug. And that's why you can do a favour for your old friends the filth. You don't have to. Just like we don't have to clean up your little accidents. Does the name Rashad Jazin mean anything?"

"Rashad. Arabic: good judgement."

"You're worth twice what anyone pays." He stretches to one of his filing cabinets. They keep serious stuff on paper. He sets an old school manila in front of me. "You can follow along in the book. Mr. Jazin works through the embassy of one of our favoured allies. He enjoys semi-official status as a dealmaker. Trade, investment, getting people together. D.S. Bell reckons he's raking it, all over. He represents one of our most lucrative markets for weapons."

There's accounts, surveillance dockets. Chloe's the conscientious type.

"Of course the spooks are on this. But they have their own agenda. Pest control, know what I mean?"

Pictures of a handsome man, profusely pleased with himself. Well-cut suits, crisp shirts, shades. They always wear shades. "You want him disrupted?"

"I'm not telling you how to do it. MI5 love this kiddie. Strong on law and order, is Mr. Jazin." As he leans in, his breath smells of, unmistakably, Vanity Rocks. Wonder whose ear he's nibbling. "But if you have one of your accidents…" He gives it the papal hands.

I told myself, no more of their dirty deeds. "I'm on my own?"

"You never was a team player."

Excitement. Not the kind I like. "And if I say no?"

He presses his wrists together.

"Bastard."

"Actions have consequences. Even for beautiful women."

There's a nice hotel round the block. The doorman hustles to usher me in and I'm shown to a gorgeously gaudy lounge where badly dressed tourists struggle with pyramids of dinky sandwiches—salmon and ham and other dead souls. A squat little gent offers cake to a smart-looking blonde. Black suit—American ready-to-wear. Tahari maybe. I had one of his Madison jackets. I don't know where half my clothes have gone. She has a sharp chin and quick fingers, and I think: she'd do for Roc. Old girls in respectable prints enjoy a sesh with the bubbles. And always, in places like this, those solitary geezers in pinstripes who look like they've been here since the fall of Singapore.

If I'd taken a different path in life, if such a thing could be imagined, I could see myself run one of those dining clubs for successful women. Hosting celebrity auctions, all for the kids. Spend half my life in venues like this, raising funds for the unlucky. Maybe get a gong out of it, bump fists with royalty. "Oh yes," I'd say, "in the Blitz, the late Queen Mother, god rest her, she visited my Grandma's house down the old East End." That's true, and the Queen Mum got away with her pearls. She told my Grandma they were paste, on account of the war. But she knew the Hepburns.

A tall lad in a flunky suit asks if I'm ready. Energy passes between us, swift and unmistakeable. "You have Darjeeling?"

In the strip-lit stockroom it's hard and fast. He has my skirt up and knickers down without words. Bends me over a shelf and I shake with the rush. When his fingers close over my mouth I taste icing sugar. He thumbs my foreskin over the glans the most careless way. He jerks and I spunk on the shortbread.

He works me. Grips my buttocks. Slides me over his cock. It spatters right up. I collapse on the shelf, legs shaking. "I love you, I love you, I love you."

Enjoy tea and cake in soaking knickers. Skirt hitched so it doesn't stain. I leave a puddle on the chair. I don't pay.

Competence

Too short notice to see Mr. Miller so I make do with tie-less Tony. We meet in the bar of a slab hotel in Park Lane. Deeply vulgar, which is why he chose it. Best cover for private business is the minted, bovine crowd.

We drink gin and he calls me Ms. Hepburn. We share chargrilled vegetables with hummus. He asks how work is going.

"Excellent question, Tony. I've arranged for a top counter-intelligence specialist to install detection equipment at the office and provide personal anti-surveillance kit to you and your colleagues. My specialist is based on site, to monitor traffic and understand the parameters of disruption."

He's polite but puzzled. "I thought you were the specialist, Ms. Hepburn?"

Smile like I'm pleased about something. "The expertise I've brought in is technical. Spectrum analysis, anomalies and so forth. I will deploy in the field, for aggressive pursuit. That's my value-added."

"You surmise, an organised intrusion?"

Tony's good-looking. His lips dainty. But I'm too old to fuck men older than me. "A working hypothesis, Tony. The focus of our friend's affairs makes it likely this is corporate. Testing the water, maybe. Ahead of stronger interventions."

"You make it sound like we're being played."

"It's possible our friend isn't the ultimate target. I need to consider all angles."

"Where's Freddie on your Gantt chart?"

I blush, because I love a Gantt chart. I'd like Freddie out the picture. I don't fancy a GCHQ—specially a busted one—checking my homework. "Our friend's staffing is not in scope."

Tony runs a delicate finger round his glass. "Do you think the bumbling duffer is an act?"

This is dangerous. Outfits have hierarchy. In any hierarchy are people who matter, even if their work is shit. "I don't make snap judgements."

He cracks a grin. "I'm aware of your work, Ms. Hepburn. You're the queen of snap judgements." Laughing, he covers my hand with his.

"Our friend puts a great deal of trust in your expertise." He fixes his lips to mine. He tastes of gin and olives.

I respond because I wouldn't let a man hang. There's empty bedrooms above us. But he's older than me. "Tony. This is business, remember?" Pet his hand, as one does a bed-bound aunt.

Reluctant, he disengages. "Another night." It's not a question.

Agnieszka doesn't meet anywhere normal. She drags me to this shopping centre at Stratford. A place with more cameras than a streamer's bedroom.

Back home I'm highly domestic. Shop in the market, make bean stew, wash the walls, my hair tied in a scarf. Give tourists directions in broken English. But now I'm spinning along the Embankment in a red blizzard of noise. Men shout the menu of sex. Long ago, I learned to manage men, to shape and love them. Let me get put down by a shooter better than me, while I'm all this.

Bag on my shoulder and sex in my hips I hit the casino. The casinos of the Côte d'Azur are classier than Monte. I got done by a particularly skilled sommelier in Cannes. But this is Stratford. The motorway carvery of casinos. Machines and streaming. No live games, except the nuts in the poker room. Roulette is a fine occupation, but not with digital balls. I glide, dismayed at such sparse glamour. And there's Agnieszka at a gaming terminal, joining a coup of baccarat, apparently live at some waterfront place in Newcastle. I been there once. Them Geordies are robust. I wait till she loses, then sidle over. "The roses bleed in the snow of the Urals."

"You are lucky." She taps the chrome of the terminal. "I see you reflected. Otherwise you would be bleeding."

"You know even dead people find punto banco boring."

"It is high risk. I like that." She's brushed her white-blonde hair and now it has life of its own. Her eyes are horribly clean. Her smooth, well-tempered skin hasn't taken much product. We go upstairs to what claims to be East London's top bar, though I doubt it. She stabs her fingers around the fun-seeking crowd. "Toy people," she says. "No form." She has the smooth assurance of a murderous robot.

We sit on the terrace. A sharp and breezy night. Punters huddle under patio heaters, talking shit about gambling. We must look like we're on a date.

With no malice, she says, "Why do you think I want to help your Mr. Miller?"

"Someone shot at me today," I say pleasantly. "In Chelsea."

Her face gives nothing but the circuits are whirring. "Many people hate you. Now you're in London they will chance their arm." She drops the lingo like the name of some artificial sweetener.

"So it's my fault?"

"Your enemies would kill you in plain sight, to prove it is done."

The view is apartment blocks for the maxed and socially useless. Who's watching at those windows? "Here's to fame."

She seems confused. "In our business we advise clients on the risks they are facing. Usually they act to manage those risks."

"Are you doing Toby Archer?"

"Perhaps we can discuss professional matters?"

Clink my glass onto hers. "I thought we were."

"I am not interested in you sexually." She's deadpan. "I understand many people are."

"Many men."

"Of course." She necks her scotch. "You are a woman."

This is pissing on ice. "I met one of Mr. Miller's lieutenants tonight. He's keen you install the stuff and train the troops. I talked you up as an expert."

"I am an expert."

Inspection reveals no irony in her flat, blameless face. To avoid those irritating eyes I check the bar. Brentwood and Chelmsford, here for a laugh and a snog. The boys have slick shirts and pressed trousers because it's a night out. The girls are cocktail numbers and sparkly jackets. That cerise fake Armani, I'd wear that. Who is this Polish tart slagging them off? "What I'm saying is, you don't work for Archer on this job."

"You are paying me?"

That cocky habit. "I have contingency. And I'm sure Toby won't stop paying you because he has to buy a temp a week or two."

"You would not be in London so long. You would be dead."

The method is obvious. A little something from Daddy's spooks. "Get the drinks in. I'm going for a Geoff."

These toilets are all gloss. I empty out, clean up and stare at the stiletto-scarred floor. Somewhere, I know how to manage the next few days. I'm not conscious of it yet. As a young girl I'd end a life and that was my success. Paid to kill, you can't fail a little bit. Now the well-placed bullet gives way to more quality metrics.

The dryer is low on the wall. I bend to it. It makes a needless amount of noise.

Choke. My head wrenched back. Can't breathe. Sharp, blinding rage. Claw my throat. Cutting. Cutting me. Fight for air. Shove my elbow in her gut. She's solid. Pain rips my arm. Head yanked up. See the mirror. She got a wire round my throat. Her knuckles white. My skin red. She's blank. Doing business. Jab her gut. Punch her cunt. She falters. Smack a blizzard of pain at her. She slacks the wire. I spin. Punch her into the wall. Crack. Her skull meets the tiles. Shakes her head like a cartoon. I touch my gun. A sequin sheath walks in. Looks at us like we're mad. I snatch the wire. Launch Agnieszka at the door. "'Scuse us. Lovers' tiff."

Stood on poxy gravel behind the shopping centre. My throat's bruised. I'm coughing oysters. Agnieszka holds her head. She has blood in her hair but won't let me clean it. "You could have finished anyone else."

"I should have snapped your neck."

Put an arm round her shoulder. She elbows me away. "Is this a thing, you trying to kill me?"

She's groggy. I hold her, till she punches me. "I will kill you." She spits a juicy wad. A ruby in streetlights.

This ambition is commendable. But she must grasp I matter more. "Early start at Mr. Miller's tomorrow."

She stares like I'm in a cage without a label. "You think I will do that?"

"Even I can't be in two places at once. And you're the expert. I'll take you home."

"No." She's horrified.

"I need you home safe because I need you to work."

"You call me zero-six-hundred. I say where to meet."

"Did you take a shot at me with a big gun?"

"You have many enemies."

Watch her to the edge of the light. The blood, the pain, the shame: it's a handsome deceit.

Drive to Bow Creek. The artsy wasteland of Trinity Buoy Wharf. Walk out on the pontoon. Up and down the river, lights shine. Taste the sea on the wind. Boats go by: canned parties—people fling their limbs to music I can't hear. Like they're being delivered to some unspeakable purpose. I have no fears and no regrets. I'm a singularity. In this gleaming swill of lights and water, my dead come and go. Stricken faces. Angry last words. I wait their vengeance. Anyone who doesn't expect to die deserves to.

By the time I stash the car and walk to Chelsea it's one in the morning. The same river. But here, mansion blocks and bridges reflect a faint gentility, old and hand-me-down. Draw aim on the Peace Pagoda across the water. To feel the kick. Hear the shot. It's warm milk and a blanket.

The night manager's heritage may be Pakistan. Black hair, cut close, neat beard, stern brow. He smiles with his tongue on his top teeth. With no words, I straighten his tie. He catches my hand. We go in the back room and it's simple and fun. I walk to the penthouse. Eighteen floors. My legs in bits but I need it.

Call Agnieszka before six. She's hoarse, like a night hard smoking. That flatness to her, it's appealing. But Mr. Miller's an old-school woofter; he equates competence with vigour. Black coffee, warm pastry, and drive up to Eversholt Street. She's outside a bankrupt escape room. The bailiff notice flaps on the breeze.

Agnieszka doesn't like this car. "Your statement, yes? Your signal for attention?"

"I deserve nice things."

"It is German."

Gun the engine through streets lively with morning. It's not eight o'clock when we arrive. While his doughboys valet the car, we're delivered to Tony's presence. Calculatedly casual in a loose Turnbull and linen kecks. Myself, I'm immaculate in a high collar monochrome Hermès, bare legs and tan Jacquemus knee-highs. A high collar, thanks to madam. She's a black fake Chanel and bargain bin courts. Unremittingly prêt-à-porter.

Tony kisses her hand and tells her she's charming in French, which is crackers. She acquiesces to this nonsense. It's a grubby performance. "This is Agnieszka," I beam. "She's skilled in counter-surveillance and grey man tactics."

"I find it hard to believe Agnieszka could grey man."

She stirs. "In the field I blend to my environment."

Tony wants to do her. Awkward, as I turned him down. If she turns him down—and likely she would—this crucial link will be ill-disposed to the both of us. I bring the chat to equipment. Agnieszka talks the talk with reassuring, excessive detail. Till Tony says, "You should meet Freddie."

Dexter blinks before shaking hands with her. Smitten and incapable, his Yorkshire vowels maraud the room. Yet beyond that painful sexual flush, his reaction to Agnieszka is instructive. He treats me as a knowledgeable but uninvolved bit of fluff. He responds to her as someone in the business. While they trade jargon, Tony and me share looks. He's elegantly seething. "Certificate fraud." Say it loud, but Freddie doesn't stop. "Fraudulent contact from real addresses."

They look at me. Agnieszka's face messy with annoyance.

Tony considers the pair of us. "I'm not aware that issue has been explored. But it's a good point. I'll have the team check client feedback. If no one has raised a red flag, our adversary's experiment may have been successful. You give us a lot to reflect on, Ms. Hepburn."

The noise in Agnieszka's throat is angry machinery.

Her and Freddie set up the equipment. I excuse myself on the alibi of another line of inquiry. Tony walks me to the basement. He likes the motor and I take him for a spin.

By now the morning's established. Mummies and nannies manoeuvre big cars filled with kids and organic veg. Every girl on the street totes a yoga mat. Holland Park feels secure in its affluence. With charm and persuasion I could get a gaff round here. The heart-stopping, stylish woman who talks so amusingly common. But my man won't leave Catalunya. And here, I'm a target.

Tony's hand slips under my Hermès. "I'll drop you here," I say. "Things to do."

His fingers are in my Etam. "I want to fuck you."

"Then dress right."

"What?"

"How would you strap my hands, if you don't wear a tie?"

"My belt."

"Amateur." Cuff his arm away. "Belt for ankles. Tie for wrists."

He leans on my shoulder. "I'm getting coffee. Will you join me?"

Nudge him to the kerb. "Don't try it with Agnieszka. She'll have your throat."

Proximity

A caff with yellow walls and women breastfeeding. A local headline: popular bloke killed in a shed at Park Royal. Industrial accident. That's a warning. Rotheray wants results.

Over a tall latte I track Rashad Jazin. He's everywhere: conferences, trade shows, grinning at expat parties. A welcome, proactive man. He signs opinion pieces in big-word softbacks. Praising stability, growth, reciprocity—something for something in a connected world. Here's a profile in one of the glossies. 'Business sheikh' they call him. 'Business sheikh invites us to his desert hideaway'. Heavy hints the place has a 'woman's touch' but no women to be seen. He speaks of relaxing with family and friends, also not pictured. In sugary text he says London is: 'Buzzy with hot energy.' Without the shades, his eyes are sharp and direct. Eyes that say who lives and dies. Comfortable in the West, he never mentions religion. The type who says, 'I'm a simple businessman'. There's less-flattering stuff on lefty sites. The strict contingent ain't fond of him neither. He must have a goon army, to sleep nights.

The waitress likes my Hermès. She hasn't seen this print before. It's a Paris exclusive, part-payment on my last job. Tell her it was a lucky find on a Eurostar shopping binge. She's got a couple of pieces, bought with grandma's legacy. When you're poor, she says, you buy good stuff, not tat. I leave a ridiculous tip.

Drive up Queensway, past the memorial to Saint Diana of Versace. Us Cockneys love the royals and she could swish a tall dress like few others. That was one of the nastiest set-ups I seen in this business. We all wanted the bloke who cut the brakes.

Stop for a dekko at this embassy where Jazin has no solid job. An unimpressive white plaster townhouse. I'm already matched and scrutinised. A big worsted comes out of nowhere. His deep voice asks do I need help.

"Sorry," I simper. "I'm trying to find Paddington Basin. I think I took a wrong turn. I looked on my phone but..." A blonde couldn't be more helpless.

He's not impressed. Strong men don't like dumb girls. With rigorous good manners he directs me to Praed Street. Try to peek round him, but all I get is limewash and chandeliers. He gives a slight bow and goes back inside. As the door swings, there's voices.

I call an acquaintance in Barcelona, a gentleman best unnamed. It's lunchtime in my gorgeous city. His wife chivvies him to the table. A beautiful woman with wine-dark eyes, she always has a kind word for my figure. Her husband's a dangerous man with fine manners. Though the call's encrypted I don't say much. Just ask where in London to meet friends. He says, "Friends from where?" in Arabic and laughs.

"Is it that obvious?" In Català, because my Arabic doesn't stretch to sarcasm.

"Good luck with it," he says in careful English. Then in Arabic, "Try the Tihamah Lounge." His wife shouts that the greens are wilting. He laughs again.

It's too early for any 'lounge', so I drive up Hampstead to work the engine. A car like this needs distance. Pick up a salad and drive to Highgate Cemetery. Sit on Tom Sayers' dog to eat lunch. The stone hound has a groove to its back that cradles my cheeks exactly. Tom Sayers was a fighting man. Short and slight, he took down much bigger fighters. King of a lucrative trade, he died of TB, as poor people do. His funeral was a riot. The lower orders smashed up graves and started fires. My grandad told me his grandad was there, picking pockets with everyone drunk.

Take a piss up the obelisk and work my calves on the hill to Highgate Village. A bric-à-brac place, middle-aged posh, decked around estate agents' windows. There's a nice five bed for ten million I wouldn't mind a look at. But they'll want paperwork and that gets me irritable. By now, whoever's tracking me is vexed with dicking about.

Walk down to what was once St. Pelagia's Home for Destitute Girls, where nuns forced young women to give up their babies. Which is funny because my Auntie May said the Christian god was the god of love. Pop in the toilets at Lauderdale House but no one's around. It's a fine day and my bare legs gleam. But every sporting gent is elsewhere. Have a smoke walking back. Though Miquel's not here, I ration the tar. He cares about me. That's what I struggle with.

Scan the car for bugs. Loose plugs. Resealed connections. Anything less clean or less dirty. If I had time, I'd strip it. I'm good with my hands. It's a family thing. Roc built her motorbike from bits online. I worry about her riding in traffic. Check underneath. A simple explosive might not scan, if there's no electronics. A plunger, jelly, bits from a watch for the balance. Old school. There's enough want to kill me.

Cruise into the City. Leave the car in the underground lot at Queen Victoria Street. Catch a bus to Westminster. These tourists had a great day buying crap. There's nice-looking lads littered about and I do some leg-crossing. One kid tries so hard not to stare, bless him. The sun's long gone and glorious night opens out. Coming down the Strand to Trafalgar Square it's so much a postcard, just needs a few pearlies having a knees up.

Get off at the Banqueting House. Cut through St. James's Park. Couples stroll round the lake, fingers in each other's waistbands. Old boys scratch on benches where they'll drink and sleep tonight. Mums steer their kids to Charing Cross after a day out in town. It's ordinary and worthwhile. And me, with deadly eyes. That bloke on the bridge: even in this light, I could have one in his head. Tip him into the water, propelling a cloud of dozy geese. His body rolling with impact and slick with bird shit. It's hard to find reasons not to.

Cross The Mall. Green Park is stripped, functional. The lights of Mayfair reach through the trees. If I'd taken a different path in life, if such a thing could be imagined, I might have married some noble gent. Lady Felicity. I'd love that. A hideous country pile and Mayfair town house. Wear pearls and tight, well-ordered dresses. Host gala lunches and shag like a polecat. A rewarding life. But I have a vocation.

The Tihamah Lounge is handy for Savile Row, and Chanel for the mistress. Miquel gets amusingly socialist, but Coco was bona fide working class. This Lounge is five-storey Georgian. Three steps up to the double doors. Black doors, shut tight. Lumpen Greek portico. Bonsai hedges in iron planters. 'The Tihamah Lounge' on a brass plaque like an upscale gynaecologist. Through dense net curtains, the twinkle of electric chandeliers.

"Good evening. Could you open the door please, sir?"

"Who are you?"

Detective Inspector Lynda Temple's warrant card gets pressed to the camera.

"What's this about?" His tone suggests he doesn't need manners with flatfoots.

I don't know posh Arabic. I can order a meal and get a bloke's thawb off. Hoping I get the syntax right, I say in the language of kings, "Don't you think it looks odd, me stood here?"

The door opens on a tall, gaunt man with a tight cropped beard. A slim grey suit, bespoke I reckon. Grandad-collar shirt. No tie. That means something with this lot.

I like a man taller than me but he's too tall. Needless height, emphasised by his lean frame. He's not impressed with what he sees.

"Thank you, sir. Do you mind if I step in?" The warrant card gleams between my fingers.

"What is the purpose of this?"

"I have news." I feel the rush of an unsupported lie. "A gentleman. He might be here."

The building is quiet. These places have thick walls. Warrens of rooms no sound escapes. "You are armed?"

Show him my gun.

"This is not a police gun."

"Depends what police you mean."

His look says that was rash.

A pair of young men drift through the hall—suits, open-neck shirts. They stare.

As though activated by a sudden order, the doorman says, "We can talk in the conference room."

The décor is what I expect: cream paint; plain, expensive wallpaper; dado rails; console tables dripping flowers. Old prints of sand dunes, date palms, and a fort with a ragged French flag. A nice painting of the Great Mosque of Damascus at sunset, yellow stones and long shadows.

Firm, without fuss, I'm brought to the conference room. A dark-panelled space. Long table and stiff chairs. Equipment: no lights or motors running, but I can't know it's switched off. A spider phone squats on the table. He sees my suspicion. "We are serious about security." He gestures me to sit. "Any trouble is dealt with."

It's a fraught and fractious game. That I've been let in is curious. Unless my friend lied, to get me killed. "And you are?"

He takes a moment to think. "Mehdi." With a slight bow.

"Rightly guided."

"It is a popular name."

"You understand." I clasp my knee to look earnest. "This is a sensitive matter."

"There are police we work with. You are not one of those police. Why are you here, Detective Inspector…"

"Temple."

"Indeed."

"I have news…"

"No. No." He shakes an elegant finger. "You told me you have news for someone you think might be here. I am saying: I do not believe that. Try again."

That he knows who I am flickers like fire. "I have reason to think your friend's life is in danger."

Mehdi reaches into his neatly-stitched jacket. His hand fills with a SIG Sauer P320. "You see this, Detective Inspector? A nice gun, would you say?"

"The US army thinks so. And popular in France, I believe."

"I find it graceful. Especially with the bronze grip, do you see?"

"Very nice."

"The grip." He points at the brassy handle. "You understand, I am just showing you this gun."

"It's a nice gun."

"It is a nice gun. It has front and back slide serrations. The three-dot night sight is steel."

"How's the reset?"

"Smooth. Low recoil."

"Sounds good."

He flips it around. The snout finds my chest. "And while I show you this nice gun, you might have the courtesy to tell me the truth."

Give it wide eyes. "Would I deceive you?"

"I do not know, Detective Inspector. The police have objectives. We all do. This 'friend' who is in such danger. Will you tell me or shall I guess?"

"I'm concerned for his safety."

"This is a recent thing?"

"People want him dead." This video kit. Why plant me here if no one's watching?

"Detective Inspector. He has more enemies than hairs on your head. Another here or there is no matter."

"These are powerful people."

The gun pirouettes. "Your reach is small. Any disruption is already in our sights."

Lean forward, hair over one eye. "Give me the comfort of warning him."

"Comfort? That is good."

"You can't ignore what I say."

"Why should this thing matter more than any other thing?"

Behind this man stand men with shorter tempers. "Don't you think it might be prudent to investigate?"

He smiles. "Have I told you about my gun?"

I get escorted outside. A drunk grabs me and I break his wrist.

Three in the morning. A sound, before waking. Traffic and sirens, in the deep hours. So quiet I hear my blood.

Draw my gun from under the pillow. Slide out of bed. Bare feet make no sound. I have excellent vision. Eyes are key. Curtains frame a slash of sky, to warn of suspect lights. Through the gap, faint echoes of ship lamps below. Nudge the balcony door. Ease back the handle. Cold air gathers me like an old friend. Water sighs and glistens. A girl's wicked laugh travels further than she'll know.

Like some marine creature, the hook shivers, testing the ledge. A clawed beast, mauling cement. Someone urgent, to climb so high in plain sight. How flattered I am. Take aim as the head appears. My finger a hair's breadth decision. "What in fuck?"

Agnieszka's eyes are glittering stars. "Do it. I will make a spectacular fall." Her pale fingers crest the ledge.

"Fuckwit."

She has no concern for soft spots, an indifference I'm forced to admire. She drags herself over the ledge—whole body, propelled by her arms. All in black, hair siloed in a beanie. She hides exhaustion well.

She hauls in the rope and I hit the light. Her eyes constrict without blinking.

"You have vodka?" She handles the bottle of Grey Goose with disgust.

"Les français sont nos amis."

"Poland is a better friend." She pours big measures. "Freddie Dexter is a man of unexpected skill."

"He didn't feel you up?"

She scowls. "They are all homosexual. You know that."

"I had my suspicions."

"You think Dexter is some buffoon, marched out of GCHQ for technical blunders. I am not surprised if he still works there."

"You reckon?"

"Stop being foolish. I have pictures on microfilm."

"Microfilm?"

"In my vagina."

"Pop it out, love. You're at no risk from me."

"You are distasteful." She flings a look over her shoulder. "And, still, you do not kill me."

While she winkles out the footage in the bog, I swap my teal velour David Nieper nightdress for yesterday's clothes. The safe at the back of the wardrobe is a regular armoury, with the knife I took off that fascist twerp, the cheese wire Agnieszka tried on my head, and this AK, oiled and assembled. It's a while since I had such mischief. "Here's something you might find amusing." I pose with the AK rocked on my shoulder.

"The magazine is empty. And the gun is old."

Punchable and adorable. "Deduction, Sherlock."

"It is Serbian. The sights are iron. Now, look at this." A thin metal cannister glistens between her fingers. She cracks it apart and out slips the tight-wound spool.

Copy her solemn stance as she carefully unrolls the film and sets her phone camera to enlarge.

Necking a big lick of vodka, she says, "At first, I think Dexter is stupid. A man who has served should not work for crooks."

"I thought he'd been rash with his winkle."

"Well, you are the expert I think. Dexter showed me Mr. Miller's communications room."

"And you had your tiny camera."

She gives me an icy look. "Do you work without your gun?"

I make some sulky noise.

"You see, here and here, the age of Mr. Miller's equipment. These are his servers, his load balancer. I ask basic questions in my foreign voice and Freddie Dexter is very patient."

"Did you ask about SSL certificates?"

That hiss of a habitual angry cat. "Obviously I probed authentication. Dexter has patched holes where data might spew. That is no great skill."

Four a.m. A sense of day emerging. I want to go out. Find a man. I'm ablaze with potential. But I must do this. Not rich enough to be free. Not secure enough to leave the field.

"My suspicion was watching him monitor traffic." Her voice is ordered, precise. Yet there's excitement. How clever she is. "I make pretty moves to engage him."

"That's what I do."

"He explains and I take pictures. Now, here." Her fingers prise a scrap of screen, split horizontal. The upper pane is a crawl of timestamps, sources, status of every device on the network. The lower pane has global utilisation, IP addresses by bytes consumed, traffic speed, regional load. This data isn't surprising. Mr. Miller deals mostly in Europe: there's pins in all the expected cities. Bit of action on the US East Coast—his nephews and ex-lovers. A blip in the Caymans, most like his retirement fund. "I ask Dexter," Agnieszka flips her phone around, "what is this?"

A pin transacting from an empty slice of the Middle East. "You know where that is?"

"The country, yes. It is hard to be more exact."

"Business sheikh invites us to his desert hideaway. Why not suppress the signal? Are they dumb?"

She empties the bottle. "An authorised user. Dexter shows me times this user connects. The pattern is opaque but Dexter is persistent. These logins correspond to certain events." A flush to her snowy cheeks. This is how she gets off. "Dexter's database records these events. Dates, locations, participants. These details come from inside."

"Spooks?"

"This meeting." She stretches the image. "This format, the abbreviations. This is an internal document."

"So Dexter's still on the inside."

She gives a pert look. "What better cover for a spy than to be an ex-spy?"

A barge horn sounds, and we turn to the window. She tips back the curtain, a signal to someone. "In Warsaw you hear boats make their way in the mist. That voice bounces from walls of old apartments. From place to place they take cargo. I would push my toy boats on blue ribbon, from place to place in my head." She flexes on tiptoe, like she might run to the river. How thorough they've been with her.

Because I'm a bitch for big gestures, I uncoil the rope. Eighteen storeys of rope is a good weight. My biceps twitch with pleasure.

Looking over the ledge, I see how she positioned herself to scale between windows. Audacity is admirable. "Let's go the pretty way." The rope hits the wall with a wet smack.

She stands close. She smells of nylon. "You cannot climb in that dress."

"I'm a girly girl." I unclip the grappling hook, measure twelve arm-spans down the rope, loop six coils over-shoulder and under-arm. She watches with the disinterest of a cat. There's no carabiners or quickdraws or harness, so my weight will hang off my breastbone. But this is business.

She loops six coils over-shoulder and under-arm. If one falls, we both fall.

She reattaches the hook and I play down the rope. Can't see where it lands. We'll know when we get there.

Inelegant, I dip one leg over the ledge. The climbing I do is swift getaways from unglamorous situations. Alone, where I can indulge apprehension. As I move, she moves, drawn on the rope. She doesn't blink for minutes. Her contrivance is what I resent.

The hook shifts and tightens. Now my weight's on the rope. Cold caresses my calves. My legs stretch on the sharp indifference of concrete. The depth of the drop sparks my erection.

Her pert arse slings over the ledge. Long legs slip down.

Retreat to avoid a kick to the head. Take one step, and another. My boots find nothing to like.

Walk backwards like clowns, by seventeen and sixteen. No sense of achievement checking them off. Cold data. Way above, early arrivals stack over Heathrow. A ship horn stiffens my spine.

Pass fifteen and fourteen. I've got no gloves, my oil-smooth palms chafing. Whatever I wanted to prove is small, next to raw skin. Her trainers close on my head. She's a long, lithe bitch. For friction, I say, "We could drop. Just go."

"Talk is too much noise."

"I'd be dead. What would you lose?"

Eleven is the first lit window. My shoulders sting. Cramp haunts my knees. The rope hangs fifteen centimetres from the bright rectangle of glass. These apartments are used by people with interests. People who hear noise at night.

She toe-pokes my head.

"Fuck off."

"Keep moving."

Balconies draw the inquisitive. A shadow crosses the light. Try to move easy but my muscles are done. Loss of glamour is a sharp wound.

Windows blaze like a dancefloor. Early rising mischief. Phones and voices. Delicious spills. Alive and alert, not like the spy above me, who goes hand over hand with precise, identical moves.

Stop between eight and seven. Maybe Londoners, blind to strangeness, won't see us. But someone will. "Where did you launch?"

"What?" She's angry. Good.

"Inside or outside the railings?" The ground floor rooms have concrete yards with railings a metre from the wall. These yards are swept with infrared. "How did you fire the rope?"

"A grappling gun, obviously."

"Eighteen fucking floors?"

"It's a powerful gun."

Rest my forehead against the wall. Feels good. Cold abrasion. "Inside or outside the railings?"

"Outside. Now move."

A slip to ground would set the infrared singing. I still don't know who shot at me. The one person in town I can trust is getting up now, brushing her lilac hair, doing her makeup. Each day I'm here she's in danger.

Starlings flicker after sluggish, early flies. Rapid and artful, the birds dodge the watchful beams. Hitch my feet on the wall. Uncoil the rope from my chest. Agnieszka unbinds herself. It's clumsy business. Elbows and knees telegraph information. Below my feet, proximity sensors promise tedious interactions.

Poorly-balanced dancers, we flap till our backs are against the wall. Some bloke with a dirty brown cockapoo stands like he's waiting for us. Want to shoot him so bad my hand forms a gun. Agnieszka takes charge, the breezy blonde. "We do aerial aerobics. Is great fun workout. You join us?"

"No thanks, love. I prefer to watch."

She jiggles the rope, cutting into my fingers. "You are naughty boy."

Give a killing smile. "Sometimes we do it with pom-poms."

He scowls and his dog walks him on.

The yard is one-point-two metres wide. The railings one metre high.

I'm three metres off the ground. The geometry's not encouraging. I'm gone to flight. The air is soft and heavy. Starlings loft up. One so close we make eye contact. Its gaze is curious pity. My left foot strikes the railing and the ground rears with concrete indifference. Whatever bruises I catch are nothing against humiliation. A girl clopping by tries to help and I hiss like a snake. The grappling hook clatters down, beside Agnieszka's feet. She unhitched the rope on take-off. Made it look easy.

Motivation

Cab it to Queen Victoria Street to get the motor, the driver under the misapprehension me and her are a thing. It's early yet. I take it slow and scenic. With my banged-up leg and foul mood I'm glad she's not talking. Her hair blows about. Her eyes shine. She's misleadingly dolly. "You want to meet rich people?"

"I know rich people."

"Then you know how to behave."

Maybe the Square Mile ain't the whole world, but it fires me up. In another life, I might have been a trader. I got the instinct. I eat risk. But working in buildings, watching screens—that ain't me.

Though the car suits this corporation, the co-pilot and me rouse interest. The outdoor guard—a nice Essex lad—pleasantly blocks our way. There's parking for authorised guests. He wants to know: are we authorised? "A quick stop to see an old friend." I pick non-existent lint off his lapel. "Perhaps someone could valet it for us?"

Agnieszka says nothing, makes no gesture. Her self-containment is disruptive. I brought her because she's useful. But I want to know who's watching behind those eyes. "This is to help Mr. Miller. Nothing gets back to Archer."

Her blankness is vast and insolent. "Of course I look to resolve Mr. Miller's problem."

"I'm trusting you."

"It is interesting. To be arrogant and paranoid."

We're in a waiting room with coffee and croissants. She says it's a trap. I point out they didn't know we were coming, unless they routinely poison guests. She sips coffee like it's razors.

"And I'm paranoid?"

"I have a high regard for risk. I don't shoot every shadow."

A small noise, like a sapling sprung back, and this young girl asks if we're for Mr. Vogt. "He has white space," she says.

With this crew, seduction is to stay busy twenty-four-seven. Activity is determinative, which is why they're no use with a gun. They don't appreciate the slow patience to watch and do nothing. There's no algorithm for it.

Me and Stroppy get a lift that's all mirrors. Neither of us looks well. The little secretary says, "Have you come far?" like it's a job interview. We ignore her. This lift doesn't serve all floors. A visitor lift, the numbers jump over gaps. I'm pleased to realise the gaps have a pattern.

Corridors branch into areas rammed with desks. This bulk of suits are traders, chasing margins that exist momentarily on goods not yet produced. It's a sport with rules that mean simultaneously different things. Schrödinger superpositions. In the old days it was stripy jackets and shouting. Now they drink chai and press buttons. Same as war. The place has an oddly-specific smell. The scent of people and process in organisation.

Here's a frosted door, among a dozen in a frosted wall. No name plate. No ID. Knowing where people are is tradable data.

The girl knocks then opens the door just enough to peek inside. This is ritual action. "Mr. Vogt will see you."

One of the astute, sandy-faced men who could never be fat nor look older than thirty-five. Across the Western world, exotic investment teams are home to brains like Gernot Vogt. Precise, engaged, smarter than anyone who doubts their vision. Though he doesn't know me that well, he bounds forward, sawing the air. "Felicity." His accent makes it a technical term. "A pleasure always. And this?"

I present him. "Gernot Vogt. Gernot, from the old German 'to brandish a spear'. Vogt, from Latin I think. Same root as 'advocate'. This is Agnieszka, Polish form of Agnes, from the Greek for 'purity' possibly. She doesn't have a second name."

Agnieszka freezes. "You are German?"

This I hadn't foreseen.

Tactfully, Vogt says, "A fellow European." That bromide dies against her blank stare.

Before we're all back in Treblinka, I say, "Good of you to see us, Gernot. What's hot?"

With a chuckle he gets his phone. Thumbs a video of pod-like vehicles intersecting each other. "Remember when this was new? One vehicle has a human driver, tasked to make erratic moves. The others are automated, learning to avoid the random factor. Now we have this." A clip of people walking across London Bridge. Summer, by the uneventful light. "Not all are who they seem. When you ask people to consider this technology, they think of mundane tasks. Assembly lines and paint spray. Or higher-grade routine work: personal care, minor surgery."

"More golf for doctors." I'm ever the perky girl.

"These can play golf." He's serious. "But where most might you want this technology?" His teacherly gaze moves between us. "What is the optimum use?"

Agnieszka snaps out. "Where there are crucial decisions in short time. In such circumstances one wants a consistent response."

"In high risk, high value business. In strategic decisions. In war. But I am talking shop." The phone goes face down on the table. "Felicity, what brings you here?"

A stolen car. "Our client is suffering unhelpful disruption. I'm thinking certificates: old tech. And a healthy interest in weapons."

When he smiles, he's the well-formed grad, stepping out to lead the seminar. A boy too golden. He tells Agnieszka, "Felicity sees baleful systems. Everything to her is interworked."

"That might be true." My girl sounds strained to admit it.

Sensing friction between us, Gernot Vogt moves behind his desk, swiping screens, fingers tinged with their glow. "There's a quantum of fake certificates. But you do not mean that." The screen he pivots to face us shows an EV SSL server certificate, the checkpoints and blocklist and what not. "This is registered to this bank. It is subject to a chain of responsibility. It is real. If I copied it, the copy would be real. This is what we used to think an advanced solution. It does not mean the site is secure. It means traffic between the server and your browser is secure. If the site has malware, the malware is secure between those points. A real certificate could rob the bank."

"This is not Russian schoolboys." Say this for the baggage: it's the truculence of her spine.

Vogt's keen not to downplay her. "Those entities fund much work. As for armaments, that pie is too tasty to ignore. Adaptive cybernetics. Command loops in mutated insects." That quiet laugh lights him up. "Not so much need for women with guns."

I pity those killer robots. So lacking fear and pride. Let me die by a mind that plans, doubts, replays that squeeze of the trigger time and again. The difference between honour and waste disposal.

And Agnieszka, like a drill. "Who do you fight for?"

Something, perhaps ancestral, takes hold on Gernot Vogt. "Are you interested in violence?"

"I am a specialist." Those eyes, firm as stars. "I prefer that to some procedure of warfare."

That clean gaze completes its analysis. "You are something more, I think."

Cold anger swings onto me. "Why are we here, Ms Hepburn?"

This wall is coated for drawing. It's been wiped, but ghost ideas cloud its surface. Take a pen from the rack. Make spiky shapes, linked with knowing arcs. "From steady state, our client found his communications disrupted. Why is not clear. But it's methodical. Would you say?"

Agnieszka gives an impatient wave.

"The possibilities are domestic, overseas, or both." Tread careful. Jazin's my little number. But Vogt needs a shake, to see what rattles. "Let's say." Add more spines to my puffballs. "One of Britain's more reliable customers wants to broaden its portfolio. Betting on future returns, they need to test discreetly. They got money. They need the right partners."

Vogt's clever. Stood still, he messaged one of his strappers. A neat, nervy Hindu lad, whose knock is followed by his hesitant presence. I say Hindu—a gold Shivaji maharaj kada slips from under his shirt cuff. Memories of a wet job in Mumbai, dodging storms and modelling saris. Without alibi, he stares at Vogt.

Losing a bit of front, Vogt says, "We should prep for the ten o'clock, I take it?"

The poor young lad—there's latency. "Yes, we should."

Rudely, I think, Vogt goes to Agnieszka first. "Fascinating to meet you." His hand goes out but she gives him the freeze. Pivoting deftly, that paw comes my way. I'm civil because it's business and he did get me out of Frankfurt that time, when things got a bit Günter Grass.

Down in the lobby, my unlovely assistant makes for daylight. "Where are you going?"

Her blank anger unsettles me. "To work, Ms Hepburn. I lose two hours productive time."

Yell at the porter. "Oi, I got a car."

"I take a cab."

Scurry to catch her. "Are you off your head?"

"You let go of my arm." She pulls away. "You think I am stupid? You take foolish risks." She flounces into the morning.

Roar through the City, braking hard between lights. It seemed smart to get Archer's bint on the donkey work. Now I need her to score, or face Rotheray's not-insubstantial threats. All I want is to solve some problems, pocket a wedge and knit bootees. Dig out my phone to call her.

"You put that down. Slowly."

Go for my gun. But that tickle at the peak of my spine. "Who the fuck are you?"

"I suggest Whitechapel. You know where that is?"

"'Course I fucking do." Check the mirror. Can't see his face. He leans on the seat, like he's nibbling my ear. The gun between his chest and my head. I didn't check the car. I take foolish risks. "Did you target me off the river?"

A heavy sigh moves my hair. "If I kill you the car will crash. But I will kill you."

"Who do you work for?"

"To Aldgate. Then the Whitechapel Road to Sidney Street."

"To kill me on my own manor? How artistic."

The gun digs in. "Silence is preferred."

St. Botolph Without swings by, its elegant spire alert to the morning sun. Aldgate station spills young techies. "Looks moody, you hugging my shoulders."

"You want me to trust you?" That little chuckle is a sweet sound. "You think these Londonistanis notice anything?"

"I'm a good-looking woman."

"The light is green, Miss Hepburn." But he slacks a little, air moving between his warmth and my neck.

Hug the line down Whitechapel High Street. "What gun you got?"

"Browning, point-forty."

"Bit classy for a jacker."

That chuckle again.

"Don't the fun-loving Saudis use those?"

The muzzle licks my neck. "In your word, classy."

This place is mine. Commercial Road, Altab Ali Park, though we used to call it St. Mary's. The rather fine mosque where I had a nice mint tea once. The Royal London where I got stitched, that time me and Roc were practising knife work on Weavers Fields. My poor little sis, distraught, thinking she maimed me. Pain is a matter of character. These pound shops and Chinese supermarkets were boutiques and Bangla tailors back in the day. It was our playground. Our world and our home.

"I want to do my eyes."

"There is no…"

"If I'm kidnapped, I should look good."

The gun taps my shoulder. A modest, encouraging touch.

Slam left into Brady Street. Burqa girls turn at the squealing brakes. One points at the car and they're laughing. A pretty girl in a grey chiffon shayla—such a feminine scarf—tips me a wink. She's seen the bloke in back.

Betting he'll go careful with all this surveillance, I act surprised that he's one of the men from The Tihamah Lounge. Ridiculously handsome. Smooth beard, nimble lips, wide, cheerful eyes. He tucks the gun in his pecs, arm casually cocked on the headrest.

As I whip up my high strength mascara, he says, "This ruse of being police will not do."

"What ruse?"

"It's easy to spot glamorous troublemakers."

I giggle. I'm a kid for flattery. "See that green van? Behind that is Durward Street. It was called Bucks Row, back in the day. That's where Polly Nichols was killed. She was Jack's first. Throat slit twice, left to right. He slashed her belly when she was dead." Me and Roc used to act it out. She was the tart. I was the killer.

"Who was he, this Jack?"

"What's interesting is why the Yard didn't find him. They tried new things—profiling, psychology. They couldn't try fingerprints, they had no system, no comparators, though he left a bloody mess. It was girls, you see? Poor girls no one cared for."

"Sidney Street, Miss Hepburn."

As we shoot across traffic I say, "On your left is The Blind Beggar. A tourist haunt of the old East End. The Salvation Army was formed there." We were raised with a sense of place. We were people who came from somewhere. "Where you from?"

"You are cargo, Miss Hepburn. I am delivering you."

We bowl past neat council places and hokey new builds. "Makes me sick, this gentrification."

"You prefer decay?"

"I prefer community."

Above the traffic and windy sky his laugh is a sweet-tinged thing. "I did not know you are so activist. Left here." Stepney Way is dull and unyielding. We slow to a block of flats by Jubilee Street. Metal kisses my neck. "I want you to understand what we're going to do. We walk to that building. You do not run or make rumpus. If you think I will not shoot you, you are not listening. Park here."

"It's resident permit."

"It's not important."

In a neat culture reversal, it's me walking two steps ahead. Drive action to my hips, show the good we could be doing. In yesterday's dress and bruised knees. Jubilee Street is yellow brick and unremarkable. Dumpy concrete balconies with rusted iron struts. Net curtains. Average cars. We had a house when we were kids because the Luftwaffe missed our street. A tiny terrace. Dad was too smart to flash his cash. Our castle, that house. Nothing could hurt us.

Steering me between parked cars and bins smelling of mortuary waste, we get to one of those bulletproof security doors that are always broken. Inside, it's the usual concrete stairs, scoured like someone scraped something heavy across them again and again. The lights are on, the fittings putrid with mould.

He slides the gun in an achy dance down my spine. "You are like silk."

Jog upstairs, my calves grumbly with bruises. His breath pursues me. His smell is flesh in its prime.

At the second floor he grabs my wrist, leads me through a hallway speckled with shredded paper.

"Like blossom in Beirut," I say.

"You know Beirut?"

"I'm a glamorous troublemaker."

This door. Unremarkable. Council blue. 'No Junk Mail' on the letterbox. He lets go, my wrist reddened and needy. Shouts an Arabic word I don't get. Then we're in.

First, it's the smell. Chicken with cinnamon and lemon—kapsa I think they call it.

Men talk in another room, the didactic strike of Arab debate. Get one word in ten, not even that.

"Do nothing foolish."

"I won't if you don't."

The gun strokes my spine.

On the floor, in a fortress of pillows and rugs, a man in a loose white thawb bubbles shisha. On the couch, two lads in shirts and chinos look moody. A shot would stay in this tiny room, its walls thickened with rugs and pictures of men who look a hundred years dead.

The man draws on his pipe. He watches the water settle. Coconut scent swirls off the coals. "Your picture has something missing."

That tone of weary danger encircles me. "What did you expect?"

"Your picture does not show your stupidity." He spends time with the pipe, smoke drifting, the water a clotted murmur. With great care he hooks the hose on the stand. Everything he does, he watches himself do. It's unnerving. "You have caused offence and annoyance." So quiet, so gentle. "You have no business with Sayidi Rashad."

"And you are…"

The young men stir.

"It is not for a woman to interrupt. Nor you."

Clench my fingers, to stop them dancing. Patience with enemies knots my gut. "Your spare parts here could have told me. What do I owe the honour of hearing it from you?"

The shisha bubbles. Serpents of smoke uncoil from his lips. "We follow the path of justice. I would not come from that place to this place to despise a body that is not clever enough to know its actions," he picks a thread from his robe, "cause a reaction," and drops it on the coals. The cotton shrivels and is dust.

"I'm honoured." So used to the gun at my back, its absence is ice. My delivery boy moves around. Keeps me under the muzzle a casual, confident way.

The old man examines the patterns that form his den. "It is not from vanity I come here. Sayidi Rashad is serious beyond your knowledge."

An engine fires up. I glance to the window.

"Pay attention. It is not from vanity I teach you lessons." His tight, bare gesture gets one of the boys to his feet. The lad brings a phone cupped in his fist.

A line of men kneel on the sand. Some are sobbing. Others stare with shattered detachment. Alive but corpses. Of course the old man carries the sword. Deceptive strength drives the blade. As each man falls, he spills like an upturned jar. The crowd raise old-looking rifles, chanting and praising. Scheduled vengeance, between meals and exercise. "You are a noble shaikh."

His hand scatters smoke as sand scatters bones. "This is not vanity. But you think in vanities. I'm sure you could tell how many you killed, how much money you made. I'm sure you think people weigh your character by that."

"I'm for hire."

"You have many masters." He sucks the pipe. "I have one master."

Outside, kids kick a ball. Cocky Jafaican voices rise above the plea of sirens. The lad on the couch scratches his stomach, languid. I engage the old man's unhurried, ruthless eyes. "So what happens?"

"Your business is not our concern. Your sin is not our problem. Our responsibilities are above," he demonstrates with wizened, killer's hands, "your worship of earthly matters. But if your pride misdirects you, the sword will find your neck."

I've been here too long. They're wasting my time for a reason. "But if I want to meet Mr. Jazin. To praise his good works."

That gesture, slight and world-destroying. "If you meet, you remember this."

The handsome one takes my arm, snugging his gun in my kidneys.

The old man waves me off. "May you find wisdom, before you find death."

Delivery boy nudges me down the stairs. His scent makes me frisky. "What's he about?" Sling a smile over my shoulder.

"A man of great faith and severity. You should be humble he travelled to see you."

"Where from? Wembley?"

His laughter scatters the sour air. "You have no concern for danger."

"Au contraire, I'm a great respecter of danger. But avoiding it doesn't make it less likely."

At the door he turns me to face him. "When you shine a light in a dark place and see things flinch and flicker, you have a choice." He kisses my cheek. First kiss today. "Go quickly. Others are watching."

"You got a number? In case I need guidance."

He gives me a friendly pat with the gun. Arab blessings catch in my hair.

Feel quite soft and sweet. Till I find someone stole my car.

Kids playing football jump and curse when I stride between them.

"What you do bitch? This is our game."

"Where's my fucking car?"

These spotty cartoons gawp at each other. The tall one gets defensive. "We done nothing. You say we stole it?"

"Listen sunshine." The back of his head hits the wall. "What I'm saying is you were here when it got nicked. Kraut ragtop. Right there. Who was the last living piece of shit went near it?" Bounce him off the wall. His mate gets cocky, punches my back. I pivot and settle his jaw.

"Crazy bitch."

"That ain't no bitch."

"Who said that?" I'm cold and firm. "What cunt stain was it?" They ache to scatter. But they're fixed in my orbit. "You."

An ordinary boy in cheap clothes who, one day, will go to prison for something dumb and avoidable.

"Say it again."

He can't fail. He's a man in these streets. He doesn't yet know each defeat is a lesson. "You ain't no bitch."

He smells of fake Hugo Boss. He breathes like a horse at the gallop. "Thing is. I am a bitch. And you're a pussy."

No surprise, his Beretta 9 mil. Tidy street gun. Good for blokes with big hands. "Now what you do?" He doesn't sound sure. "I ain't no pussy."

The others fall to the shade of the block. Scared and energised. For some it would be their first kill. The essential step to manhood.

He holds the gun like it's precious but alarming. He has no relationship with it, not yet. In the point one of a second it takes, he stumbles: no aim, just trust in proximity. "Now what you do?" This means more to him than me.

He's sweaty. "I don't care what happens."

"Then you're an idiot." I'm locked on his chest. He'd be gone easy. "Kill me today, what comes tomorrow? You be running, hiding. Enough people owe you favours? Takes a lot of favours, going on the run. You got money? Ways to get money? You got strength up here to keep going? You get caught. People get tired of lying, they make mistakes. Then what? Prison? Young boy like you? Those men don't mess. They're doing twenties, thirties. They have it and walk off laughing. So you duck down your head and you be a good soldier. Spend the rest of your life getting fitted up. Till you land in some hostel with schizos and junkies.

'Oh yeah,' you tell their bloodshot eyes, 'I'm a killer, man, know what I mean?' So do it, blud. Shoot the gun."

Breath so hard his body's clenched. Air whistles between his teeth. His eyes burn. Unsure and embarrassed. He can't lose. But he can't lose himself. "Fucking crazy bitch."

The gun in his sweats, he turns and runs. With a crack of trainers on concrete, the gang scatters like goats from the wolf.

I sling the car keys down the drain.

Models

A room, somewhere discreet and stupidly posh. It's kind, she takes time off. Time's money.

Covent Garden, drifting to dusk, the light near gone. The lad on the desk ran out to get chocolates. A nice box. Her favourites. I'm a businesswoman or something. Unexpected overnight stay. These versions of me have their moment. Living and breathing and gone.

Take half hour fluffing about, retying my hair, doing makeup. I bought a new dress, just H&M. A disposable knee-length in green velour. And a pair of peep-toe heels. No time to paint toenails. Just buff them. Nothing to be done with the bruises. She'll worry. I'll make a joke of it. She'll worry more.

Who wants me dead should have done it by now. Not Agnieszka, she's directed by complex calculations. Not Jazin's boys, more subtle this side of the desert. More reason to duck down my head and be a good soldier. They could ventilate me anytime. They haven't.

That knock rouses my gun. As I check the entryphone, I'm nervous and excited, even after all these years.

My darling Roc. So kicky in that lilac hair. That nice cerise Emporio Armani barely contains her huge tits. A black shantung shirt shimmers and gleams, popping open. She has Love Hearts cufflinks: Lick Me and Bite Me. Her low-rise courts are dazzling. A pink Birkin and the warmest smile. "That a Springfield or are you pleased to see me?"

We eat each other's mouths. Her cherry gloss is delicious.

"That suit's fantastic. Thanks for taking time off."

"Like I wouldn't. Cool dress. That colour really does you. What happened to your legs?"

"Spacewalk. Re-entry didn't go as planned. Good day at the orifice, darling?"

She flicks her bangs. "My dear. Wall to wall German anal."

"German anal is a thing?"

"It's not quite as efficient as you think it'll be."

More than desire, her tough, feminine presence banishes harm. "I got champagne. And these."

"Yum." She hangs her jacket and lays on the bed. "Mind if I slip the shirt? I have trouble getting nice things to fit these monsters."

"46H?"

"You're too kind."

Lay next to her, caressing the dragon that curls beneath her sports bra. So much is darkness. Roc is a dazzle of sun on water. "It's been an interesting week."

"On a scale of shit to sugar how much danger are you in?"

"Well," keep my voice cheerful, "there's always challenges."

"Whom should I curse?"

We grew up the same. But somehow, she got this West End voice—even as kids it was there in her rounded vowels. No one in the family talks like Roc. Kiss her cheek, to see her smile. "There's filth. Arabs. This Polish bird. Spooks. Hackers. They're on me like the clap."

"Will they come after me do you think?" She's not selfish. She understands risk.

"Whoever does is hellbound."

"Don't worry."

Her left shoulder is crossed flintlocks. Beautifully done, the brass fittings inked to catch enduring light. "You're a canvas for your dreams."

Her hair washes my cheek. "I love that you remember things I tell you. No one else bothers."

"They're fools." Lick the flintlocks from grip to muzzle. Lay liquid kisses along each bone.

"You can do that all night."

She tugs back the shirt and I pull her towards me, dabbing kisses across her breasts. The bra is tight as skin. It sighs at release, and I marvel at these things I know so well, which are so strange to me. Latch to her left nipple, its flesh alive on my tongue. Its taste of latex on the cocks of nervous men. Dense flesh spills around my face. Her strong arms draw me in.

"Bite it."

I do as she wants. A skittering sigh explodes. Dents from my teeth flush with blood beneath the skin. She struggles her trousers. I slide them off and the plain black knickers hooked high to her waist. I search her eyes. "My reflection." So alike and not, our faces the same and distinct in ways we can't describe. Everything of her face is my face, deflected.

She surges like the sea.

I'm a girly girl. I give to men by receiving. To ride is strange. She's a fevered summer. My hips recall this inside-out manoeuvre. She frets and groans. Stripes her skin with finger burns. A strand of spit worms from her open mouth. Every piece of her chases the moment. Extraordinary vehemence digs her fingers into my arsehole. "Make a baby in me." Whatever I give is swept on her rolling tide. And all I can think is I should have done more. To be as effortless as I expect my men to be.

With sighing regret my skin parts from hers. She smiles. "I love you, I love you, I love you." Which is kind, because she's not done.

A man fucks me and walks away. Roc's the same. But she can adjust to the moment after, when random gestures and faltering kisses fill the awkwardness of two bodies spilled together. She can settle, while I have too many limbs.

To ease the moment, I feed her chocolate and champagne. Minibar fizz with an oversweet finish. "How's dating?"

That sigh before she speaks hangs like smoke. "Saw a nice girl the other night. Tall. Muscles. Black as the Devil's eyes. We went for a Moroccan then back to hers. She gave me a fair seeing to. No plans to meet again."

I don't know to say sorry or what. "Hope she knows how lucky she is." Which sounds stupid.

"It's all luck, who turns up on the apps. I got nudged by an ink queen. At least we'll have something to talk about." Champagne swills through her throat. "There's a girl down my street I fancy."

"Pretty?" I can only say dumb things now.

"You wouldn't believe. Long, shaggy orange hair. Real marmalade. Down to her waist. Very pale. Black frame glasses: proper Michael Caines. Skinny as fuck. My clit goes hard every time I see her. I tried saying hello, just casual. She sort-of smiled."

I'm sad for Roc and hate this girl. My sister is something amazing. This girl should be honoured. But she just sort-of smiles. "I'm seeing a copper tomorrow."

"You minx."

"Business. Detective Sergeant Chloe Bell. She's a lez. I'll put in a word."

That laugh, too keen to be true. "And how exactly do you pitch me?"

"Bright, attractive, tall, strong. Talks posh. Good sense of humour and excellent career prospects."

"I fancy that myself." Before silence drifts too far, she says, "You up to go again?"

"Of course." What else does a woman say?

With an upheaval of decorated flesh, Roc reaches to her Birkin. "Look what I brought."

A beautiful strap-on. Black leather belt with bright steel rivets. Hard-pack genital pad and ten-inch PVC cock, crowned like the Eiger.

Relieved to step back from emotion to fact, I get on all fours and present. The possessive sneer of leather adheres to my skin. I shake down like a wet dog. Slap the wall as she pins me. From slow, her hips gain rhythm. Drawing out. Bringing back. Controlling.

"Look at you. Keen little bitch."

This is my religion. Everything comes to this. I pant. My arms and legs shake. Hard plastic commands aching flesh.

She laughs. "I want that orgasm."

"Wank me." My voice tiny, fissured. "Please."

"You."

Take our momentum on one hand. Reach under and pull my little stump. Scrape its slick crown. "Please."

"You."

She sinks the cock again and again. I flail, desperate as a schoolboy. Never used to take so long. I could shoot three times, straight off. Now obstinate valves frustrate me.

She bends forward. Rigid plastic bites my gut. The derisive slap of her tits on my back. "Whose bitch are you?"

"Your bitch." The convulsion starts in my stomach. Through my colon to my anus, gathering force. "I'm cumming." A submerged splatter. Discharge wets my balls. "I love you, I love you, I love you."

Roc rides till the wet on my arse grows cold. We collapse, the dildo lodged inside me. Her tits spread round my spine, nipples hard as thumbs. "Whose bitch are you?"

"Your bitch."

Though we've done this many times and find comfort in each other, I know what she's thinking because nothing about her is hidden from me, no more than me from her.

She unstraps and disengages, a bit sullen. We shower and make scented, sudsy love. She cums, quick and decisive. I take too long and she's kind, and all I think—all I think—is how much time she spent getting tattooed. How many hours she laid in hard chairs to make breathtaking art of her body.

We don't dry our hair and I love how hers looks: dark lavender arcs behind her ears. There's average white in the minibar, that Chablis the French pump through pipes. I offer to call for nice stuff but she doesn't want anyone at the door.

Though it's early, the city feels shut. We're in a bubble. A fragile place.

"Have you called Miquel?"

No and I should. He doesn't call because he understands delicate business. He knows I call when it's safe.

"He might be worried," she says, because we're inside each other and she knows what I think.

I glance at the landline by the bed. Only hotels have landlines.

"I never get between you and Miquel."

"Never, babe." Miquel matters to her. The rest are sex and nothing. "I really want you to meet him." The end to that sentence—'I'm sure you'd get on'—reminds me of cold afternoons, off school, watching TV dramas where people do ordinary things. Of course she'd be witty and charming. Of course they wouldn't get on. "I'm grateful. About the baby. He will be too."

"You'll be a fantastic mum."

The life of the gun is a pure life—straightforward, no distractions. Ambiguities that make life unbearable are absent from the gun. In any room, I'm the certainty. People know what I want. These tangled emotions upend me. It's hard to stand when gravity pulls strange ways. "Miquel won't get between us." Words become fact.

"This week is the first time I've seen you in three years. You'll sort this business and go back to Barcelona. I won't see you till the wedding."

"I've been here a week and there's maniacs at me. In Barcelona I don't have to be on the whole time."

"That's nonsense, Flick. You don't have an off switch." She lays back, resting the wine on her tits. "'The fruit for the cuvée Saint Pierre, named for the church in the town of Chablis, hails from vineyards in the lieu-dit of Les Chaumes, in Maligny. The soil is rich in clay, which gives a concentrated, age-worthy wine.' What's a 'lieu-dit'?"

"French wine-talk. A scrap of land with the name linked to a vineyard. You know the French make a big thing of place. Being from 'this place'. What happens in 'this place'. Fréchet the mathematician was born in Maligny."

"What's he famous for?"

"Probability and calculus. Background to computing."

"His wine's nice. Maybe we could go down to Chablis. Last holiday we had was a dirty weekend in Hastings."

"We had to cough up for the damage, remember?"

"I remember every time with you. It's not about Miquel. It's you."

She's everything to me. But a man, strong with passion, is everything else.

Because she knows what I'm thinking, she says, "You would still have your men. Like I'd have other women. There's no limit to sex."

"It's about me putting you first."

"It's about me having certainty in love. You want to marry Miquel. Same reason."

There's density to this silence. We risk getting bound with it. I'm not brave. I make decisions on the probability of not waking up tomorrow. I get away with more than I should and one day I'll pay. I'm not friendly or kind. I don't suffer fools nor wise men. I don't want regret, the rest of my life.

She reads the bottle again, the curly writing, the hand-drawn map that gives it that artisan feel. The hand-drawn map is a setting in a graphics package. Dorothy knew there was no magic behind the curtain.

"Roc. Will you marry me?"

Shrewd wonder shapes her intelligent face. But there's no hesitation. "Yes, Flick. I'll marry you." No commotion. No easy claims. Streetwise and sharp, she takes nothing for granted. "You'll still marry Miquel, of course."

"I'll marry you first. This week."

She gives me a narrow look. "Nothing hooky. I want a real marriage."

"Takes paperwork."

"But you can fix that."

"I can fix it." This idea that seemed so vast ten seconds ago is now project management. Shake her, so her pictures dance. "You beautiful little lez."

"If you marry me, you're a lez too."

We laugh. Till the knock at the door.

Instant, she's all attention, looking to me for instructions.

"Bathroom."

Frowning, she shakes her head.

"Go on. It's me they want."

She scoops her clothes. Shuts the bathroom door quiet as a whisper. Ten seconds, I'm dressed.

Another knock. Not loud, but demanding. The entryphone shows only shadow.

Braced, I unlock and step back.

An irritable man in poor skin, brown bomber and dad jeans, kick shuts the door and pulls a Glock. A Balkan fake Glock. With an ugly suppressor. He aims on my pelting heart. "You alone?" His rosacea and Brummie accent suggest a contract operative, in town for one night only.

"Who the fuck are you?"

"I heard laughing just now." He sounds offended.

"Who are you?"

Rude, his gun dents my velour. "Well, it's not important, is it? Get over there."

Step to the window, to get his back to the bathroom door. "Ain't you got people up north to piss off?"

"Less mouth. I got a headache. Give me your gun."

"Go fuck yourself." As I draw, he skims a shot over my hand. The suppressor makes it no more than a door slam. A bubbling wound furrows my skin. My gun hits the floor.

"Kick it over." He snatches it up.

Disquiet turns to grief. I've been made small. Blood on my fingers its own sad story.

Keeping me under his sulky eye, he backheels the bathroom door. It opens with a squall. "Who's there?"

"Two sailors and a sea scout." If he sees her, I'm on him. Hands, teeth, everything.

Trying not to commit skin to the move, he flings my gun through the bathroom door. Something breaks.

"That's seven years' bad luck."

"Shut the fuck up."

Grip my hand. Pain dictates me. "At least say who sent you. That would be sporting."

His voice makes everything dreary weather. "You understand you're in the last minutes of your life?"

"Yes, bab, I understand yow."

That unfussy way he takes aim. "There are times people look the other way. And times they don't."

"Is this about Rashad Jazin?"

"Everyone I have the other side of this gun thinks it's about someone else."

The bathroom door opens. "Don't the spooks do their own pest control?"

Roc steps from the dark, so quiet.

"Believe me, there was a queue for you."

Insane. She's no business in this. "I'm sure the taxpayers are grateful."

"I'll enjoy not hearing you anymore."

Roc wobbles on tiptoe. I scream inside.

That stillness. The stop-go decision. His eyes bug. His lips make an ugly shape.

He squeezes the trigger.

So does she. The full-throated screech of my gun drowns his muffled shot. The wall ruptures where I was standing.

She falls back from the recoil.

Point blank in the brainstem is instant. Face down between us, the back of his head laid open.

She's shaking. I think, 'Don't scream'. And I'm ashamed. I know she won't.

To focus her, I say, "You saved my life."

"No one takes you from me."

She drops the gun in my open hands. It stings but that's not important. Get the safety on and my arms around her.

"I never thought I'd do that."

"It's okay."

Tense light in her eyes. "I'm like you."

"No, sweetheart." I dust her hair. "You did it for love." Her tears scald my neck. We hug and kiss. And I think: someone heard that shot. We need the place clean and him away before they draw awkward conclusions. "We can't be found, love. They'll keep us apart if we're found."

"What do you need me to do?"

I wad him with towels so he doesn't fuck up the carpet. She digs his bullet from the wall. There's no exit. My bullet is smothered in the gunk of his brain. A bullet is DNA. I need it back. But I can't expect Roc to watch that. Again, I've got to shift a corpse before it gets stiff and selfish. The dead shouldn't make so much grief. "We need a car."

"Didn't you have a car?"

"It got stolen."

That look in her eyes. "What?"

"I stole a car. It got stolen."

"How do you do this every day?"

There's no time to waste but she's crying. I cradle her. "Same as you, darling. I couldn't do what you do."

Her breath comes harsh. "I go to work. Do my moves. Go home. I do this many fucks and I'm done. But you." She writhes in my hands. "Any day you could be dead. Who would tell me? I want a family. I don't want to tell our children Mummy Flick got shot by some headcase."

What does she expect from me? She could get killed by some creep with a grudge. Does she think I don't care about that? But excuses make me wretched. "I'm sorry." At this angle, the hired man is topography. "We need him shifted."

"Who is he?"

"No one. He's dead."

She gives me that look. "He might have kids."

"He would have killed me and killed you."

"Without you that wouldn't matter."

There's no progress when she's like this. Simple certainties grow grainy as old Polaroids. "I need your help to get him away. Our DNA's on everything."

"I killed him." She picks up the Glock. "Should I have this?"

"The safety's internal. Don't touch the trigger."

"I'll keep it. In case. How's your hand?"

Blood makes ruby knots. Bullets crush and stretch. Velocity shapes what a bullet does. Oscillation shapes the wound. His trick shot skinned my hand. It's ugly. If it's septic, I'll soon know. "It's nothing." What we do should be quick and effective. Unpack the towels from his head. Fold them in a laundry sack. Can't find a way to carry it that doesn't look like stealing towels. Shit like that gets you caught.

We haul his dead weight upright. I'm worried she'll get squeamish. Then ashamed because she gives herself to everything with generous candour. Take an arm each on our shoulders. "It's like this. We're models. Fun types. We picked up this lad. Had a drink. We're taking him home. As a cover it's weak. It relies on a casual assumption he's alive. We need him moving."

We practise working his feet. There's a window for this, while he has flex. We walk him, rehearse our steps. Prop him against the wall while we do our makeup. Fix our handbag straps to clench his arms to our shoulders. The laundry bag is awkward. My hand bleeds with the weight.

"Why do they want you dead?"

Already I sense his legs stiffen. "Digging dirt on their fair-weather friends."

The corpse slumps as Roc tries to face me. "They'll send someone else."

Heave the body upright. "Yeah, they'll be grumpy."

"Have I made it worse?"

"No worse than I would have made it."

She snuffles and I think: is it safer, fucking strangers in windowless rooms?

There's always cameras. The calculation is no one's watching. Chasing our alibi, we weave and stumble. Slap the meat sack dragging between us. We're models. Fun types.

There's bastards in the lift. A mid-range German couple, giving earnest thought to dinner. 'Abendbrot,' they say. That's casual supper, I think. Or is that 'Abendessen'? Roc knows. Her German's stronger than mine. The couple work hard to ignore us. We're clichés to these people. The woman has a nice pair of tan zip-up Riekers. I can see her in some mall in Düsseldorf, saying she must get trendy for London. The Brummie's head hangs down. We keep his back to the mirrors. The hole in his skull plain sight. Point blank and it didn't come through. He's got the fattest brain.

We let the Germans get clear before we step out. The woman looks back with a face I don't care for. These ordinary types are trouble.

One deep breath and we're gone. We bounce off walls, slip, get loud.

Blow through the lobby, jigging the body like a prize at the fair. Smart lads on reception, unofficial couples, business arrivals groggy with cabin pressure turn as I shriek. Guide Roc and the stiff in an arc, barging tourists out the way. We whoop and shout. It's vital everyone sees us.

The doors slide back and our carnival crashes the night. Down the street, around the corner, in sticky shadows. We sag with the dead man's weight. "Can you hold him till I get back?"

Her face sinks as adrenaline fades. I don't know what life she dreams we'll have. Don't guess it's this.

Prop the bones on the wall and scout options. An average motor, nothing flash. I'm checking locks, and there's eyes in the dark.

A chubby sort—recessed brow and wild tufts. His shirt open too many buttons. He's fat, but his coat came off a bigger man. His bagginess is, no doubt, deceptive. "You interested in this?" He nods at the car.

Across the street, Roc puts on a show, pinning the stiff with her body. "Here first, were you?"

His meaty fingers circle the road. "No bother to me. I can take my pick."

The superstition that he knows me kicks my veins. "Best crack on."

"Them electrics. Very smooth. But you don't get the performance." The streetlight silvers chest hair twined from his gaping shirt. "You don't see women, much, doing cars."

"Glass ceiling broken, eh?"

"You know that girl there? With the fella."

"Should I?"

He licks his lips a nasty way. "Wonder if she's doing business."

Hate fires through me. "They're drunk."

"Careful," he says, nodding at the car. "One mistake makes all the difference."

Kill the alarm—these things are just toys. Couple of snips from my nail scissors and the immobiliser's dead. The engine, polite and well-kept, seems keen for a spin. Pull across the road. Roc's got the beef up the wall, an awkward, one-sided embrace. She snogs him to make it look real, her face pale, eyes behind glass. "Come on." I grip the lad's arm. "Some creep's watching."

She laughs, loud and synthetic. "Of course. We're entertainment."

I know how tough my sister is. I want to comfort her. But I'm owed to a corpse. The dead have too much claim. "Help get him in the car, sweetheart."

We jolly the bollocks. Shriek and laugh. Make a thing of tumbling him in the back seat. Roc's pretty face is cement. This bastard's beyond retribution. But I'll punish whoever had hand up his arse.

I tell her, "Get a ride home."

"I want to come with you."

"No need, darling." Hold her tight. "Further you are from this the better."

"Won't your wife have to get used to it?"

Kiss her, because I don't know the words.

Her ride shows up. An unremarkable Toyota. A pleasant Turkish guy who's smitten with Roc on sight. He gets out to hold the door for her. I wave till the taillights vanish. Punch the wall, to shift the pain.

Dissolution

At casual distance it's any crap stuffed in a car. The car's underpowered, disposable. Head south, to the muddy luxury of Deptford Creek.

A missed call from Agnieszka, narked I'm never there to suffer her wisdom.

A message from Roc, to say she's home. Her place is average safe—a concierge and cameras. Nice little gaff up Lisson Grove, its location a prudent secret. Anyone tries it for what happened tonight will meet with extreme terror. My sister is sacred.

It interests me, this traffic. My assumption is anyone driving at night is a wrong 'un. Like men who wear Tweety Pie socks. It's the coppers' dream of a future where everyone's suspect. And me, the girl with the most cake.

Slow across Tower Bridge, to gorge the night city. Silver water, sequin streets, the promise and the cost. Graceful, indestructible city. No one can break this. Not the King of Spain's men in their tall ships. Not blackshirt scum. Not hell-bound martyrs. Swing down Tooley Street and away south. Old warehouse fronts, tacked to apartment blocks. Bare brick and black window frames. Onto Jamaica Road. Get momentum into the night. These launderettes—amazed they still exist. These mags 'n' fags. The Chinese chippy. The tool shop. These people stay in their shops all day. Hardly see daylight. Hardly break even. What dreams sustain them?

Southwark Park, a mess of darkness and sex offenders. Joggers bust through the lights, lycra and phones gleaming. Lads at the King's Stairs roundabout, tight as a fox on a vixen. Men tune to me. I'm a carrier wave.

Lower Road opens out, empty and peaceful. A bus goes by, the bodies unclaimed cargo. People always believe they have reasons for what they do.

Hang a left to Surrey Quays. Used to be shit round here. Now it's students and dockless bikes. A leisure centre gleams like a scar as I spin into Redriff Road. There's a dress waits for me in Barcelona. Need to shave a kilo to fit. Miquel's lovely mum is designing the invitations. A huge propulsion of travelling aunts, handsome cousins with trim little beards, nieces with pubescent racks testing the seams, cava and dancing and extremes of tradition. I'll make a speech in flawless Català, so that means more lessons. Miquel's kid sister will catch the bouquet. And the maid of honour will be my wife. How to manage a complex future.

On the A200: terraces and towers, a school fenced-up like prison, a camp of old huts promises car auctions daily. Down Evelyn Street to Deptford Creek. A tinned-up Irish boozer on the corner. Used to be The Thames. Then it was Bridget's or some shit. The obligatory 'céad míle fáilte' a tad ironic.

New buildings block the water. Scrape round to a concrete slip by the festering creek. Black as arseholes. Stagnant mud and rotting gulls. To kill the stink, Ducados smoke. Miquel and Roc will make me quit. They'll change me. They'll go on changing me. No one in love can stay the same.

The smell of the creek. The fatty air. The suck of water through mud. Generations of killers lost bodies down here. When that old spook Marlowe got done in Ele Bull's room, a Hepburn settled the body. This is what I want my baby to know. What we do we do well.

Light from high rooms draws a boat on the shore. Stranded behind squat bridges. Its cabin rebuilt with house windows. Its hull rusty and stained. I could lose the stiff in the mud, but a weak tide would be my undoing. A rotting boat is misadventure.

He's deadweight. Hard and unhelpful. Dragging him and the towels racks my muscles. Try not to smash his head on the ground. I don't need some eager plod ruminating on skull fragments.

The boat sits off from the wall. Manky ropes hitch it to cannons. With the rigor in his sorry bones, I swing him onto the rail. Step back far as I can. Hitch my dress and jump. Land like a bomb and drag him inside. The door's open, which is moody. But there's no other manoeuvre.

Set my phone next to his head. Get the tweezers. This hole in the back of his skull, cauterized by the blast, collapses inward, a creamy meteor strike. When he first picked up a gun, his lifetime odds of ending here shortened to near evens. It's where we live. That margin just beyond evens.

Shine light in his head. Send my tweezers after the bullet. It matters, retrieving this bullet. I'm unpopular with this fool's masters. So I keep my prints clear of his skin and follow the shaft of damage into his brain.

Takes a bone-numbing fifteen minutes to find it, snug in his cerebellum. Blobby with tissue that reminds me of mushrooms. Then I strip him. He's hairy and going to flab. His cock is unkempt. A few tarts might know him but he's no Casanova. Bung his clothes in the bag with the towels. They'll be casual garbage by morning.

Death by misadventure. He tumbled onto this boat—bollock-naked, confused. Lost balance. Smashed his head on these metal stairs. I make it happen. I destroy his face and break his skull, a casualty of night and circumstance.

"You don't know what you're doing."

Whirl round. The door's all shadow.

"From intense peace comes intense power."

Tall and slender is all I see. Aim clever—I'm on him.

"What are you doing in my home?" Ignoring the gun, he makes for the bloody wreckage.

I backheel the corpse downstairs. It lands with an untidy clatter. "I'll blow your fucking head off."

"Did you kill him?"

"I'll kill you."

"Do you think I'm impressed with this?" He's calm. More—he's serene. "What are you doing in my home?"

"Look, sunshine." He doesn't move. "It's business, yeah? You go to the filth, you're dogmeat."

"You're a woman."

"Of course I'm a woman. Now fuck off."

"This isn't accidental, is it?" He gestures at the stairs. "This is the outcome of complications."

"Are you on meth?"

"Out of intense complexities, intense simplicities emerge."

"You quoting Churchill?"

"Seek straightforward solutions." He looks downstairs. I can't see much. But he can, it seems. "Who's going to clean this up?"

"I don't care."

"Well, that's no answer. In the five minutes since I got home, it's clear to me you don't put a great deal of thought into your actions. You reckon with each individual occurrence, in preference to examining why your life is off-balance. Whatever led to this could have had a less complex solution, if you'd taken a holistic view."

"I am aiming a gun at your spleen."
"Can you say with confidence where my spleen is?"
"Anatomy is my hobby. I'm gone now. You keep shtum."
"Or what?"
"I kill you."
"I have no fear of death. From intense peace comes intense power. Your gun is meaningless to me."
"You're a headcase."
"I don't break men's skulls."
Grab my bag and the laundry sack.
"At this height of consciousness your bullet is ineffectual. Go on," he says. "Try."
I back to the door.
"Reflect on your chaos. The path of clarity brings priceless rewards."
On the rim of the deck, mud seeps and smirks beneath me. Jump, and crash again on bruised knees. As the laundry bag flies to the water, it catches the light of a phone from the boat. Lay my hands to the roof of the car. Count ten, to stop them shaking.

Sound through quiet streets is antagonistic. Three motors blend out from the dockside. Slam the hatchback into reverse, stones slopping down on the mud. Headlights come at me, my face in sickening brilliance. Floor it to a service road, blocked with a chain-link gate. The car's not much but I cane it. Leave the gate on one hinge and a chunk out the offside wing. Sparks beneath the wheels dazzle the night. The three cars lumber behind. Resourceful predators don't waste energy on the chase.

Run to a tower block, my seams protesting. A gunshot follows. What's surprising: it's such a bad miss. Crash the door as boots kick over the cinders. Run upstairs, snot clagging my throat. Another shot. In public. They really don't care.

By the sixth my lungs are fucked. Dodge down a corridor, boots behind. Four or five of the bastards. Skittle round a corner. A run of identical doors. And one, wide open. Bundle in and close it gentle, alert to bottled gunfire from a room at the end of the passage. Smell chilli and unwashed nylon. The boots rumble by.

This flat is rancid junk. Broken drawers spill tees and baggies. Busted fans and sandwich makers, boxed off the shopping channel. Drink cartons with candy-stripe straws. Aerosol cans and jars of jam, with little faux-muslin lids. Energy drinks. A broken bong. Packs of Camels. Bike magazines. A plastic jug with a spoon embalmed in yellow gunk. A set of weights. A skull in a cage. This is just the hallway.

The room at the end is the nest. The carpet—what's visible—burgundy red. Purple walls. The curtains are black sheets, thumbtacked to the frames. The floor is pizza boxes, clothes of unknown label, bits of tech, split plastic bags, a restaurant ice bucket, duvet and pillows, mugs and cans. The walls are plastered in waifus, their bug eyes and cute skirts between fat-arse sci-fi and games.

In a corner, staked by craft ale and vape cartridges, sits the most fuck-off PC—twelve core overclock processor at least. Flashing lights, for badness. And the starship commander, a vast bearded man in kaftan and flipflops, propels his big-breasted avatar through apocalyptic real estate. Voices leak from his headphones. He's playing live with nice guys.

He doesn't see my shadow. Careless, for an alien-slayer. "I been sent by god. She wants you for a sunbeam."

At impressive speed, the chair hurls back through a jubilant scatter of bottles. His avatar falters. I grab the keyboard and take out a fuck-ugly swarm. Just for jokes I shoot his mate through the head. A blizzard of warnings scold me. Outrage howls from the headphones. Try to spin the gun cowboy-style but I'm rusty. After she drops it, she stands blinking like a girl not sure she got touched up.

"You shot Jeggsy."

"He was a traitor." Terminate the program. In the silence, a siren far off. "I'm borrowing this, alright?"

He scrapes his beard like that's enough to unstick it. These guys have insane ability to sustain themselves. While I run my pretty pins all day, he does tech support, hacks on game boards, bit of innocent astroturfing. Makes just enough to maintain this Aladdin's cave of filth. He gawps at my legs like the sun coming up. "You play?"

"A bit. I'm more covert."

"You a spy?"

Smooth my dress over my hips. "Some bad men have the wrong idea about me. I need a white knight. Got a beer?"

He hauls off to a kitchen I don't want to see. I'm hammering keys when he comes back with something oily from Devon. He takes a moment to enjoy my shape. But his interest is tinged with alarm. "What's that?"

"Security Service operational database. I like to know who I've upset."

No fool, this boy. "They'll track me."

"In theory. But I notice you use endpoint security management, which should hold them these two minutes." The beer's warm, of course. Craft ale. Dad was a pale ale drinker. Watneys, back in the day. Always a crate in the sideboard, in case the mother-in-law came round.

Though concerned, he's fascinated. "That for real?"

"Old credentials and a bit of deductive logic. There's no names or dates. That would be stupid. These codes describe event, operative and target. That character string is me. That's my code. Click that, you get the interactions I've had with these people."

"It's hundreds." Bless him.

"What's interesting today is live operations. That one's a hygiene visit—a hit, if you will. And this one started when that one went wrong. See the dependency? Why was your door open?"

His reticent pride might be laughable in less shambolic conditions. "My door is open to damsels in distress."

I don't know whether to hug him or boot his jacksy.

He says, with earnest logic, "I await a damsel. And here you are."

A fun interlude from nuts with guns who bear no personal malice. "Let's close this now. Before the orcs get restless."

"You leaving?"

Pain only goes so deep. "Good sir knight, it's enchanting here. But I'm not the sort to dodge a battle."

"You are brave as well as beautiful." Words with absolute conviction.

I can't fancy him. He wouldn't know where to begin nor when to let go. But men are special to me. How fragile they are, weighted with doubts. "You're brave, with your door open, leaving things to chance. You understand risk and reward."

"To be loved is reward worth any risk."

We must read the same fortune cookies. "Risk is where you put in and hope to get back. But today's reward is tomorrow's nightmare, is what you need to remember. Don't hang your fedora on love, when what falls through your door is a loony with time to kill."

"I don't care about danger," he says, like some stoic idiot. "Virtue is sufficient."

Comically, he attempts a bow, too thick in the middle to make it.

And it's not comic. It's a guy in a dead-end life who believes the things that pester me through nightmares. "I'm sorry I shot that other player." I'm ashamed of it now.

"Jeggsy's alright. I'll do him some mods."

There's soft skin beneath his cluttered beard. I don't guess he goes out in the rain. In another life I might have been the girl next door. A friendly, unfussy presence with no urgent business.

"At least tell me your name."

"I'm the angel of death. There's none like me."

Of course the goons took the car. No doubt some eager retard is stowed down Chelsea now, waiting to make war stories.

Quiet, late, cold. A nasty breeze from the river. My bare legs prickle. These fathomless shadows. This pointless road. Cars swagged in tarps for late frost. I can steal a car. Drive till they find me. Die like a good girl. I know why my sister puts faith in love. A safe home. A warm body at night. Why she never tires of worry. That belief in a time when things will be right. When accounts get settled.

Nelson Road, named for the man of Trafalgar. Shot through the spine by a sniper at fifty feet. Don't sound much, fifty feet. But the guns they had then makes that a good take. He wasted three hours dying. They packed his corpse in a brandy cask, so it wouldn't rot on the trip back to Blighty. Can't have your heroes all maggots and pus. He got a big statue and this road. Nothing for the fine shot who got him.

Get noodles from the Chinese. The counter girl stares like I'm from Mars. The woman in the mirror has rumpled hair. Skin shows through makeup. Ripe looking hand wound. Stain on her dress. Speck of blood. I see it. That boat freak called the police. He's giving them zen while they clump about in waders. When the stiff gets known there'll be words between filth and spooks. Somehow, it'll be my fault.

These noodles are slippy with oil and gritty with soy. Sugar snap peas so green they must be healthy. I recycle the box and chopsticks. I want my children to have a nice planet, long after I'm some fucker's Nelson.

Walk the length of Romney Road, not liking how the trees whisper. Feel the lights vanish behind me. Old London has murderous roots. New mischief resolves from old blood. Trees and fields, moonless clouds, murmur as I pass. At the pier is a chain hotel—the most rooms on the least ground. Drive swing through my hips, to catch purpose I don't feel. The lad at the desk is unattractive and wasted. "I want a room."

"For now?"

"I'm here now."

"Don't get walk-ins this time of night."

"But you get walk-ins?"

"Yes."

"So we're not outside the parameters of the possible, are we?"

Struggling with whatever dope he's taken, he makes a big effort. "Single?"

"Double. I sleep diagonal. En suite?"

"We have en suite." Like a confession. "On the premium floor."

"Well that's splendid. Minibar?"

"What?"

"In the room."

So slack I could mould him like putty. "Not here."

"But you got booze?"

He waves vacantly at a sad little closed-up bar. I've no clue how desperate a person would be to drink here.

Cradling an armful of miniature G&Ts, I examine this premium room. There's a bed, a shower, an okay bog, and one socket works. Tony messaged. He's worried about me going dark. He actually says 'going dark' like we're some crack-brain army. To tempt a response he tells me there's been 'developments'. I reply I'll be at Mr. Miller's by ten—a hideous deadline from Greenwich. Of course he comes back to offer breakfast. Tell him some other time, so he's sulking.

Scan police channels. The good folk of Deptford getting disturbed by gunshots. But not gunshots. Fireworks. Launched by feral toerags. So I know, in the pastel rooms of Scotland Yard and the dingy back halls of Millbank, recriminations have started. No doubt I'll get summoned to Rotheray. More in sorrow than anger.

Pull up the radio on the TV and settle to a soft-talking DJ playing quaint jazz for insomniac wives still regretting they didn't go when they had that offer. I want a cigarette, but the windows are sealed and disarming the smoke alarm is too much manual labour. Dip in and out of sleep to cocktail music. A few bad dreams—nothing I don't expect.

When I surface at some thankless hour, a man sounds like he's reading the news to himself. There's been a fire in a tower block at

Deptford. Nothing major. Confined to one flat. Fierce but quickly controlled. Not quick enough for the bloke who died. Suspicions of overloaded electrical circuits. It's what these bastards do.

Take a piss in the dark, alert to silence. I don't flush and my warm-bread smell fills the room. Miquel loves my smell. He loves everything about me.

Sleep till the lousy scratch of day brings me to cold life. The radio plays breakfast pop. The fire has dropped from the news.

Get a shower, wash my hair, do my makeup twice. Mascara won't sit on baggy eyes. Strip my face to its pale self, the lines and abrasions only my loved ones know. Still a few years before I go under the knife. If I'm careful. Drink water and eat well. Give up smoking. Get quality sleep and healthy sex. Manage my anger. A few significant paydays, I can take out the firing pin. Let it sink to the mud of the Llobregat. Become an old donya with grey in her hair. All my little ones round me.

When I check out, the lobby's clogged with early-rising tourists, their immature needs implausible in this grim light. A trans cutie works the counter. Nice blonde hair and good skin. She reacts visibly to me. "Did you enjoy your stay?" She filed down her accent along with her cheekbones.

"Lovely. The bed's like sand."

Good teeth in an uncertain smile. "Are you in our loyalty scheme?"

"Loyalty's not my thing."

Wary vixens, we gauge each other. She stands, to show a vista of mint boobs. When she leans forward I get a lungful of Jimmy Choo. "You know you have a stain on your dress?"

My default is attack. Biting it costs. "Yeah, I'm embarrassed about it. Where can I get new schmutter?"

"There's nice shops in Greenwich Market. Nothing's open yet." Struggling with kindness, the way people do. "I'd offer but…"

"We're not the same size. You look lovely." Virtue is always sufficient.

Call Agnieszka. When I ask is she alright, I get sulky silence.

"Tony says there's developments."

"We discuss when we meet."

"And how's your love life?"

"You are coming to work? Or shall I give another excuse?"

I don't want joggers and early pervs to see me shout at a phone. Such an uncouth look. "Yes," through gritted teeth. "I'll be there by ten."

"I'll be there at eight."

I'd put a bullet in her head, if I thought it would make a difference.

Find a caff for veggie fry up. Check the latest Middle East rumpus. Anxiety is vital to a healthy flow of guns. These stories of strike and counterstrike show Jazin's hand everywhere. And I'm warned off from that direction. Which is interesting.

Message Miquel in my charmingly flawed Catalan. Tell him a few more days. He understands the job. He's faithful, I've seen him turn girls down. He'll be writing music, arranging a protest, planning the future with his crew of earnest beards. I dream sometimes we take down the Spanish state. How we might do that. Miquel thinks I'm working my way out the business. Wonder how I'll feel, the first year I go without killing.

Go looking for clothes. This clobber-shop—what once might have been a boutique—has polka dots, flower-print, this silver dress like something from Star Trek. Paisleys and rainbows because everyone's queer nowadays. But the time-honoured cool of houndstooth mini and black shirt can't be denied. I got young girl inches. I fit this stuff easy. Smile at the assistant, like we might be from the same planet. Head for the change room.

The yard door spills lukewarm April light. This bloke's unloading a van. Black polo, black slacks, like a jazzer. Dracula hair and a smooth goatee. Boxes piled on his arms like they weigh nothing. He says, "Get in the van."

Among boxes of clothes and nylon cord, the ceiling light casts stunted shadows.

"What's your name?"

"Felicity. Flick."

His fingers sift my hair. "It's real."

Up goes my chin. "Everything about me is real."

He knuckles my cheek. "What exactly are you?"

"A woman."

I know he's pleased. "You're a sissy. Get undressed."

"Please."

"Do as I say."

No menace. No threat. The masculine voice of restraint. Quick-flowing desire laps my skin. Slip off my jacket. My fingers shake as I pull up my dress. I fumble my boots. My panties get snagged. My cock, hard and needy.

"You see," he says, all reasonable, "you got a sissy dolly. Don't touch it."

"Please."

"All fours."

A clumsy move in a cramped space. The metal floor dusty with rainbows.

He holds his hands in front of my face. They smell of oil and work.

Lick his fingers. I'm shaking. My cock pulses.

"When did you find yourself?"

"Thirteen. I stole a dress. Midnight blue. Flared with frills. Put it on and I was flying."

"And the eyes?"

"My sister made me up like Cleopatra."

"A stylish woman, with a little dolly. Very little."

"It's good with clothes. Smooth." My cheeks flush hot. These are intimacies.

"Hairy pits?"

"My boyfriend says it's feminine."

"Your boyfriend?" His voice mild and steady. His hands still. Only shooters hold their hands still.

"He's manly in every way."

"You fuck often?"

"Two and three times a night." Through warm dark hours, Miquel is always in me. I wake and sleep and he's in me.

"You're self-made."

"I'm good and obedient." My body tingles, flashed with heat. "Please." I lick his hand. He holds me off with one finger.

Sudden brightness flushes the air. He sits on a box by the open door. "Here."

My naked arousal a public event, I lay cradled by his tall knees. "You're open." His knuckles sink home. "So are thieves rewarded."

Writhing. Slimy with sweat.

"Whose body is this?"

"Yours."

He deposits me on the floor. Traffic, machinery, sounds of the street, flow over my flesh. The whole town could take me.

He brings the shop girl, talking a relaxed way. "She's a thief. She wants nice things for her sissy body."

The girl laughs. "That won't do." I'm surprised she's Scottish. I thought she'd be whelped off the Polthorne. Her boot strokes my thigh. "She has good skin."

"She's very aroused."

"That thing looks fit to burst. Too titchy for me." She giggles. "I like to see what I'm eating."

There's a rustle of clothes. He strokes my back. "Ask nicely, Felicity."

"Felicity?"

"Her name, she says."

"Felicity." The girl swills it over her tongue stud.

"Ask nicely."

"Please fuck me. I've been good." A shiver cracks me like lightning. "Please."

He's in. I ride back, weepy with gratitude. He pins me like a butterfly.

The girl says, "Her little prick's leaking dew drops."

I move to touch but he slaps my hand. "Whose body is this?"

"Yours."

"My god." The girl laughs. "She wets from her arse."

He's Caesar with the voice of a dove. "It's her pussy. It wets."

He's barrelling deep in my guts.

The girl's hand under my abs. "So tiny."

I don't want her to, but it's not my body. With a move that tears me wide he fills me. She brings me off, pain spiking my groin. "I love you, I love you, I love you."

The man laughs.

"Oh," she says. "The little girl made a mess."

They make me mop the floor with my dress but let me keep the clothes I took. Wipe myself all I can and put on the shirt and mini. The Scots girl kisses me, biting my lips.

He drives up west. Makes me sit leg cocked on the dash. "A trucker's slut." At every red light his hand's on my cock. He pulls me off on Tower Bridge and again at Marble Arch. I cum pressed against the window, wailing at civilians.

With a fine sense of my needs, he boots me out. I sprawl on the pavement. "Slut," he shouts, a big grin on his lovely face.

Transmission

I'm late and Agnieszka's in charge. I wiggle into the meeting, dumbstruck at her appearance. She's modelling a man's suit—charcoal, Paul Smith or something—a bleach white shirt with silver cufflinks and, insanely, a Carlton Club tie. Her hair, ironed flat, in a vicious tail. No makeup. Swear I see wires in her skin. Tony and Freddie Dexter sit either side. Tony with his collar gaping. Dexter gleaming with sweat. The impression is a ventriloquist, up the jacksies of lacklustre puppets. And they think I'm the oddball.

Tony's eyes fix on my legs. I didn't try this skirt before I nicked it. It's short even for me. My legs are bruised. There's this nasty bullet welt on my hand. Possibly, I'm a distraction.

Agnieszka draws breath—or pretends to. "I have been here since eight."

"I said I'd be here at ten."

"It is ten-thirty."

"Traffic." I get coffee from the filter, and I'm not at all surprised they're still staring when I sit down. I've never done a civilian job because that would fuck me. But there's a nasty interview feel even I recognise. "So…" I give them the smile. "What's occurring?"

Mr. Miller pays these men well. A generous sort, he does right by the boys. But even handsome Tony, scruffbag man about town, defers to Agnieszka, while Dexter studies his fingers like they've undergone some change he can't place.

The blonde masterpiece speaks. "There have been developments. Two developments." Her hands lift and settle. "A transmission. From a node in the Middle East. An anomaly to regular traffic."

That blip in the desert she tipped me about. "What's the score on this anomaly?"

"That is one development," with a kind of robust emptiness. "There is another, concerning yourself."

Overriding the urge to slap her takes unhealthy effort. "What's that then?"

"The British Secret Service. It seems you annoyed them."

Dexter goes off like a nodding dog. "Oh yes. Definitely miffed."

"Since what occasion? We've had several tiffs."

Her unblinking eyes, cruel as the moon. "Decisive action has been authorised. It is inconvenient."

This sensation, I'm loath to admit, is embarrassment. "This anomaly. Got a trace?"

Tony weighs his moment. A tussle of lust and duty. "The equipment is helpful." Judicious prick. "As is Agnieszka's expertise. Our immediate need is progress." That soupy voice don't suit him. "I believe delivery is your key metric."

So they go on, like I didn't get broomhandled up the tunnel. Dexter's worked the coordinates of this communications outlier. Obvious it's my boy Jazin, up to mischief. I been shot enough not to believe in coincidence. The puzzle is what came first: the interference to Mr. Miller's business, the spooks' interest in Jazin, or his interest in me. I'm everyone's kamikaze.

Goes without saying, Mr. Miller's deals with the Middle East are strictly Dubai bag boys. Dubai being the auto erotic asphyxiation among criminal pastimes. I preferred Aden, for all it got lively. This signal from the playboy oasis got tangled with Mr. Miller as part of some ongoing attack, says Dexter. Which is bullshit.

Tony gives me a look horribly close to pity. "This is context." He says it loud, to shut Dexter down. Dexter blinks like a punched spaniel. "You understand, Flick, my focus is to regain control of our communications capability. We've lost money because of damaged interactions. You know the value of reputation."

Is this the same Tony who bad-mouthed Dexter while eating my hummus and veg? It's all a bit pally-arsey. "What do you suggest, Tony?"

"Why don't you take time to examine the situation." Anticipating I'll throw a strop, he squeezes my arm. "It's your expertise we need. Route your input through Agnieszka. She's here full time."

My muscles flex and his hand slides like something stunned.

Agnieszka thinks she's unreadable. But her eyes are clear glass. She never said how she'd kill me.

"I'm going to powder my nose."

These toilets have coy figurines for Gents and Ladies. He's a sod for effect, is Mr. Miller. Have a piss and throw some shapes, snarling in silent rage. To have the shaft put in is unconscionable—they know all I've done for their boss. Not that I blame Agnieszka. It must be murder to be her. This is saccharine Tony and bung-ho Freddie Dexter. And no choice but continue.

When I leave the toilet, a bearded black lad relaxes in the corridor. Jeans and plaid: not one of Mr. Miller's boys. He shakes his hand—a loose, casual greeting—then I realise he's priming an asthma inhaler. He jerks powder into his mouth. The hiss of gas fills the quiet hallway.

"Nice day for it."

Self-satisfied, that smile. "I don't swing that way."

"But if you did."

"If."

It's dirty to pull a gun this close. Poor taste and poor planning. I nuzzle my XD into his waist. "Why so much energy, chasing me?"

Nice laugh. Manly. "People hate you, sis." Shrewd and reproving. "You take a simple moment, make it drama."

"What about that bloke? The fire?"

He shrugs, a world of power in his shoulders. "You care now?"

"Second-rate violence cheapens us all."

"Hepburn." He moves away from the gun, light as a step on the dancefloor. "You had your warning. People stand vexed, get me? You run with this batty brigade, do their bidding. What Rotheray says is nothing. He be next."

It's rare to hear it so blunt. "You know the Polish girl?"

Then he insults me. He taps my gun with a big, firm finger. He's a pulse in my veins. "You don't mean this, do you? Not here. You draw in a time you can't fire. I tell you. You bring vexation and damage. You bring it yourself."

He walks, knowing I won't drop him. Take a moment to fix my eyes. Unkind light gilds my lashes like tears.

Everything's decided. Agnieszka talks trace and triangulation, while Tony snugs my shoulders to guide me to the door. I'm the glamorous guest who got squiffy and pissed on the cat.

Tony tries dropping honey. "Just a few days. Stay in touch won't you." He strokes my cheek and I think: you'll never know what it is to fold me double in a filthy van. Big girl thoughts; no one likes to feel small.

To get married in England requires twenty-nine days' notice. So the notice of my nuptials must already be given. Wedding plans are a welcome displacement from setbacks. So I go looking for Spike. At a pub on the shit side of Hampstead, a woman with miserable skin says she can get him a message. If I show a bit, for her trouble. Everyone's down on their strings these days, which puts getting shot in perspective. Those of us from the wily side know money can always be found. But for regular punters, poverty spreads like arthritis.

Spike is lanky and dangly. Arms too long for his body. Legs like spaghetti. In grubby jeans and a Harrington specked with paint. His cover is shiftless decorator. He's a no-show maestro. He's lost hair and his face has canyons that make a man wise and disgraceful. He's casual, like it hasn't been years. "You're looking well."

"Not bad yourself. How's the painting game?"

"Up and down." A thin moustache of beer froth tags his lip. "What brings you back?"

Do hopeless girly shoulders. "Business. Friends."

"Trouble?"

That's a tad forward. "Paperwork." Try to frame the logistics. "Birth certificates."

"Not too hard."

"And notice of an upcoming marriage. Backdated."

A sly reaction moves his chops. "Aren't you hitched in Spain?"

"Catalunya. Two birth certificates. Parents' names, occupation, all that. Young ages. Thirties."

"Needs full names."

Something clogs my throat. "Leave the names blank."

"Not really. The authorities expect it."

I'm used to secrets. Their weight doesn't slow me. But unfamiliar reticence makes me awkward. "Private business." I sound unconvinced.

In the instep of his thumb is a blue star. Shaky ink, uneven colour. He did it himself, when he was inside. For his daughter, Star. She must be eighteen, nineteen. Spike rubs the tattoo. It's habit. "Who do you trust?"

Women are the ones who care, where men are cramped and simple. Care, concern, trust—these baubles we hang on our tree. But I don't care. I trust no one but Miquel and Roc. I need a favour from Spike and he waits with absent sadness. He's not seen me in years and I'm telling him lies. He's disappointed. But I want what I want. "It's not that." Do the coy dolly thing. "Just business. I got to keep schtum." When we've done the money, I ask, "How's Star?"

"Working her gap year."

"Yeah?" Make sure to look interested.

"She got into Cambridge. Girton. Doing natural science. She loved all that at school."

I don't remember his daughter repping the test tubes. But I don't know her—or him—that well. Like any dull-witted civilian, I say. "You must be proud."

He looks over the rim of his pint, a walk-on man, too hard to show it.

Call a ride back to town. The driver's west African by his accent. Ghanaian, I reckon. White vest and suit jacket. Lines at his brow from squinting and worry. The radio's locked to a talk station, and he's on the phone the whole time, mixing English and one of those languages I'm too ignorant to know. "Yes, oh yes, yes," and "No tell him, no you must, no," mixed with what could be Akan or Dagbani. "You must tell him." Then a blizzard of consonants.

The radio says a corpse in Holland Park. Tell the driver: "Change of plan." He watches the rearview as I cross my legs, this skirt short as a tea towel.

The usual clowns point and film. Every crime's a circus. White tent in the park; techs in puffy suits; the explosives mob, in case it's terror. Pump my hips towards a young plod at the fluttering tape.

"'Scuse me." Give him soft eyes. "Can I cut through? I'm meeting someone."

He stares at my bruised legs, the black shirt flush against me, my nose-wrinkling flirtation. "It's a crime scene." He points at the tape. "No access. Miss." 'Miss' with a little cough.

"It's my girlfriends." A true ingénue. "We're meeting for tea." The tent and its slow-moving supplicants, creased suits and powder-white hazmat, beguiles me. Death gives thrust to those without traction in life. "I'm just going to the restaurant."

He makes some formless gesture.

People press to the tape, filming. No one has much to fall back on, so they film what they find. The Alhambra or filth poking a corpse. 'I was there! I'm someone!' The young plod's distracted with the crowd and his radio's inaudible demands. He shouts at some bloke bending the tape. I slip sideways, tagging the ribbon from tree to tree.

A tight mesh of spring leaves and I'm silky sly beneath stoic branches. I like it outdoors. Me and Miquel are in the yard, on the roof, at it like foxes in the Parc del Turó del Putxet. I love that view across El Raval while he bites my neck.

Slide to the edge of the woods, the tent blinking between leaves. I need the source of this. Nothing's coincidence. I've an eye to the corner where canvas panels are rigged with metal clips. Unhitch a couple, chafing the wound on my hand. Pain says I'm alive. Inside the tent it's a tableau. A weird, steady thing. Noise drops. Faces turn. The crumpled detectives. The bright-eyed forensics. The pathologist with her dreads knotted back. Her look measures me for her slab.

In the sliver of time before bedlam I reach for the corpse. Beneath a waxed sheet, a thing out of use, an intention for someday. I expect Agnieszka's hollow eyes, content at a sacrifice she engineered. But it's Tony. Handsome Tony. Still with his top button undone. The bullet hole in his neck so right for him: roguish and scruffy.

Then hard hands keel me over and I'm arrested.

Professionals

Shepherd's Bush cop shop has dismal views. Can't see any decent shops. I'm in a room, not a cell, because Detective Inspector Jack Marsh—a young and eager fellow who knots his tie in a Van Wijk—is intrigued at my interest in Tony's death. He calls Tony 'Mr. Hazell' which, clearly, was his name for one-night hotels. I'm sorry for Tony. But sorrier for me, sitting in this hard chair, drinking cardboard coffee.

D.I. Jack Marsh knows who I am. Who I am 'explains things'. He calls me 'Ms. Hepburn' in almost a shy way, like I might hurt him and he might enjoy that. When they booked me in, a sharp woman plod gave me a proper frisking, lingering, oddly, on my calves. They took my gun for tests. I want it back.

Now I give Jack an impressive length of thigh, which I stroke with delicate candour. "Why would I shoot Tony?" I'm purring. "Mr. Miller is an old friend." Jack has one of those black tungsten wedding rings that look like machinery. I imagine his wife is a smart, practical sort.

"You kill for money. That's your trade. Perhaps one of Mr. Hazell's enemies made you an offer."

"And I left him in Holland Park? And went back to check he's still dead?"

"Things didn't go to plan."

"Oh, please." I signal to the filth at the door to bring more coffee. "What is this 'plan' things didn't go to? My job isn't knocking off sidekicks. I bring focus and expertise. You could do with my help."

"Why don't you enlighten me?"

"Bodies don't get dumped in London, you know that." Lean forward so my pheromones dance him in. "Strange things are happening lately. Some bods are unaccountably upset and I catch the backwash. There's nothing of me to this death."

A junior flatfoot seeps round the door. He holds a laptop like an offering. Jack Marsh asks me to wait, while him and the lad pick at words onscreen. Cross and recross my legs, so the girl guarding the door gets a flash of my knickers. She's a dull sort but, no doubt, someone loves her.

"Well," says D.I. Jack Marsh. "I should ask what you did with the other gun."

I wriggle with pure delight. "Let me guess. Ballistics says he got shot with a whole different piece. Of course, you could tell that from the entry wound." They're staring, so I push the boat. "I would say you're looking for someone in a hurry. Who wanted to make a point and ain't bothered about the mess. Me or anyone like me, we're not so blasé. Who you're looking for is who I'm looking for."

The door opens. D.S. Chloe Bell has a thing for grey-blue jackets with unnecessary stitching. In motion, her shirt shows a pretty little pot belly. She washed her hair and let it dry on the wind. "Thank you for looking after D.I. Temple." Mischievous cow.

Jack watches his power thin like ebb tide. "Ms. Hepburn is under arrest. She compromised a crime scene."

Everything about Chloe Bell speaks of striving to master compulsion. She stares at Jack Marsh, her stance wide and centred. She doesn't have rank. This isn't her manor. "The Yard has use for Ms. Hepburn."

"Is the Yard not interested in who killed Tony Hazell? Or security issues in Mr. Miller's business?"

That's not a bad punt. I haven't spilled Mr. Miller's troubles but Jack's a bright boy.

"The Yard has interests." Bell's chest and belly lunge, irrefutable. "This murder is part of a bigger picture."

"Sorry to butt in."

Jack looks at me, shiny with anger.

"I want my gun back. For emotional support."

Chloe Bell has a Ford Mustang. She'd drive like Bullitt if she had somewhere to go. I like driving. Sitting with idle hands appals me. I ask can I smoke, and she jacks down all the windows. A cruel breeze whips my mouth. "It's the spooks. If you don't know."

"Rashad Jazin isn't short of friends." She curses fuckwit cyclists. "He has grateful bodies across the peninsula. The hair bear bunch get a cut of the guns."

"I met some cheerleaders over Stepney. They seemed remarkably fond of a westernised dog."

"They're not stupid." She skims a delivery truck, jeffing at the driver.

"They talk big but the numbers are small. When you burn through ballistics, you get pragmatic. Jazin opens doors."

The streets roll by. I'm itchy. Head south through Earl's Court. Brompton Cemetery and Eel Brook Common. She's making for Wandsworth Bridge. "How's the concierge racket?"

"It's a line of inquiry."

"With shit like Declan Nolan?"

"Alcohol is an expensive lifestyle. And that AK of yours cost more than a dinner. What? Of course I know about it. And one day the Provos will knock on his door to discuss how he invested their money. You think you've got problems."

"I have opportunities."

We glide around Sands End, scrubbed and well-behaved. She takes a nice strip of black silk from the glovebox. "Turn your head."

"What?"

"I don't want you to know where I live."

Saccharine suburbia gets blacked out. "Watch it, you're pulling my hair."

"Big girl like you making fuss." She gives the knot a mean tweak. "It's just till we get there."

I despise a blindfold. "Won't it look odd, you carting me round like this?"

"You're not the first."

Not that I like the sound of that, but she has got more intriguing. I always hate it. Scarves and bandages slapped on my face, by big egos with not much to hide. What she's thinking: I get caught, I can't lead anyone to her. Weak assumption.

The tyres say we crossed Wandsworth Bridge. The way the car leans I know we're on the gyratory. East, I reckon. Battersea. A main road, by the sound. Then a right and, nearby, trains. Clapham Junction. Curve left, then sharp right. Not much traffic, we don't wait at corners. Quiet. Maybe near Wandsworth Common. We shunt at the kerb, the big engine suddenly still. A bit of late birdsong. Residential street.

She gets round the passenger side and levers me up. The trick to walking blindfold is to ignore it. Life punishes hesitation. I get the scrape of wood and a key in a lock. Not a door, the sound's too hollow. Maybe a side gate. We're still outside, my heels feel damp gravel. "Up," she says. We're on metal stairs. One flight. Then two. Steps bolted to the side of a building. There's give in the metal. Fire escape? "Wait." Now she's at a door. Turns one, two, three locks. Every noise reveals her. "Step." I step too far. Lunge into a hallway. The door shuts. She puts on the light. It glows behind the silk. The blindfold's gone. My eyes contract but stay open. I'm no beginner.

A narrow hall. Grey carpet. Bare walls. Steady light. Three doors to the right. Door at the end. Where the wall meets the ceiling shows damp painted over. There's a burglar alarm. A smoke detector. A carbon monoxide meter. Cameras watch from high corners.

The kitchen is cramped with big furniture. The table seats six. How could she need that? Old cooker, chunky fridge, washer dryer—clean but drab with disuse. She doesn't own these things. She minds them for her replacement.

She lifts a bottle from the rack. Holds it flat like something dead. "Red's all I drink." She nods me to sit, and I pull out a chair, watching for a reaction in case it's her chair. But the seat's dusty. They're all dusty, bar one.

She opens the wine and pours tall measures. Merlot, firm and fruity. She tries not to shudder at my lipstick on the glass.

"Indian or Thai?"

"Indian. Vegetarian."

"South Indian Ayurvedic?"

Rice cakes and lentil rings. "Lovely."

"Half hour." She tucks the phone out of sight. "They cook it fresh." She sits sideways from me. "You know Superintendent Rotheray?"

"Someone tried to kill me. I thought he'd like to know."

Still no eye contact. "Aren't you used to it?"

"Not with a bazooka at tiffin. People in my industry generally have some finesse. Which reminds me." The wine is fresh-tasting, smooth. Hard to imagine her choosing this, flicking options, reading up on terroir. "I had to dissuade a bloke yesterday. Spooks. And they tried it on down Deptford. Civilian got toasted. It's what Jazin means to them, innit? What that lovely gun money means."

She dumps me what's left of the bottle and gets another. I consider poisons that lay below liquid. Heavy molecules.

Turn the bottle around. Not sure looking for what. "I don't generally do a bottle before dinner."

"You've had a busy day." There's something impressive about her. It flickers through her evasions like fire through trees. No noise. We're far from traffic. That scratch, I guess, is birds on the roof. Or rats. There's always rats. "Rashad Jazin." Now she looks at me. "Jazin has interesting business. Cash goes out, cash comes in. Investments pay off, contracts prosper. His diplomatic status gets him through doors. He's tireless over the canapés. But there's something less than tangible about his tangible wealth."

I'm in a strange place with a filth I don't trust. "He must have substance. You don't stiff blokes in that business."

"Oh, they get paid. As you say, they're irritable people. Jazin maintains a bright gloss of influence and utility. A perfect suspect package."

"The business sheikh."

"Felicity. Can I call you Felicity?"

"It's my name. And I'll call you Chloe. From the Greek: blossoming, fertility. A goddess name."

"How many languages do you speak?"

"Four or five well. Bits of others. Just stuff I picked up."

"Your file says you're a primary psychopath."

"I'm just a girl. What makes the drip-dry brigade so keen on Mr. Jazin?"

"Access. He brings the right people. You've been to the Middle East?"

"Yemen. Dubai. Bit of Saudi."

"How did you get on?"

"A lot of lovely men with free time."

She stands and I realise her phone vibrated. "Stay here."

She unbolts the door. Then her shoes on the iron stairs. Check the kitchen drawers: old cutlery, string, electrical tape. Cupboards mostly empty. Cups and plates look like they've been here forever. Jolly patterns, mazed and weathered. Someone bought these. Was proud to get them. Used them with a sense of good fortune. Long gone now and the plates still here, forgotten till they get dumped.

By the kitchen door, cameras dare me to something unruly. "Can I help?" All bushy-bright. She ignores me and dumps the bags, their sloppy sides translucent. She palms forks and spoons from a drawer, remnants of larger sets. I know this is how she always eats. Functional and that's it.

We scrape the cartons. There's pongal, a good stomach liner; hawaijar, as nice as fermented soybeans can be; eye-watering jackfruit chutney; and parottas to wrap it up. How a person eats says a lot. If they like food. If they're tidy. If they had hard times as a kid. Kids who grow up hungry understand food. I don't have those credentials. Dad's work kept us comfortable. Chloe Bell interrogates each grain of rice. Every cashew is examined. A creature of plain utility, she deliberates each mouthful. I'm thinking about my hips. About my wedding dresses. But for her to get fat would be a betrayal of some skinny childhood. In the killing game, we read people. Her behaviour is consistent. The tight posture, the downward looks, the sparks of interest that die away, the movements centred from her pelvis using minimum muscle power. I chat and smile: she hasn't mirrored me once. Those neural niceties don't feature. She was so much more alive doing her concierge act. Getting here was an act: shouting at truckers, laughing at her own jokes. She's shown me more than she meant to, showing me her habitat.

"You don't mind me coming in on Jazin? Rotheray thinks I'm useful."

"You're avoiding prison." That chilly matter-of-factness. "I'm sure to someone like you that's a sensible choice. Besides." Wine ripples down her gullet. "I'm a fraud specialist. I'll be at the inquiry with spreadsheets and accounts. I take it you plan to kill Jazin? That is what Rotheray wants?"

"He wants me close."

"Do you smoke?"

"Only these. Like Gauloises but Spanish." I stay put while she thumps about in the hall. The smoke alarm wails and goes silent.

She gets an old saucer for an ashtray. It's glazed with a faded picture of a sandy-haired boy in shorts sailing a boat on a pond. The boy's smile is worn and the setting is bleak. All that time, there with his boat.

She's not a regular smoker, that's plain. It's to make believe she's a real cop with hard knuckles. "If you close Jazin, Rotheray won't hand you a bulletproof dress."

I'm tempted to remind her death comes to each living thing. Propaganda of the deed is my answer to anyone who lives life for its own sake. On the fourth of August 1878 Sergey Stepniak-Kravchinsky, a talented man who walked the walk, killed Nikolay Mezentsov, chief of the Tzar's 'Third Department', his secret police. Stabbed him on the street and walked away. One of Miquel's heroes, Stepniak. A killer for reasons not money. For me, doing the king of the spooks makes him golden. And what happened to lovely young Stepniak? He died in London. Knocked down by a train at a level crossing in Chiswick. The gods just laugh at us. So I tell Chloe Bell, "Most people live too long." My breath in smoke rings. They break apart on her ceiling. She watches my slender neck, the way my hair falls to my shoulders. She sees my legs. Hard muscles through my thighs. "What are your plans for Jazin?"

"He's connected to illegal arms transactions. Some of his associates are British or wanted in Britain. He does deals through a London embassy, which is a breach of protocol. He's the vector between a spread of dubious bodies."

"Knock him down, someone else comes through."

"He's politically exposed, so we watch his bank accounts. There are discrepancies. We can't trace them all. He uses privacy rackets and offshore hideaways."

Swish to the counter to crack more Merlot. Keep my back to her, play trustful. "Doesn't every rich, connected bloke have interesting transactions? The Jazins of this world are a magnitude different to us plebs."

She stiffens, grips the table. "I can't stand people who think they're immune."

"No surprise you don't like me then."

"You intrigue me."

This kitchen is her, off-duty. See her, nights and weekends, eating takeaway, writing reports, watching the world through her phone. Busy and useful, she won't get promotion. She'll get used up and forgotten. Takes courage to live that way.

With wine in her cheeks, she asks, "How do you not have PTSD? With all you do."

I don't understand the question. "I like what I do. What's your fun?"

"I'm a numbers freak. A dyke with spreadsheets. I was with a Commander in anti-terrorist a couple of years. Did flowers, cards, surprises. The sex was great."

"You don't have to tell me."

"But you're so keen on sex. I'm methodical. I follow patterns. So I didn't want to see the shifts she worked didn't map to operations. A Commander. Of course she was busy. There were things she couldn't tell me. Safer, you see? What you don't know can't get you killed. So I put up with nights and weekends. I doubted my own suspicious nature. You know how that feels for a filth?"

"I know not to be too trusting." Try to sound nice. But people cause their own problems.

"It was a civilian. A florist. A woman whose biggest risk was blood from a rose. But she was fun. Civilian fun."

I don't guess I'll get out this building without bravado. "What did you do?"

"When I went to give her keys back she was out. I drank five litres of water and pissed all over her kitchen. I pissed in the oven, the washing machine. I pissed behind the fridge. I see her sometimes, on major shouts. I'm glad she never looks happy. Does your heart get broken, Felicity?"

"When I was a kid. Now I make the weather."

Hers is a soft little smile. "Everyone says you're submissive."

"The submissive controls expectations. If I sub, you must dom. I make you perform. I surrender control because I don't doubt my power. Do you know how hard it is to deal with someone who surrenders control? Every shred of anxiety leaves my body and piles onto the man. If he fails in his most basic task, how does he face the mirror? I terrify men through submission. I don't have safe words. I don't have limits. My partner is a man of extraordinary strength. Intellectual, political, physical strength. A man all day. I subject his strength to my surrender. I carry death in my hands. I don't recognise heartbreak."

For a long time she looks at me, this worrisome detective. "How did you become this?"

"Tell me about Jazin."

She takes a cigarette. "You drink brandy?"

"Mascaró. Fine Catalan brandy."

"I keep Martell for cold nights."

The bottle has been here a long time. Crusted. The label's damp. It rides nice on the Merlot. Old Jean Martell wasn't even French. He was born on Jersey. "You were more jolly as a concierge."

A swill of brandy hits her brain. "I was on duty."

"And this is you?"

"I'm a loner. A drinker. Hard round the eyes."

"I don't want to bulldoze your project. I respect fine-grained work.

But I can aim and shoot faster than you. Behind the trigger is the better machine." It's late. I could lay down and, possibly, sleep. She's the sort to stay wakeful, brooding in grubby pools of light. Replaying times she could have been smarter. She'll only be this. It's not my problem.

"I'm on duty tomorrow. I'm sure you have things to do."

"Is this where you send me home?"

"The door's locked till morning. You share my bed."

Rightly, she wants to be tough. To give orders I obey. In the candour of her lassitude, she's the cop and I'm the crook and that's her moral agency. She lets me use her toilet, standing guard. The bathroom's cluttered and uncared-for. Makeup and cleansers, stuff for her role-play. Old paracetamols, rusty scissors, a menstrual cup in a dusty box, half a dozen dead ants. Ants have an exoskeleton. They don't decay like flabby humans. Those ants could be here long after us two are gone.

Though the flat seems large, with those doors we don't mention, her bedroom—the room she shows me—is a cupboard. A double bed fills the floor. Simple metal frame. No headboard or bars. Plain nylon sheets, a bit foggy. Collapsed pillows. A bed where an exhausted body would fall.

I get the side by the wall, so she knows if I try to leave. Her regular side, by lines of old sweat. We drop our shoes. Of course we sleep dressed. The light stays on and a body width between us. Close enough to see, beneath the grey, her skin's alive with freckles. I picture a kid, gappy and snubbed, unsure at each moment, preferring to stay alone. She hardens her face. Everything to us is armour. But something shamefully yielding beneath her creations. That little girl, in flight from the crowd.

Because our eyes meet, I ask, "What you thinking?"

Her voice warm from drink and close surroundings. "You want Jazin. You offered me nothing."

"You read my file?"

"It's a page-turner."

"Then you know I got a sister. The most beautiful lez. Keeps herself immaculate. Intelligent, funny, tall. Tits out here. Never says no. Submissive. You can walk her like a dog."

"I know. She's on the game."

"She has to, to manage her urges."

"Your offer?"

"I get you quality time. You cut me slack on Jazin."

"What quality time?"

"Up to you, Chloe. I'm talking a girl that does everything."

"You can offer that?"

"She'll do it."

"And this gives you Jazin?"

Try not to sound impatient. "We're professionals. We know the terrain. Take three days. Three's a good number. I get you a flat, stock it with booze, she keeps you busy, I engage Jazin. You're nowhere near it. My sister will swear any alibi." It's arrows in the dark.

These sheets have her smell. Faint hairs litter the bed. The pillow's spongy. My brain wants sleep. My body twists with restriction.

She talks and I'm baffled. "We could go somewhere. Sweden. I've heard it's nice."

Fuck Sweden. She's crackers. "How does that nail Jazin?"

"I was thinking, after."

I really try. But I can't process this nonsense. She's indulging in romance because she's drunk and I smell right. What this has to do with anything I can't fathom. Try to sugar my voice. "We both got work in the morning. Let's not kill each other tonight. It's a good offer with Roc. She delivers. And it might not be three days. She's ripe to settle." Now I miss Roc truly. She tinkles her fingers and complexity melts away.

Things quiet down. Hard sheets and hard light recall less-successful moments of my career. That business in Cannes, up in the hills. That shit with the Egyptian army. The beatings and bullets that ruffled my skin. Yet through it all I'm gorgeous.

Drift to some kind of sleep. It's the mansion dream. A big house and I'm checking room after room, admiring décor, ready for death. Chasing a man whose patent shoes click against marble stairs. Who clinks the ice as he swirls his scotch. Whose clothes sound like caresses. I must catch him. But he moves like oil. Grandeur and space. Panels and drapes. Sunlight fills the windows. I can't look outside. There's a gun in my hand as I rattle down bright hallways. Pursuing a target just out of range. Dreams so real my lungs knit tight. Every thought to the mission. Every nerve to the trigger. 'I'll send you to hell,' I tell that man. Lullaby words.

Chloe Bell burrows into me, blonde against my sternum. I stroke her neck. She makes yielding noises. So easy to kill. Gone before waking. I embrace her. She responds in dull sleepiness, planing her body against me. We're born. We die. Others replace us. Not better or worse. Others. I kiss her dry little mouth.

I wake and she's lacing her shoes. In a neat manoeuvre, she draws a Glock 17. Illegal, no doubt. The Met wouldn't authorise her. "I could kill you."

"'Course you could."

"It's loaded."

"I see."

"I would have no problem ending your life."

"Alright."

"If I put this to your neck…" Her aim's a mess. "Would you do what I say?"

"Chloe. Darling." I stand. She doesn't even track my heart. "Before that touches my neck, I will lay you cold. You don't want to kill me. But I don't need an incentive. To kill is my opening move. When I play chess with my sister I lose like a bastard. I only attack. I sacrifice all my army. She beats me with foresight and patience. You will love every minute with her. The time for this was when I was asleep. Love shouldn't get in the way, sweet girl. Nothing gets in the way of the gun."

She shows me Jazin's figures. Though accountancy was never my strength, these numbers are manufactured, modelled from briefly glimpsed actuals. Jazin gets places. No doubt he says yes to more things than he inks. Most immediately interesting, he's in London this week. That pretty boy from The Tihamah Lounge will have told Jazin's people about me. But the man needs to eyeball the candy.

Chloe makes terrible coffee. "There's no breakfast."

I burn a lot of calories. I want breakfast. "I'm in shit with the spooks." Light two cigarettes, so she gets my taste.

Smoke meshes her hair. "The whole world wants you."

"I don't set out to annoy people. They do it themselves."

"You told me about the spooks when I got you out of shtuck. Or don't you remember that favour? Holland Park? Tony Hazell? D.I. Marsh will write that up and I'll get bollocked."

"I'm grateful, Chloe. Truly. What they did to Tony Hazell, that's their idea of smalltalk. They'll make any amount of mess to keep Jazin."

"If you get him more people will die."

"People die anyway."

Do my face. Get my eyes busy. Restore this look that gets me through each thrilling occasion.

We swap numbers and snog. Her lips are gritty. She blindfolds me again. Must look extraordinary to the neighbours. But she doesn't seem fussed. It's another chance to kill me—to do us both. Her heavy breath says she knows.

She drops me at Peckham bus station, of all places. Whips off the patch like the last gasp of a drab magic act. We kiss and cuddle. I tell her I'll set things with Roc. "You'll love her. She's a professional."

Machinery

Get a bus to Waterloo. It goes the long way through Southwark and Rotherhithe. A young bloke smiles at me. We flirt a bit. But he gets off at his stop. People are on and off at Brunswick Quay, Russia Dock Road, Southwark Park. What drives the before and after of this brief time together. Intersecting, traversing and moving apart. If I'd taken a different path in life, if such a thing could be imagined, I'd live in one of these backstreets. A little two-bed with a smell of damp and sullied communal garden. A lodger in his late teens, fresh from home, sharing my bed. He'd trace the lines around my eyes and tell me I'm still a looker. We'd go down the seaside in summer, two weeks in Margate. What's better than that?

On the ramp at Waterloo I check missed calls. Mr. Miller sounds in a bad way. Left a message himself, which is rare and disturbing. But with Tony gone maybe there's no one he trusts. He says he's grateful of me, he's sure I'm making progress. Call his private number but it's voicemail. Leave a breathy message, dripping with consolation. I've neglected his business. Time to take charge. Agnieszka's inbox has a specially ugly sound. Tell her I want a highlight report, jaldi. Then replay this unknown number. Its quiet rasp says, 'You don't listen do you? The grownups have had enough'. What a treat to get a threatening call. Don't waste time on how he got this number. Phones are currency.

Buy a ticket to Woking and make a big thing of getting some bloke to point me at the Woking train, which I board with a storm of wiggling so everyone sees me. Like all trains in London it smells of burnt dust. Waterloo slips behind, seamy with morning sun. Spring colours the city, the trees fuzzed green. New apartments stacked from kiddie bricks flush with light. A robot lists the pretty numbers: Earlsfield, Wimbledon, Surbiton. Places I can't imagine being for any reason than spite.

Get off at Vauxhall and swish to the spook shop. They're not as tetchy as the bods across the river. With any luck whoever followed me onto the train is gnashing their teeth in Clapham. Find a sly spot by the old pier to dial a number which beeps in someone's pocket in the drunken pyramid behind me. Then a sloe-eyed stroll to the Pleasure Gardens.

Of course he tracks me easy. It would be worrying if he didn't. He's older, his face more stringy but his body still lean. A forceful walk, shoulders forward, makes me think he's taken up cycling. His arms have that kinetic grip of pushing through traffic. He walks past me and under the trees. A walk in the woods. Real old school. His jacket has a single vent. He was always a double vent man. And tan brogues, scuffed on the heel. This matters.

He pauses under the sycamores where, once, he would have lit a cigarette. His dark curls are tamed, grey at the roots. His placid eyes hold a spark.

"The brown dog weeps at the moon, comrade."

Air moves in and out his nostrils. "If you want a war, stay in Spain."

"Catalunya."

His jaw clenches. "Our friends up the way want your head."

"They're friends now?"

Last year's leaves sift around. He kicks and they crumble. "We are not involved in this. That individual and the interests he represents are crucial to the fight against terror."

"His friends are Baghdad barbers. I've seen their scissors."

"You've seen nothing." He slips between trees.

"What you got on him?"

"I shouldn't be talking to you."

"You could say you're paying off a tart."

The man he was would have laughed. "That would be less risk." He swings around to stop me cold. A practised manoeuvre. "What you never grasp is people don't like you. At best you're a useful nuisance. This is what happens when you stop being useful."

"You'd let them kill me?"

"Our political masters get anxious at divisions in the community. They don't see this or that agency. They see a cohort of professionals supposedly keeping them safe. We're civil with the domestic agency. We cooperate. If they believe you want to pause one of their assets, we don't say, 'But she's a good girl.' You've been around long enough to know."

It's alright here with the smell of damp wood and the parakeets lairing about. Tidy spot for a bit of cock. "So why meet me?"

"In my line of work there's a premium on curiosity." He gazes at a fitness trainer putting lycra girls through their moves. "Do you really plan to kill Jazin?"

Oddly, I don't. I want to meet the man everyone's fussing about. But it's become a fact I'll kill him. "It's a favour to the Met."

"Christ almighty." His eyes follow a girl in a strappy top and leggings as she pulls into a split squat that inflates the tattoos on her shins. Her hips are like basketballs. Even I find them entrancing. "If Jazin was out of commission," he says, "that would concentrate risk in Middle East financial networks. There would be instability, in already unstable markets. Which allows a front door. The fanatics. The socialist contingent. Those discontented with a self-renewing elite. Given your fiancé's activities, the Spanish government will classify you as a foreign terrorist. I doubt your friends in Barcelona have the resources to protect you when the Madrileños come clumping around."

That stings more than it should. "I'm highly regarded in the movement."

"Of course. You're a useful nuisance. I'll leave first. It's you they're after."

"Can't nothing be done with these bastards?" Talk too loud. His shoulders calcify.

"When you were a young girl, Felicity, this naivety was charming. You're old enough now to know who's to blame."

There's numbers I could call. But people don't flow like they used to. Sometimes I think I'm the only one left.

Get a ride to Chelsea, to shower and change. Ralph acts surprised. "Ms. Delamarre." His smile is revolting. "We thought you'd left us."

This needs to be dealt with briskly. "Any messages, Ralph?"

His fey little fingers dance. "No one asks that anymore! And, funnily, yes."

A standard, white DL envelope, my alibi name in unremarkable Arial. Such an ordinary object, my body burns. "Who brought this?"

"Courier. Regular chap."

My brain says my room hasn't been searched. But my nerves are itchy. Get the AK-47 from the safe and play with the action, to calm myself. Take a shower and restore my eyes. Slip into a nice Rococo Sand sundress, tight on the waist and high at the thigh. A Japanesey print of water and shifty herons.

The envelope lays on the table, dull and alarming. Stand at the mirror and masturbate, engulfed by big, beautiful cocks. Can this envelope kill me? Doesn't feel like powder inside. If it was dosed, Ralphy-boy would be heaving. A cellular explosive maybe, thin as skin, triggered by interruption to the envelope's integrity. Smart but risky. Could go off in transit. Paper is a psychological weapon. People go mad with what they read.

Get the dumb kid's knife and slit the seal.

'Please forgive the approach. No one bothers with letters anymore. I have a research question on which you might wish to contribute. I shall be at the coffee shop near your hotel at five o'clock each afternoon. Please stop by if convenient. Dr. Frederick Dexter.'

No way to tell it's from Dexter. Nor if it was written before or after Tony's death. If it is Dexter, I'm not surprised. Finding this place is a cinch for an old spook. But he's a fool to say where he'll be.

Make coffee and lay on the bed. Let the breeze caress me. There's music somewhere. My toes itch to dance. Curtis was a lovely dancer. I call Miquel and a dream unfolds as I hear his voice again. That blunt way he answers melts me. He knows not to say much. We chat about the weather. I try to explain the quality of London light but get tangled in adjectives. He tells me I'm out of practice. The gentlest rebuke. I tell him I can't even speak English proper. He laughs but doesn't understand.

My beloved tells me his estimada mare asked about the wedding. This wedding is a fact. Strong, beautiful mum-in-law wants invitations printed. Because I love this man and admire his mum, I say, "How about eight weeks Saturday? Santa Maria del Mar. That would be lovely." He's sniffy about a church do, but his mother won't have nylon.

In careful, direct words, so I understand, he asks if I can sort my dress in eight weeks, and make the arrangements, and whether the family can gather at such short notice. He has important relatives. Everyone must be there. Though madly in love, I'm miffed he should doubt my skills. Any white dress that flatters my shape will suit me. We got cousins and nieces for bridesmaids; they can wear something festive and pretty. And Roc is always stunning. Miquel's mum will supervise food, of which there'll be truckloads. His mates in the band will play the right tunes. Everyone will be drunk for three days. It doesn't need a Gantt chart.

But my darling wants this to be wonderful. The one event I can't let slide. Santa Maria is gorgeous. I can do the full flashing-eyed Catalan bride beneath those slender arches. As for the paperwork, I'll pay a lawyer.

Tenderly, because he's tender with me, he asks when I'll be home. I tell him it's complex business. He doesn't pry. I tell him when I get back, we're staying in bed three days. He laughs and says five. Poor Miquel. He's burning without me. As I look ahead, I know I'll stay with him my whole life. He manages me, that's the thing. He makes me the woman I should be.

A message from Spike. He's got the merchandise. Another unbreakable promise.

If this coffee shop is a trap, I'll be acutely embarrassed. When people want you dead, because they're paid for that, is the same as walking blindfold. You can stumble and stutter. Or move like this is normal. By no means am I an optimist. Gamblers and junkies are optimists and look how that works. I desire the future, knowing death's at hand. Stroll by the river. Smile at men. Enjoy their instant attention. My legs fill a lot of eyes. They're strong, defined. They lead men to my heat. I knew early what a pretty girl I could be. Now I'm ageing exquisitely. So do I go on or stop.

Swing into this dreary coffee shack. Slab tables and fake bygones. Freddie Dexter pretends to read his phone, twisting a paper napkin to ugly shapes. His suit is average and rumpled. His hair hasn't seen a comb. Grey, on some men, is distinguished. On Freddie it seems forgetful.

"Miss Hepburn." He says it too loud.

"Freddie. I got your old school communication."

He bends the napkin like a ruptured cock. "No one bothers with letters. They've become more secure because people assume they're unimportant."

Gift him a smile. "Always one step ahead. I hear there was asset loss."

Takes him a second to twig. For a SIGINT he's slow. "Oh, yes. Most regrettable. The usual offices are looking into it."

"Tragic for Winnie-the-Pooh." I'm so pleased with that my shoulders shimmer. Milne, Scottish surname, synonymous with Miller.

It takes Freddie too long and when he gets it his laughter's messy. I avoid the pitying looks of young men. Finally, he asks if I want a drink.

"I was wondering how one gets served. Vanilla latte. In a real cup."

Attempting gallantry, he booms, "Sugar free?"

"God no."

While he lumbers to the counter I check my phone. Nothing from the Warsaw witch. She's been quiet too long. Message Roc that I love and miss her. Get a bouquet of hearts within seconds. She must be between fucks. Tell her I need a favour. She says: Anything. Rotheray knows where she works. So do the Morlocks. The fallout from that hired clown will get messy. Either I sacrifice myself or destroy all our enemies. Whatever it takes to keep her safe.

The booth upheaves as Freddie settles. Latte spikes me up. "What's this research question?"

He takes off his glasses. His eyes are soft and wet. Their skin reminds me of jellyfish. "I hope this won't sound outlandish."

"I'm broadminded to the point of obscenity."

As expected, he doesn't get the reference. He folds and unfolds his specs and plants them back on his face. "It's about a colleague."

The notion he's fallen for Agnieszka and wants help navigating her knickers fills me with glee. "No names," I tell him.

"It's awkward." He fiddles with his coffee. "Seems grotesque."

An adjective I wasn't expecting. "What does?"

"I made observations. Discreet, of course. I think that one is machinery."

Innocent face, with a tongue full of sugar. "Meaning?"

"It's very well done," he says warmly. "Smooth work."

I think of Gernot Vogt. The blood and the heroic. "Who'd do all that and use it like this?"

"Maybe ask her employer."

Freddie might be smarter than he dresses. But it's a rash deviousness I thought Archer too cowardly for. "What tipped you off?"

He hunkers close. The eager schoolboy. "Her speech. The overlay of an accent to mask hesitant diction. To explain uneven word stresses. And her eyes. The blink cycle doesn't work. Her eyes would be too dry. And that capturing stare. She doesn't merely see. She assimilates. Her temper's well-built."

"She's physically strong. Mentally tough. So am I."

"But you're all woman."

He's too clumsy to make a play. "Perhaps this individual has something of that."

"A hybrid." He sucks his lips the most unattractive way. "Even now, having one so refined would be serious progress. I know people," he says, coy. "Something like this, you can't keep secret."

He wants my blessing to call in the people who hate me. "Probing the subject would bring a robust response. Let me try, before we waste your friends' time."

"It's not a waste…"

"It would be. If all they find is burnt skin." It's after six. Young men head out for high times and soft landings. I want so much to be with them. "You leave first. It's me they're after."

A soft, spring evening, mild and still. My dress skims my thighs. My jacket locks warmth in my armpits. The soft black hairs Miquel loves. Take a stroll up Danvers Street to see Alexander Fleming's old flat. I've been grateful for his microscopy more than once. What would my blue plaque say? Lover, engineer and assassin. 'Assassin' from Arabic 'eater of hashish'. Some in the business do drugs to fence their emotions. But I want to feel everything.

The King's Road is all married couples, fluffing each other's beards. The garden at Carlyle Square is locked. But not in a meaningful way. The Sitwells used to mooch here, doing whatever they did. Sort of neighbourhood I aspired to. Before Catalunya.

Sit under the trees, blending with the last light. Legs folded like the Copenhagen mermaid. I'm a lucky bitch to go places. To get paid to go places. All I must do is take someone's life and that's not hard. Watch sunset flush the sky. The windows of posh houses glimmer. Not long till someone's with me. A presence of stealthy intent. "I don't bite. Much." He's only about sixteen. "You on the rob?"

He stares like I'm some forest creature, transformed by dusk and witchcraft. His noisy heart the rhythm of distant machinery.

"You can tell me."

He gestures beyond the roses. "Basement window. Might have a look."

"And they got motion sensors. And a big nasty poodle."

"I'll be on my toes."

"Get off. It's not eight o'clock."

With adolescent looseness, he folds to the ground. His eyes swallow my face and legs. "You won't tell?" He wants to make it a threat, but it's a boy's question.

"My dad and his dad were proper. Post Offices, banks, security vans. Anywhere cash was moving. My grandad went down but Dad never did. A patient, diligent man. Knew where everyone was meant to be. A job had to be worth it. When other kids learnt football and cricket, he taught me risk and geometry. Where to go in. Where to get out. He told me the steady hand wins. You're what, sixteen?"

"Soon."

"Jacking windows in plain sight. The job has to be worth it. You fall on your face. Leave empty handed. Then two years' getting kicked around on the farm. And then you're a crook. And everyone's got the knife in."

Through the dark I feel his shiver. "You been inside?"

"I saw what it did to my grandad. And he never fired a shot that wasn't deserved."

He moves close. "How old are you?"

Cheeky child. I tell him the truth.

"You're in proper condition."

"It's pitch dark, sweetheart. You can't even tell my eyes."

"They're blue."

"And yours are hazel."

That distinct separation. The sound of grass ripped up. "What you doing on the rich man's lawn?"

"Waiting for you."

His lips work hard. His tongue strives. He's kissed girls at school and round the way. Pretty things with weaves and bangs who don't yet know the abandonment of kissing. Everything the mouth touches it becomes.

Unhitch his jeans. Double down to tug his boxers with my teeth. That noise he makes when his cock's released. He's worried he'll lose this. My job is to help him win.

I take him full length, his crown smooching my larynx. He tastes of piss and deodorant, and urgent, hungry youth. He grips my hair, works my head so I gag. He tries fucking my face, comically awkward on hard ground.

I disengage. His penis paints sloppy kisses. "Strip me."

He tugs my dress over my head, hesitation too obvious in his fingers. Without conscious meaning, he claws my empty chest.

"Strip me."

He pulls down my knickers. A slender Apollo in the rich dark. "I'm not…" he says. "I never…"

"Follow your instinct." We're kissing again. He massages my

shoulders. His thumbs dig deep. His cock yearns towards me. But he needs control. "Beat me."

Strong fingers tremble.

"I deserve a beating."

He tears a sapling and cracks it across my thigh. The sting is intense. I see colours. Swing around and he whips my arse. Blood dances through ruptured skin. My breath fills the night. He stripes me, sinking surprise and discomfort in my tight flesh. He whips between my legs and I bury my scream in the dirt. Then his hand's there.

"You want this?" he murmurs.

"Please."

"I never do this."

"Please."

He yanks me, hard and dismissive.

I shiver and thrill, raised in tender obedience. "Please fuck me." Even now I feel his worry. "She's open for you."

His cock is young enough, still, to recall each time, not the aggregation of times. "It's wet."

"For you."

Nature takes hold. He finds his flow. Bounces me on the ungiving ground. I grovel and grunt and take every atom he offers. He flips me over, cracking me on my spine. Bends back my knees to my chest. He's in again, his weight on my thighs as they scorch my ribs. His lithe body hits insane speed, battering me to a shivering orgasm. Fast as a drill he splays me. I give everything. Let go everything. He cums with heat and velocity. I jolt, my body shocked. As he pulls aside, I let go a fountain of piss that clatters in the grass. He twists my soaking cock and brings me off. His mouth consumes me. All I can say: "I love you, I love you, I love you."

Somewhere, a window closes.

His voice is fractured. "I done nothing like that."

"You're fantastic." I love being naked in his arms.

"I want more."

That's the prize for me. To create compulsion.

He's hard again. The vigour of youth no experience can match. My arms around his neck I wriggle and writhe. We cum together, shaking and sweating.

A kiss like hours. I don't want this to end. That's the worst part.

Too soon, the wet on our bodies turns cold. He needs to make money and I'm always late for something. Sex is never casual. I care for these men, and leave them.

In this incomplete dark, his eyes have liquid sweetness. "I want to see you." He'd never plead with girls his age. He's learnt to be soft with a woman, while she breaks his heart.

"You know Hyde Park? Princess Di's fountain. Tomorrow night at ten." More complication.

"I'm…"

My fingers bar his lips. "I don't want to know your name. Ever."

"Your body." He strokes it fondly. "It's machinery. Goes on and on."

"Mind out for those windows, okay?"

He helps me up. Our hands part. "Maybe I just do stick up."

"Yeah." I kiss him. "Much safer."

Walk miles, to feel my bones. Up Fulham Road. Round back of the Brompton. I got stitched there once. A misunderstanding over gold bars, of all things. My dad was disappointed I never took to thieving. A man of few words, he told me once, 'If I taught you carpentry, you'd want only the hammer'. Roc was even more hopeless. She couldn't nick sweets without getting caught. She gave shopkeepers blowjobs to keep them quiet and a whole career was born. Sometimes I think we're too young to be orphans.

The German Embassy, Belgrave Square. Civilians mistake gunshots for other noise. Especially in locations where shots are less common. Civilians make two errors. They run like fools with no appreciation of ricochet. Or stand still, wondering if what they heard was a shot. Better reckon it is. This crowd of organ banks runs at full panic. While I sketch the trajectory on the dark air. To me, gunshots are an invitation.

German embassy guards duck behind pillars, bellowing at their radios. Guards at the Norway embassy over the street implement procedures. The herd is wailing, but I think that's a Heckler & Koch, maybe a G36. Crouch by the front wheel of a tank-like Mercs. Bullets spray the hood. One whips my face. A flash of gold under the streetlights. The G36 holds 30 cartridges. They clip together for continuous fire. But this individual is more forensic.

He fires again. I assume it's a man. He's bastard untidy. Shots return from the end of the street. The Met shooting blind. These premium wallahs rate clumsy protection.

As the windscreen shatters and snowy glass dapples my face, I get what's occurring. There's a wedge of green across the street. Slight, with solid old trees. I go front of the Mercs. If this is my last breath, it's all been worth it.

Three long strides and smack chest high into wire. Mash my hands grappling the fence. Fall through bushes. Thorns chide me like a martyr. Shots go on. Just the filth. Their blunt and puzzled shouts command the street. Disappointed. Robbed in their moment.

Ambulances arrive. Concrete striped a hectic blue. A paramedic shouts, "What the fuck's all this?" and the filth get shirty. Try not to feel cuts and fractured glamour as I clamber out the far end of the park, my snagged dress more precious than pierced flesh.

Take Lyall Street, Eaton Place, Belgrave Place, to get the other side of the action. There's dead civilians. Their blood will talk long after it's washed away. On the corner, the Spanish embassy squats, fat and complacent. Guards twitch, pretending they're ready. I yell, "Catalunya lliure!" and spit at the wall. A guard shouts, "Puta!" It's all they can think.

News sites blow with terror shit. Embassies attacked by the usual suspects. How it works: they label these suspects with names of dead refugees. Backdate some hooky intelligence that says they came from Syria via Naples and Paris or some mumbo-jumbo. An ambitious bunch in the Middle East claims the martyrs, because why not? That none of it happened doesn't matter. It draws a line and what's important is drawing a line. Right now, a bloke from the spooks and a bloke from the Yard are shouting at each other about how I jogged between them, and their bullets just hung on the air. My enemies have lost all proportion. And me, with weddings to dress for.

Round the corner, the Italian Cultural Institute is having a do. Young men in formal wear smoke in the porch, making gestures of kiss and curse. Women in wraps and sequined trousers hurl black hair across their shoulders. I slink up the steps, hands moving around to distract from pulled threads on my dress.

My Italian is slight and ropey. But my bruises speak for me. A lad hangs his coat on my shoulders. A Sandro Paris, double-breasted, it reaches my knees. "Excuse me," I say in my tourist accent. "I've had a terrible shock."

They've been at a private view. They didn't hear shooting. They're shocked when they check their phones and full of consolation for me. I tell them I'm Araminta, a name I use in these situations, easy for Italian speakers. Over a nice Nero d'Avola, as young men cluster to me, I explain what went when the devil cut loose and it was, "Veramente una zona di guerra," mashing Catalan into Italian. One girl kisses my forehead, like an old aunt. The man whose silk lining slips lusciously over my shoulders says it's an outrage, "un oltraggio," that one so bella should be subject to, "brutalità." His fingers suggest exquisite brutalità.

An older man with a white goatee is summoned. A doctor, his English is better than mine. He takes me to a functional office where he tells me to lay on the couch. I'm not a trusting sort but I know he's a doctor. He handles my body like an awkward problem, rather than the fount of joy. His lotion stings my cuts. He thinks I cracked a bone.

"It's nothing." I wave my dolly hand. "I'm always doing stuff."

His look is chastening severity. "You should have x-rays." Careful English makes it massive. "You may be running around on damage. You're too young to start with arthritis."

I drape an arm on the couch back. "Another glass of that lovely red would help."

He bundles the latex gloves. "Are you sure you don't want to go to hospital?"

"They have so much to do. These tragic events. I don't want to be a burden."

With meticulous courtesy he grips my arm as I step into my shoes. "I could give you morphine. But I see you prefer the grape."

"So much healthier, don't you think?"

As I swing my Chanel round my shoulders, he watches the jacket's contours. "You have a gun in your pocket." Said with mild lack of surprise.

A brisk and practical smile as I fold the young man's coat. "Dangerous days. What's a girl to do?"

"This country does not have so many guns."

"It has enough."

He fusses the clips on his bag. "I wonder if you are more than you seem."

"You seem a careful man who respects patient privacy."

He eyes the coat quartered over my arm. "You should give that to Giampaolo. He may leave without it."

"Giampaolo. Thank you."

Through contoured skin, his old man eyes seek me out. "My brother died the gun death. He stayed silent when he should have spoke."

"I don't have those choices."

He's grave and sober enough to value honesty over survival. I excuse myself to powder my nose. The toilet's nice: glass and posh soap. As my piss bastes the china, I'm concerned at this nonsense impeding my plans. Civilians dropped in the street. In Belgravia, the goons of a half dozen embassies stroking their hardware. Grown-ups will be notified. They'll be miffed.

Brush my hair and refresh my eyes. I should get the first plane to Barcelona, but I'm between stones and the sea. Sirens make fun of this ache in my chest. I don't want good advice. I can't use it.

The party's breaking up. Young people in sombre mood, their poise abashed by close suffering, hug and pledge to be there for each other. I love these close-knit southern people. This flowing and joining. Back home we know all our neighbours. All the old boys at the market and the black-shawled vellas who cross themselves when I walk by. I feel their offence as energy. Their fear invites me.

Pleasingly, Giampaolo palms a glass of wine on his way over. His hair is piled the most negligent way. His stubble is coalescing. His dress shirt collar is tight and his sporty peacock blazer a Zegna, I reckon. Hand him his coat with a gentle, "Grazie mille."

"I should thank you." He picks up my quiet tone and we're conspirators, relishing excitement in tragedy. "Araminta is an interesting name."

"It's an invention. From Congreve." I giggle. "I'm rather fond of it." I can't hold this impersonation of Roc and tighten my vowels. "And you?"

The darling boy gives a little bow. "Giampaolo."

"John Paul."

That tiny smile, his downturned eyes, that's heaven. "After the Holy Father, yes. My mother met him when she was a girl."

"You must be specially blessed."

"I feel so."

With death and mayhem around us, he does the right thing. There are kisses and hugs, warm words, though I don't catch them all. This poor young woman, marooned in the night, naturally a man should take her home.

He squires me into Chapel Street, his arm around my shoulder because he knows I'm a woman who wants that. Belgrave Square is fierce with lights. A helicopter hangs. Curiosity draws me off. But he walks me down Headfort Place, a scrap of old warehouse offices. A nondescript road smelling of window polish.

His car's a Citroën SM. With the flattened snout like a baffled shark. He's boyishly proud, which is sweet. That metallic green paint could be original. "Wow."

"1973." He's ludicrously modest. "I searched for years. Maserati engine of course."

"V6." I stroke the trim. "Carbon-rim wheels. Top speed two-twenty, I believe."

"You know this car?"

"I know fast cars." I start to ease in. "Silly me." Of course it's left-hand drive.

Obviously, he watches my legs. The doctor's lotion gleams like suncream. It's after ten. The sirens, the shouts of irritable coppers, the helicopter's churning blades, the music of this city I love and can't have. A dangerous urge to unmask. To explain I'm so exquisite a risk, people plan to destroy me. I'd relish his wonder. For now.

Piccadilly is jammed. Police block these racing streets. I ask about Italy. I've hardly been there. Giampaolo is from Milan, so I talk about things that matter: Marni, Fausto Puglisi—I have a Puglisi dress. Black, square shoulders. Cost thousands. Miquel calls me decadent. But he loves me in arse-skimming frocks. And Canali, and Ermenegildo Zegna, where that peacock blazer comes from. Peacock, referring to the bird's blue throat, not its garish nethers.

"Your dress is lovely."

"Rococo Sand."

He's endearingly baffled.

"A brand, not a person. Indian designer. Nandita Raipurani. Breezy silhouettes and bold prints."

He drops the window to let in restless engines. "You love to explain things."

"All my friends say that." I never like to deny Miquel outright. I don't want more to regret. But I'm desirable now. It might not always be this way. When I'm old and filled with hate for foes that escaped me.

We twirl into Hertford Street with its angry railings. Ride the revs at Shepherd Street while a nice pub spills rich drunks.

Giampaolo is adorably earnest. "We will go for a real drive. This car is such sweet machinery."

We barely move in this traffic. I dislike staying still. It leaves one open to upset.

"There is," he ventures, "a hotel."

The SM is a sporty thing. Its luggage compartment is trim. I'm surprised he got that nice leather holdall to fit. "Do you do this often?"

His look is the most delectable chivalry. "I want them to think we planned this."

I'm stunned. "You're worried they'll think I'm a tart?"

"Of course. Because you are not."

For the longest time, this manor was high rent brasses. Roc could clear half her mortgage tonight. But she declines to rub up to the scumbags that know me. The notion I need to give Roc a wedding hovers around my thoughts. She's fierce for tradition.

Late in the evening and news from Belgravia is much on the mind of the desk-monkey. He watches us glide through his monogrammed portal like we might be lethal minded. But Giampaolo knows the walk. A long stride, the bag loose in his hand. As we're presumed to be lovers, I loop my fingers through his belt, his spine a contagion of movement.

"You have a room?" His accent makes it imperative. "It has gotten late."

'Gotten' is old English. Ill-gotten gains and all that. The concierge might think my man's pulling a Yank. But his usage is correct. I don't get much chance to chat grammar.

We are signore e signora Montanari, which I guess means 'of the mountains'. He is Giampaolo Montanari and, quick on my pins, I say, "Felìcita Montanari. Buona sera." Giampaolo squeezes my waist.

The bloke asks do we have ID, because: security. Giampaolo ponies his driver's licence. No doubt he has a wad of licences for these excursions. I smile and make pretty Italian noise. The desk clerk lets it go. Naturally I don't need to be identified. I belong to this man.

In the lift, he explores me, falling upwards into passion. The motionless hallways are dead. A TV. A rattle of bottles. Sombre chat on the night's events. We have a serviceable king size and nifty lounge, where I throw myself on the couch in a flurry of thighs. "This is lovely," I squeal.

Under warm-tone light, he's not the best-looking, but neat and sincere. He asks if I want a drink.

"Surprise me." I stretch, so my shape is no secret. I don't lie about things that matter.

Trying to shake hesitation, he investigates the minibar, disappointed there's no Campari. No one has drunk Campari these last fifty years. There's tins of ready-mix G&T and he fusses with glasses and coasters. He asks if I want something to eat. But that means room service, so I pat the couch to get him sat down. There's painful fun in delay.

Unsure of the landscape, he grips my chin between pensive fingers. He's a tight kisser—there's panache in his lips. His hand claims my neck, old-school. He whispers words I guess are avowals of ownership. "I'm different to other women." I never say this because it never matters. But Giampaolo is concerned for my honour. Less robust.

His thumb stalls in my clavicle. "You are beautiful."

"You understand how I'm beautiful?"

"I don't care." Not the right answer. But he's trying, poor love.

I've done this a long time. Few are immune to the fire. We kiss and caress, urgency in his touch.

"Araminta. So beautiful."

His underpants are silk and long. A lady's-lace colour. He's circumcised. I suck and he surrenders. He's not toned from dance or feral nights. But authority shapes him. He grips my hair. I let go his cock when he most wants release. He curses, some darling Milanese sound. I crawl between his legs. "Fuck me."

This is new to Giampaolo. First day of school. First kill. Mine was a boy who called me names. Who thought I was weak and helpless. When they found his body in the Regent's Canal they counted sixty-nine cuts. No one forgets the first time.

I wiggle open and, hesitantly, he's in. I say words men love to hear. I draw him on, demanding, assuring. He cums too soon. I would never tell a man that. Not once does he touch my cock nor ask about it. I finish off in the toilet. He's already in bed.

We cuddle and kiss. He plays with my buttocks but nothing else. Movement diminishes, till I focus on sounds in the street. Music and shouts, engines. Try to name cars by their noise. Nearby, a window closes.

Though the room's sealed and the bed's snug, a thrill prickles my skin. In a hotel there's always people. Room service, cleaners, security. Guests come and go. But action is magnetic. Whoever's in the hall, they're not delivering snacks or fixing a spill.

Slip out of bed and get dressed. Have a piss, brush my hair, do my eyes. Dig out a fresh magazine. The Springfield XD 9 mil is a short black handgun with three-dot steel sights and a four-inch hammer-forged barrel coated in Melonite. It has a dual captive spring and full-length guide rod. It weighs 28 ounces. The magazine holds 16 rounds. Despite its American style it's made in Croatia. This model is around twenty years old. A veteran. Draw aim on the bedside lamp, to get my eyes in the mood.

"What is happening?" Giampaolo flounders up.

"Don't turn on the light."

The daft git raises his hands. "You are robbing me?"

"What? No." A civilian, poor love. "Someone outside wants a chat. Stay here."

"You are in danger?"

"Really, you're lovely. But I need to get on."

He sits up, a baffled child.

"Stay quiet. Stay here."

Hallway lights in night phase, intimate and warm. Check the carpet. Heel notches. Brogues. Not heavy enough to track. Need to get this away from Giampaolo. He's unequipped.

Swing to the lift lobby, loose and casual. Each lift faces a camera at every floor. Hand in my pocket, I ease open the door to the stairs.

Above me, someone stops. Feel their anticipation. Slip to the mezzanine, to look up through the stack. To shoot an unseen target is for nervy amateurs. In a tight space. In walls of hard echoes. And I want to know who this is, that presumes upon my troubled sleep. Quiet, I move up, a silken princess in the tower of her fate. They can't see me. I can't see them. We feel each other through restive air. It's this again.

Two floors apart. They let me make the moves. Raise my gun. Admire how light gets lost in its surface. My gun leads me up. So quiet. I can hold my breath two minutes. Not bad for a smoker. I love this panic in my lungs. This fear of no air. Every sense in my body enchants me. Draw a hand through my hair to feel its soft kick. My chest on fire. My brain liberated from fear.

Ten metre range. They own the worry. Their concern this risk is for nothing. Look up between piled stairs. I feel what they feel. This tension from shoulder to trigger. Calculations of angle and speed. Confidence they can make it. Doubt they can't.

Something shows. A gun. A face. I know who he is.

Switch to my left. Such infirmity drives my daring. He needs to shoot. He hangs too long. Ten metres. A child could do it. He's gone. A shuffle of skin and something falls. A face on the rail, splayed with blonde hair.

In death his belligerent beard floats free of soft black skin. Less assured yet more impressive, this man drew me to the edge. His throat, sliced wide, weeps blood. The wire, sharp and efficient, spun to Agnieszka's red knuckles. In that black jumpsuit, long-sleeve, flared. Black trainers. She pinches her breath not to sound excited. "Put your gun away. You need both hands to help."

"He was at Mr. Miller's. He's security service."

"He is nothing."

As we brace to shift the body, I want to ask why she stopped him. It takes serious strength to kill that way. Guns can be messy but, sympathetically used, present a clean death. This is butchery. A ragged gash of cracks and leakage. To garrotte is a cross-body move. The left hand works the target's right shoulder, while the right hand loops the throat. Anticlockwise is traditional, I believe. As the target jerks back, they sever themself. It seems too personal somehow. The full-body embrace. The warmth. The smell of skin.

The door to the roof has been forced, no doubt her doing. While she uses my wet wipes to scrub her fingers, I go through his pockets. I'll get blamed for this stiff, so I'm not fussed with forensics. His gun is a Glock 22. Commonest hardware on Earth. Some cash and a fake credit card. Driving licence, also fake. That asthma inhaler: genuine, by the powder smell. Nice wallet. Tan, with a clip. Veggie-friendly polyurethane. No phone, which is intriguing. "They've lost two, chasing me."

"I am sure you are on the wall as a major threat. With the mullahs and patriots."

We carry him onto the roof. The usual gravel and concrete. Vents like submarines. Rooftops have a distinctive smell. Waste air ducts, warmth, bird shit scrambled by rain, dead things returning to nature. There's wildness to rooftops, an audacity of height. I wonder how far one could travel, roof to roof, never touching ground.

We plant him beneath a pile of bricks, bending the carcass double while it has give. We leave him his gun for the afterlife. In cursory light, she's a busy precision of hands. Passing drones will see building material, unremarkable, stored and forgotten. By the time some maintenance bloke kicks it over, revenge will already be had.

"I had a disappointing sexual experience, thanks for asking. He's fast akip downstairs."

Those points of light—face, hair, hands—a mime of fathomless menace. Her body resolves just partly, visiting from some other place. "Why do you think I killed Tony Hazell?"

"Thought it was these goons."

"Why?"

"To warn me off."

She might bet her wire against my gun. The kill's fresh in her blood. "You make so many errors. Day and night, you make mistakes. Hazell was a problem. I did what you should have done."

"You were waiting for me at Archer's?"

"I knew you were in London. I knew you would need equipment. It was predictable you would visit Archer."

"You got pally with him just to meet me?"

"You joke with no reason. Dexter, who is not intelligent, summons you and of course you go. There is death tonight. Of course you are there. You consort with a man in a peculiar car. Of course these operatives see you. You were once so feared and hated. But now you pile error on error. You stand with your back to the edge. I could throw you down."

"You could not."

"I broke his neck with my hands."

"You didn't break mine." Step away from the parapet on some restless pretext. "That hole you put in Tony's neck was untidy."

"Close range is never pristine. You know this."

Now I laugh. She's horrific. "He had you in a clinch?"

"In desire men are unguarded. You know this."

A helicopter grinds over. Instinctively we face down, hands in our pockets. Her hair a shocking beacon. She must know I can't trust her.

"So how's Mr. Miller? Now you killed his fixer."

Ice thickens. "I settled Tony Hazell because you failed to do so. Another error."

"Didn't you make an error with this bloke?"

"Why? You are to blame. I could shoot a school of little Catholic girls. It is you that would piss in a bucket."

Tipping her out to ride the air would take muscle. I beat her in that casino bog. But brittle darkness blurs my edge. "Time to go."

Those unblinking eyes suffocate me. "You have no plan. You follow only desire." Here where light creeps, furtive, from below, her gross tranquillity is ferocious. "Yes. We are here too long."

We squabble about who risks their back. I get hissy and jog down first. She walks soundless behind. The desk-boy gives a confused wave, as I trill, "Ciao." Agnieszka makes noise like a lion with piles.

We take Giampaolo's car. We squabble about it. "It is how they followed you."

"So they won't look for it now." These vintage models have minimal locks. The door gives with a kirby. "Start her up. You do know how to wire a car?"

"It is only machinery."

Indiscipline

Three in the morning we get there. This Maserati engine gives a hundred and seventy horses. Leather seats I shouldn't approve of are dreamy for bare legs. The Citroën SM doesn't have a brake pedal, just this rubber nipple. The tilt on corners makes every move a car chase. It's gauged to two-twenty kilometres, but she gives earache to keep the limit. South of Purley, the M23 like the Valley of Death. This long, boring road pleads for speed, to rip through nowhere places. Hooley, whatever the fuck that is. Dull houses mediocre villains keep for a lay-up. Near the motorway, handy for Gatwick. Tall hedges and barking dogs.

"West on the M25."

She'll top me in some farmhouse. The unsolved bint on a true crime show. But I'll kill her first.

"Slow for the junction."

"Who's fucking driving?"

"There are cameras."

Pull onto the slip, meek, though fuck-all's about. Few trucks up from the coast. Bit of holiday traffic. Those sporty hatchbacks always around late at night. Under gantry lights, the road climbs through space. A slick funeral ribbon, squirling away to the sea. "What lane?"

"West."

We fly over the M25 like the rim of some drab, resentful planet. A place of dismal journeys and no arrival. "The myth of arrival," I say.

"What?"

"The myth of arrival. The founding deception of Western society."

She clicks through her cultural references. "Of course you are strong on completion."

The M25 yawns ahead, promising Kingston and Heathrow. "I could get the early to Barcelona."

"We take junction 9."

"Leatherhead?"

"Skórzana głowa. That is 'leather head' in Polish."

"I'm so glad I'm here."

Junction 9, the A24, then unlit, spongy sideroads. She directs us into the yard of a tile-hung gaff. Mullioned windows leak soft light. The house is modest. Two floors. Old part is fake-Tudor, 1920s most like. The matching extension maybe 80s or 90s. Lot of fussy glass and carved wood. By no stretch a mansion but here, on this land, it's twenty million easy. A triple garage with carriage lamps. The conservatory round the back all lit. Padded chairs, glass tables—predictable taste.

As we get out the car, I slot my gun to her hip. "Why here?"

She doesn't break stride. "This is not for your silly paranoia."

The front door's not locked, which is interesting. The hall's a stage for an old-time country house. There's the pokerwork chest with its big iron lock. The wooden stand for umbrellas, its lattice chipped with the carelessness of decades. A trug full of tools. A wicker basket piled with plant pots and shaved lengths of twig. A lamp made from a rum bottle. The print on its shade is Mary Quant if I'm not mistaken. A pleasantly inconvenient console table. A worked silver tray with big green goblets, fat blue candles, a ceramic quince and Arab-style teapot. An engraved map of the Surrey Hills screwed to the wall. I'm disappointed not to see a cricket bat and photos of floppy-haired lads with try-again smiles.

"What a dump."

She ignores me.

Every light in the place is on, which shits me worse than darkness. The curve-away stairs delicately shield assassins in waiting. "Who else is here?"

Light catches her razor cheeks. "We wait."

This sitting room is an angsty queen's wet dream. High-back chairs in biscuit. Glass tables with more silver trays. Vast, gilt-frame mirrors reflect fake Tudor beams. Sprigs of greenery in Chinese pots. Brick fireplace closed with an iron grille. Delft plates, lamps like balloons, glossy hardbacks, expensive garbage. I pick up a chunky volume, *One Thousand Bucket List Ideas*, disappointed that Die Young isn't top of page one. It's grotesque. "I've gone on holiday by mistake."

She fiddles with a globe that, predictably, is a drinks cabinet. Anyone who owns such an object should expect to be killed. She pours a big whisky and, again, I'm intrigued at how little she understands. Her knowledge is focused on complex tasks. Any nuance is off radar.

I sprawl on the couch, a bit overstimulated. The upholstery's hard. The cushions are punchbags. Best thing in the room is the ceiling light, a six-prong affair like the crown of a palm tree. If I'd taken a different path in life, if such a thing could be imagined, I could be the attractive chatelaine of a place like this. All tweeds and fresh air in the daytime, and dom-and-fladge by night. Local lads calling while I'm baking pies, flour on my cheeks and restless.

Night wears away to slow morning. We're across the fields from the M25. No traffic. No nothing. Just my bones as I shift around and the valves in her throat drinking. Two people, poignant with distrust. "How did you know I was at that hotel?"

"It is not hard to find you. Six died in that shooting. Ten injured."

"Don't say you care."

"Of course not. But it is obvious you are there."

"Why not let him kill me?"

"Dexter builds a database of events. This Middle East transmission correlates with intrusions to Miller's business."

That's mildly interesting. "Dates, locations, participants?"

"I see only briefly. But to find who attends these events, it is possible."

"You asked the spooks."

"They chase you. I do not want they chase me. I speak with people in Poland."

The scotch isn't working. I'm tired and hasty. "Devious bitch."

"I am expert in my field."

"And what did 'people in Poland' tell you?"

Unblinking, she stares. "They told me names."

"Who we waiting for?"

She fakes interest in these trashy books: New York people watching; balloon rides over seething deserts; life in fucking Provence. "This may entertain you."

She hands me a brick of Cecil Beaton portraits. Handsome lad, Beaton. Nice way with light. Garbo, full-face, one eyebrow raised, like she's got a Luger under the table. Grace Kelly, bless her darling heart, strength in every muscle. My distant, great-grand-auntie Audrey, getting away with the most ridiculous Givenchy dead ferret hat. We never had much to do with the Dutch contingent. They were legitimate business. Roc's got something of the old girl's poise. And her vowels. "I washed my face and hands before I come, I did."

Of course Agnieszka's puzzled. She has no reference points. She stares at these pictures like news from Mars. She shows me a spread of skinny girls modelling Valentino up some Tuscan mountain. Those villages look delightful but they're full of nutters. "You like this?" she asks, bizarrely.

"Valentino? His prêt-à-porter's alright."

"You do much shopping for clothes."

"I don't wear Chanel to scrub floors."

"You are a housewife."

"You think that's weird?"

Something along the dark lane jacks her to her feet.

Tension is the sweetest wine. "Talk to me."

"I shall see these are the right people."

"What 'right people'?"

She has that look. That blank, brittle anger.

"What people?" My gun's out.

From her jumpsuit pocket comes the dinkiest Jennings.

"You been robbing museums?"

She swishes her flares to the door. "It is the Germans that robbed museums." Her programmed patriotism the icing on this devil's mess of a cake. She's across the gravel with commendable stealth. Obvious she has night vision.

Embracing that impulse that often turns out badly, I nip upstairs for a shufti. This place is in the cluttered, narrow style. Top of the stairs, potpourri unfolds its disused graveyard smell. There's a pincushion stabbed like voodoo and chunky glassware. An old-fashioned bathroom, chipped china and spindle fittings, where I take a quick piss sat facing the dimpled window. Too dark for anything but my disrupted reflection. Limescale on the bath taps says they've been stuck a while. The mirror is foxed. Makes my face look eaten away.

Three other doors up here. Try the middle. It might be a trap but that doesn't dissuade me. Every light in the place is on. This bedroom is a sparse affair. The ceiling slopes and dips, tracking vagaries in the roofline. The plaster's off-cream and old. A double bed with an iron frame, dressed in stale linen. A blank wardrobe, not even hangers. Nothing in the drawers except dead beetles and this book of watercolours, cracked with age. A magpie on a snowy branch. A river beneath autumn trees. The house, unfinished, its outline sketched in dark pencil. A strong-faced girl in a raincoat, wet, matted hair flailing around the collar. Neck like a birch tree. Greenish skin, reflecting the storm sky. Painted in thin lines: 'Chrissy by Chrissy'. Something grisly to it. I know, because I'm an expert, it's the face of someone killed.

A soldier in civvies is still a soldier. The younger of the two men, he stands by the fireplace, his fawn suit premature for the weather. His hair's short, balding a bit. There's energy to him. The older man already helped himself to scotch. His dark suit sparkles from morning mist. Old bits of hair clutch his oval head like a life raft.

Their eyes on me the second I'm in the room. Before I can drop a silky bon mot, Agnieszka declares, "I told you she would be snooping. She cannot be left for a moment."

"Well." Talk loud, to own it. "Who have we here?"

"This is a colonel in the Polish army." The younger man gives a little bow. "This is someone familiar with communications."

"From headquarters?" I ask brightly.

"The doughnut." His voice dredged through gravel. "Alright here?" with heavy-jowled candour. "No pricked-up ears?"

"I did a sweep." I didn't, but it seems remiss to admit that.

"I also." Agnieszka is one kitten-killer. "The house is secure. Is why we use it."

The Polish lad nods, clearly knowing who 'we' means.

The big spook pours another drink, back turned like a priest at the blood. "I must be in London by seven."

"Miss Hepburn." The young man's English is smoother than Agnieszka's. "You must think me careless not to declare my interest in these matters."

I wiggle to fix drinks. This globe is a hideous thing. Not even old, just antiqued. Who keeps this place and why? "You have the advantage of me. To what 'matters' do you refer?" I serve drinks, achieving my aim to leave Cheltenham man with a glass in each hand. Though he doesn't look unfamiliar with that.

The Polish officer tilts his glass. "Za piękne panie," to herself and me, "Za nas," to the big man, who lofts both drinks with heavy humour. "For some time I work with our comrade here." The officer nods to Agnieszka, who twitches in a mime of goodwill. And I'm thinking, 'Comrade?' "She is a sure ally to those who do difficult work."

"I seen that."

He treats me to a tight smile. "Our comrade has my confidence.

Naturally we have discussed her assignment. Your activities are unusual, Miss Hepburn."

"I try to keep boredom at bay."

"Recent events show how well you succeed." He laces earnest hands. "We are here on a mission of comfort. In the current hurly-burly."

By now, the old dodger has downed one scotch and raises his nose from the other. "You piss people off. Understand?"

"I understand short-sighted morons are trying to kill me."

"It's not usual for a stop to be put on home ground. Not the job the boys like."

"I'm aware what they like."

He hangs in mid-grab for the bottle.

"Is this about Freddie Dexter and his boys' book of Middle East conspiracies?"

Real diplomat, my Polski colonel rides in. "This is about several things, Miss Hepburn. My comrade has briefed me on various matters. The geography is material, yes, and to a particular high value asset…"

"You've been told to knock it off," Cheltenham man bludgeons in. "Told in strong terms. My colleagues in another branch have lost assets. They get irritable with widows and orphans. You've been spoken to. They struggle with why you don't listen."

"Maybe I don't like their manners." These girly shoulders pack a fierce wiggle. "Nor do I like getting dragged to the middle of nowhere." Throw a look at Agnieszka. "I'm going back to town. You can come or stay with your real friends."

"You should listen," she says, thickly. "You never listen. Is why you are always in trouble."

The colonel moves close, so I get a good look of his off-the-peg cloth and a good sniff of his Lalique. "This is a mission of comfort. My colleague," he gestures to the blimp, "has presence in certain discussions. He could, perhaps, have this enthusiasm for your death scaled back a little."

A rumble of sour breath from the massive man.

"For myself, I am persuaded by my comrade's observations that an asset valuable to us—by which I mean, the greater 'us'—might perhaps be making moves to 'cash out', as gamblers say."

I get it. I don't like it. "So, with your lukewarm blessing, I get shot by both sides? And I do this, why?"

"Did you not explain to your policeman friend why?"

"She is frightened of prison," Agnieszka chirps. "She is frightened to wear nasty clothes."

Ignoring that gravely insulting truth, I tell the men, "What if I say 'fuck you' and go back to Barcelona?"

"Barcelona?" The older man's jowls make it a bronchial fog. "Barcelona isn't a bubble. Colleagues in Madrid have ample on you. You may find yourself back here anyway if you marry this Catalan terrorist."

Miquel is a man of honour. A prince of ethics. A devastating lover. But I swallow my rage, stoking the hate. "You're ready to do what's needed. These rules we all understand. Scratch me and go back to your better agendas."

I turn, ready for the bullet. I don't know why they take so long. Go upstairs to the toilet. My piss smells of whisky. Daylight behind the stippled glass, faint but unstoppable. Think about taking the sketchbook. But that's for another time.

I'm not surprised the big man's waiting. A big bastard who smells of scotch and too many crunch decisions. His deep blue worsted is quality. That attractive gaminess wool suits have. Double-breasted. Stretched tight on a life of second helpings. Catch his eyes. Not mere hate, I expect that. The precise contempt of deep understanding. "Care to escort me downstairs?"

"Serious people are talking about you. While you stayed away, you were a curiosity. A freak useful to us once. Before you followed your cock to sunnier climes."

I rile. But his voice is a jackhammer.

"When that cretin Rotheray offered, you had no need to jump. You could have sorted Miller or failed. It doesn't matter. But this is you. You compound things. Involving that Polish bitch wasn't clever. She has a serious screw loose. Now the Warsaw boys are having a go, and even you must remember what happened when they pissed about in Iraq. And because there's a stop on you and because my colleagues lost assets, they can't say to the widows of those good men, 'You know, we weren't really serious about putting an end to that fucker'. It's Jarndyce and Jarndyce."

As he goes on, his skin rolls about, shifting his tufts of hair like boats on a swell. A lifetime of frustration fires his rage. But I don't want advice. What would I do with it?

"Your mouthy, no-consequence fucking around was amusing when the Middle East was Russia's problem, and we were shitting allies for breakfast. But now the ragheads are up at Buck House and the world's gone queer, you are exactly the turd in the jam. We left that spiv's body in Holland Park and that didn't put you off. You blundered in for a bloody look-see. Then where did you go? Vauxhall. You call someone you shouldn't call. Drag them to a public place…"

"He warned me off."

"No he didn't. He told you to kill this fucking bod, because they're working a double-blind you dozy tart. Even if he had warned you off, that wouldn't lodge in the candyfloss in your head. And as for that embassy caper—you were meant to die, you thick bint."

"You stand there, dribbling on your cheap suit…"

"Anderson & Sheppard. You know that."

"Go for your gun. I go for mine. We settle this like adults."

"Christ, you're stupid." He glances down to the Polish lad. "Two minutes. Tell the driver, will you?"

Agnieszka appears behind him. Booze makes her spastic.

"What's this got to do with their lot?"

That noise in his throat is an earthquake beginning. "If you say to a reasonable person: 'Russia or Germany?' which do they choose?"

"I was surprised at Germany. I thought it would be cleaner. What do you want?"

"You kill Jazin. We kill you. Win-win."

"And if I don't fancy taking up the harp?"

Spit froths his lips. "You bloody pansy. We give you a new identity."

I'm too startled to be outraged. "Are you off your Chinese? How do I have a new identity?"

"Change your hair. Bit of surgery. It would solve problems."

"Not for me."

Giving himself to gravity, the stairs beg at his hefty tread. "Then short-sighted morons will continue trying to kill you."

Both men are outside in the morning light, grey and resolved. The Polish colonel is at Agnieszka, kissing her hand. She does hair stuff, tucking blonde thatch behind one ear. She's a stereotype. Blonde hair, blue eyes, rounded chin, that sulky muscularity. None of this is accident. She's the pattern of her tribe.

The men's car melts out from a hedgerow. A young oily rag gives the windows a shine, looking busy. I know he's clocked me. On the ride down, his passengers no doubt said much about me. They'll have more to say going back. He's distilling what story to tell the boys at the factory. I make moves for him to latch onto. Swing my jacket against the sharp morning breeze. Gather my hair in a tail and let it fall. I don't care how smart or wily they are. I'm Felicity Hepburn. I'll die as I am.

The SIGINT merchant meets my gaze. Though he's got years on me, we've played this game long enough to value what we despise. Everyone comes back around. Different jobs, beliefs, bone structure. But always back around. George Orwell had blue circles tattooed on his knuckles. In Burma, where he was a cop, the old boys did that as protection from bullets and snakes. When I read *1984* I was taken with the Chestnut Tree Café. That way it appears. A useful nuisance. Jones, Aaronson and Rutherford. The fallen heroes. Fitted up. Banged up. And there they are, in the Chestnut Tree Café, 'relics of the ancient world' as Orwell says. The chessboard set up but no game. That's the business this man's in. That's where they want me. Crying till next time, in the Chestnut Tree Café.

At last, the Polish contingent finish their farewells. The men walk to the car. The young driver stiffens, shows a bit of respect for his cargo. He gets them aboard and they fanny off into the blue. Agnieszka stares at their dust. "You ungrateful bitch."

I presume she's not sober, but still it's a shocker. "Was that why we came here?"

"They offer help. But you have only indiscipline."

I'm amused and appalled. "So it's a good thing I shill for the spooks?"

"Or be killed by the spooks. I am not concerned."

"He wants to change my identity."

Those unyielding eyes survey me. "Of course, your present identity works so well."

Convergence

The house is far behind, its door unlocked and lights burning. I yearn for regular pleasures. Pastries from the market. Figs from old Agustí's dark little shop. His hands deep in the barrel. Wizened fistfuls of obscenely succulent fruit. Shopping for dinner, my hair in a flowery scarf, my hands too full for a gun. I want all of life, not glimpses. "Can I leave you somewhere?"

"We have much work."

"Who's 'we'?"

She seems baffled. "You work for Mr. Miller. He is paying you. And you are paying me."

"Everyone is paying you."

"We have much work." She checks her phone. "Rashad Jazin arrives this morning."

Eyes wide and burning. "Right. Heathrow."

"You should not make assumptions."

I can't fathom how no one's killed her. "What assumptions should I not make?"

"This is a powerful man. He would not set down in a zoo. His plane will land at Northolt at eleven hundred. No doubt he will be taken to his house at Regent's Park. He will remain on ground that is cleansed and defended."

"But you, sweetheart, are concerned with Mr. Miller."

"I am concerned with my country. The colonel did not visit just to see how you wear dresses."

Because this car has a hydraulic brake triggered from a simple plunger, braking is faster than standard models. Its brake force derives from plain pressure, rather than the travel time of a pedal. The stopping distance is short. As we just found out, as I crunch the brake to take a swing at Agnieszka.

She's up to meet my punch with impressive spirit. Fighting side-on, in a car, is not graceful. We're locked, spitting vulgarities. "Cunt."

"I have a cunt."

Punch her face but she traps my wrist at viper speed. Her unholy strength probes my bones. Grab her throat. It doesn't constrict. It resists.

Wholly abnormal. Cars swerve and squeal. I spit in her face, she spits in mine, and we subside, fixing our hair. A sports job skids around us. The driver yells: "Lezzas!" Point one of a second later, his rear nearside tyre explodes. He's across three lanes, arse-up in a ditch.

"That was stupid."

"It's education."

We don't talk till the chianti lands of Streatham. Pull over by Tooting Common. Victorian villas emerge, grudging, from sleep. I don't get that English thing: sleeping till seven. Before dawn is the cream of the day.

She looks round with minimal interest. "We are here for some reason?"

"What do your friends want with Jazin?"

"You think there is a conspiracy?"

"You know his flight plan. You know where he lives. Does your dashing colonel have something up his rękaw?"

She corrects my pronunciation. "My country has many concerns. Including how to work most effectively with our allies. This is not of relevance to you."

"It is if I'm going to get killed."

That nannying look. "This neurotic belief everything centres on you. This continued insistence your death would make any difference. We are components of the large machine. A component fails, it is replaced. No one holds a wake for a component. No one makes speeches what a fine component it was. If you cannot erase and be erased you should not do this work."

Spite claws inside me. "I'm successful in this work."

"You are successful through reckless choices, not through genius of tactics. I see the files. You are hard to manage. You are called on precisely because you are expendable. I am sure you would have the most pretty funeral and serious people would say most eloquent things. It would be a most predictable affair."

Agnieszka drops the window. Settles her gaze on the bus stop over the road. Between the trees, a woman pushes a buggy. In a coat because, maybe, she thinks it might rain. Blonde hair tied back because, maybe, it's not had a trim in a while. White t-shirt, horizontal blue stripes. The type Matalan knocks out by the million. Jeans do favours to her wide hips. With a label that says Ralph Lauren I bet, badly stitched in some warehouse. Who cares? Ralph don't need her money. The kid in the buggy is a bright little spark. Brown curly hair, I guess from his dad. Those stripy denim kid clothes that all look the same. He wrestles the strap, banging forward and back, leaning over to pick at his shoes. That splash of red I guess is one of those chewy books. That's me, plus a couple of years. Pushing a buggy round the Plaça de Catalunya. Getting advice from all the old fusspots. She must be taking the kid to nursery, on her way to work. Her entire day built around drop off and pick up. Rain or shine, winter and summer. It's a long job, being a parent.

Agnieszka clicks the safety off her Jennings. Draws sight on the woman's head. She drops aim a centimetre. "Is better. The child first. A moment to reflect. Then the woman." She's steady and holds a clean line. Her finger licks the trigger. It clicks to position.

I punch her hand and the shot sings out. The car it hits is a disco of flashing lights and wailing alarm.

Agnieszka looks at me, satisfied. "You are selfish and weak."

For appearance, I throw a tantrum. Flounce off. But I can't shake the doubt. Her taking that shot meant nothing. It's not my business. I jumped into what didn't involve me. I proved her right.

Light a smoke and walk down Thirlmere Road. For a successful woman I spend a lot of time like a tramp. There's nothing wrong with these streets. Brick houses, trees, bit of front yard. Okay place to raise kids. But nothing connects. I don't understand how these lives build to any crescendo. Like the Netherlands. The Netherlands is beautiful, practical. But flat. Nothing leads the eye skyward. These people going to work. Those kids off to school. Work to earn money, to stay somewhere between going to work. School to learn things that don't matter. Not in the long run. Miquel, who knows music, calls it the symphonic pace of life. The upbeat, the lyrical, playful even. Scherzo, I like that word. Nimble and wholehearted. I don't feel that here. I feel barely a heartbeat.

A raincoat at the corner. One of them beige jobs, always creased and stained. Flasher mac, me and Roc called them. When blokes used to flash us. He's not tall. His hair's half-gone. He's crumpled and not having fun.

Before a man talks to me, I feel it. That tension, as need makes its move. Though he's no prize, I don't stop being grateful. To be born provocative should not be worn lightly.

"Doing business?"

"Yeah."

He's unmade and unattractive. But I'm pissed off, so why not. This nervy, neglected, sallow man. He'll do instead of self-pity. As we walk, he flaps his coat. It's buttoned, so the coat is dancing. A nervous habit and I think he's had times of living on his nerves. No one looks that beaten that hasn't fought.

Obvious, his wife's in charge of interior decoration. I don't believe a clean house is the sign of a dull woman. I'm fastidious about our apartment and I don't think I'm dull. Here's everything, neat and regular. Grey sofa, grey chairs, small tables and overbig lamps. The sideboard's pine but dumpy.

"It's normally lunchtime," he says, "before I find a girl."

"Is this what you do?"

"My wife's at work. She won't be back all day."

"What about the neighbours?"

He glances at the drab nets. "Everyone's working."

He makes coffee. Just instant, but better than nothing. He's Bernard. He can't help saying his wife's Mary. Says her name three times in two minutes, to establish her as fact. He says, "That's her," and I squint at the framed picture of big shorts on some beach that could be Torquay or Torremolinos. She's neat, well-aged, unremarkable.

"She works with architects."

Only after he's made coffee, he takes off his coat. I'm surprised he wears a suit. But its averageness is what I'd expect. Beige and creased, it doesn't sit well on his frame. He's the geezer who visits Fitzroy Square and takes the airhead tarts because the sight of Roc shrinks his balls. He talks too much, cums too soon and stays exactly the same. "So," I say, "where you working?"

"I got interests."

"Picking up girls? That your interest?"

"I can pay."

Maybe his wife gives him a tart allowance. It's tiring, watching him do nothing. I beckon with a take-it-easy smile. "Tell me about these girls."

As he sits, he takes out his wallet. A tsunami of creases grind the nap of his jacket. He has actual notes, tatty, stuck with tape. "What I pay an hour."

Roc is five times that. But I'm a street girl. "How you want it, Bernie?"

"I like that. 'Bernie.' What the boys used to call me. Mary says 'Bernard' is distinguished."

"Well it is." I search for one. "Bernard Bresslaw."

"Was he famous?"

"Not really. What you want?"

"I like a bit of talk first."

I'm not surprised. "Hour starts when you're ready."

It dispirits me, how he bustles to the kitchen. Not on principle: Miquel is an excellent cook. His mum brought him up admirably. But we're a couple. We share everything. Bernard's a man left fallow. Filling the kettle and rinsing the cups. He has no other arrangements.

Cross my legs to give him a thighful. This lovely dress needs a clean and a mend. My knees are scuffed. I can smell myself. My eyes are late for mascara. His knuckles stroke my leg as he sits. "What you do with these girls?" My voice all seduction. "Every detail."

With clumsy modesty he parks his hands between his knees. "Some don't want to talk. It's time, you see. Time's money."

"I got other income."

"It's good, having income."

It's like we're in sales, gauging prospects. "I'll strip. Give you a dance."

That perks him. But it's memories, not anticipation. "I loved the old clubs. Drinks on the table. Notes in the G-string. Going out back."

"You stud."

"It was different then. I could say, 'I'll have that one and that one and that one.' They'd line up."

"Those girls were smart."

"I wasn't here then."

"What you do for cash, Bernie?"

"You mean: do I go out for it? Can't, can I?"

I tug him close. Surprisingly, he resists. A sulky resistance. Like he feels a bright light upon him. "Have you got trouble?" I can sound kind, when it suits me.

"You're different," he says. "Most want it done quick."

"I'm known for my sensitivity."

"When I'm there. Y'know, having it. They're thinking how quick they can get to the next one. And their pimps, watching the clock." He looks startled. "Where's your pimp?"

"Getting beer. He likes to start early."

"Treat you okay?"

"It's protection. What's on your mind?" I'm not keen to find out, no more than I want sex with him. He looks old. I don't fuck old. I only come here to use his shower.

He makes more coffee. A busy girl wouldn't put up with this. My pimp's a nice guy, but how long would I get off the leash? "I'm ready. If you want to get cracking."

His head jerks out the kitchen. "You want a macaroon? Mary makes 'em with coconut."

So we eat his wife's macaroons. They're sweet. I feel my hips bloat.

"It's like this," he says, spitting crumbs.

He's going to tell me he's got no dick. His wife took it for an architect's model.

"I did time."

"I'm listening, lover."

"Armed robbery. Did a ten in Long Lartin."

Many years ago, a bloke called Gareth Connett made a working handgun in the metal shop at Long Lartin. Caused quite a fuss. There's a good tradition of improvisation. Scrap metal, bedsprings and matches. Not accurate or reliable. But enough to drill a hole. A ten stretch is mid-range. Premeditated, with shooters, can rack a twenty. My grandad didn't get life. But they finished him. "Were you the triggerman?"

"It was this factory. There was meant to be no one there. I'd done a bit—shops and offices. Had some cash tucked away. We planned a night out after, with the tarts from the massage parlour."

"You got caught?"

"Night before, I had a win at the tables. I used to like it, the casino. That job was an extra. Like you doing one on your way home. It felt wrong from the start. These were blokes I hadn't seen. We got told: this is easy—goods and cash. I went in with 'em. I have a deceptively soft personality."

Bits of coconut frost my leg.

"Some blokes took liberties. These other blokes didn't like it. Then the filth came and I was running. Tripped over a fucking box."

That's my fear. Something dumb, like falling.

"Me and these mugs got lifted. Those other blokes were nowhere."

"You mind if I…"

"Not here. Mary won't have it."

I could stay home and get told not to smoke.

"I get ten with lifers and hard nuts. And I never done more than show a gun."

"They do that. Filthy bastards."

"Then one of the blokes that stitched me gets done for murder. In Long Lartin, isn't he? He's a name, though, so I stay clear. Come visiting day, I see my sister. We've always been close. We're chatting and this bloke's in the next room. With his missus. Mary."

"Your Mary?"

"Not then. Not for years. 'Course, he has lots of visits. He's a name. You know how they straighten the screws."

"For a price."

"He wasn't the only one with money. My sister kept mine. So I got messages passed across. Mary was waiting for me when I walked."

Frankly, I'm horrified. "How did you get away with that?"

"She was looking for the door. Gone off him. I had money put away. She had hers. We moved here."

"This other bloke. Is he looking for you?"

Bernie shrugs. "He's still inside. I don't know he's that bothered."

"You reckon? You fucking shamed him."

"He didn't want her. So she says."

"So what is it?"

His eyes are black pits. "She thought we was going away. Proper away. We could have. But I wanted a house. Something secure, y'know. Then she finds out that's it."

The fucking mug. His woman chucks a dangerous man to be with him. And he blows it on a house in Tooting. Now she must make money and him… "You can't work, can you? You have to keep low." I'd kill a man did that to me. "She works and you get tarts in."

He looks slapped. "Thought you understood."

You have means and incentive. Go down in flames, or waste away. "You put a roof over her head. That's handy when it's raining."

"I like your eyes."

"They're my defining feature."

His lips twitch. He can't find a nice way to say it. "Have you got tits?"

"Yeah, but ever so small." He tastes of antiseptic and too long indoors. He's not sure how to kiss. His lips poke at mine like tasting some strange delight. "I'm having a shower."

As my sweetheart Roc tells me, men are not gourmets of love. As women we do all we can to nurture their talents. Blokes are preoccupied, rushed and clumsy. Unschooled. Funny, says Roc, the best are often the posh lads. Rich sorts that grew up with nannies, whose brisk hands would stiffen a boy under the bedsheets. Trained early by a stern woman, they know what to do.

I soap him, but he can't manage it in the shower. Seems scared of falling. He lays towels on the bed not to wet the sheets. Obviously, he expected something different. Some men do. But they succumb because I have power that flows from deep affection. With Bernie, I don't make a fuss. Displace away. Take a spank and he brings me off with a screwdriver handle. Of course he keeps a screwdriver under the bed.

As he fondles me, I know this is every girl he brings here. Can't manage it but she's had the money. He never sees her again, that's the thing. So I say nothing. I squirm and spunk the towels. I stick this screwdriver up my arse and give him a show. Lick his body. His face says his nipples never got licked before. He tastes of his clothes, that old coat, too long on the peg. He can't relax, his body a torture of worry. Work his thighs, licking and stroking. Teabagging, just gently. Get a mouthful of soap he forgot to rinse. His legs grip my head. I feel his stress. I can't fancy him, not after what he told me. But a man should have this, because death is the end, and all the years before. "Tell me about your work."

His voice clouds over, like night talk through the cell wall. "I done a bit. Shops. Places with cash on the premises. I hurt no one. Got in easy. I'm compact, y'see?"

Lick his thigh.

"I was big in the clubs. Lined up, dropping their knickers. I could have two or three. I was at the casino. Money all sides. I didn't need that job. But I could do no wrong."

"Some days I feel invincible."

"I didn't listen to myself."

"You got set up."

"I got Mary."

Kiss his cock. "When did you get her?"

"First day out. My sister let us have her house for the day. Legit, you see? Me visiting my sister. Mary climbed in the back gate. We fucked on every flat surface."

Rub my nose between his dick and sack. The scent of a male. "She's beautiful, your Mary."

"I'd come home at night and she'd pretend to be sleeping."

"Did she struggle?"

"I always won."

When he starts I can't stand how hesitant he is. His Mary was a saint, to keep up the act. He tussles me. I use a twelfth of my strength against him. I belong on all fours, it's my natural position. But he drags me up to do cowgirl, a dominance I find awkward. He's barely hard but I steal a rhythm.

For no reason, he says, "I forgot the condom."

"Don't matter," I say. "Fill me up." But he's thinking what if he catches something. How to tell Mary.

Though he's nothing to do all day, he wants me gone when he's done. He doesn't say that. He says, "You must be busy."

I've lent more than the hour but I don't ask extra. He looks at the window, and I say, "It's alright. He don't know where I am."

Bernie says nothing. Scared of a pimp that don't exist. When I'm gone, he'll put the towels in the wash. Have a wank for Mary. For how she was. Before she knew this is it. I'm not sympathetic. We all suffer our choices. He doesn't ask if he'll see me again because he never sees us again. How could he when he can't see himself.

Meet Spike in a caff and I'm tanking on rösti and beans, in busy and vaguely shit North London between Hendon and Brent Cross.

He chomps toast, which he doesn't seem to enjoy, and smells more than usual of turps.

"How's the decorating?"

"Up and down." I can't tell if he's joking. His face is concertinaed. He rubs that tattoo the whole time.

"Heard from herself?" I could bite my tongue. 'Herself' is what he called Judy, his wife, before she left in a blizzard of Benzedrine. That's the thing with addicts. Death doesn't impress them. To cover up, I gabble, "What's she doing for her gap year?"

He looks at me like I'm mad. "In Cambridge. She works at a lab."

Star, who I haven't seen since she was a dazed little kid, has bound herself to science in hopes of a different life. She'll call him, visit at Christmas, get drawn inexorably away like stardust to a black hole. She'll meet people, learn stuff, map her own direction. She'll achieve things she won't tell him about because he won't understand. My dad was disdainful of professional killers. He thought it a poor career, compared to the splendid complexities of an audacious heist. Dad valued craft over outcome. When he was successful, the money was an afterthought. Getting the scheme in his head to work in the world, that was his delight. Spike won't even know when his daughter succeeds.

We talk about the Belgravia business. He reckons the cops cocked up. He doesn't think spooks were involved. Like lots of people, he thinks the spooks an exotic 'over there' thing. Shooting up foreign blowhards on no-knock warrants. I'm too busy and full of potato to explain the feuds, the jealousies, getting visited on me for no reason.

From his paint-spattered toolbag, Spike takes a folder. Scuffed and scribbled—something a painter would use for receipts. He's fastidious, is Spike. Inside, two birth certificates and a notice of upcoming marriage given at Islington a month ago. The certificates are beauties, with the lines and big fat crown and the names of four people, parents it seems. Mr. Stephen and Mrs. Laura blank on one. Him an insurance broker, her a nursery teacher. Birth registered in the London Borough of Redbridge thirty-one years ago. On the other, Mr. Michael and Miss Julie blank. He's a computer engineer—nice—she's a dress shop proprietrix. Birth registered in the London Borough of Wandsworth thirty-six years ago. There's flattery.

"Handsome."

He stubs his finger at the blanks. "Should have let us finish the job. And this," he points at the marriage notice, "no names, no venue. It's one step from empty paper."

"One step's all I need." Dig around in my Saint Laurent. "Get Star something," I say, all sincerity. "Something nice."

Hit Brent Cross, as this gorgeous dress is now rank. I haven't slept for days. I'm at the stage where the world is soft silver. This venerable retail temple has the diffused abundance of an alien city. Get a good black dress, knickers, and shoes, and regretfully drop the Rococo Sand in the clothes bank. Hopefully, down the line, it's some use.

Dip into the bogs to make a call. Urgency in my voice, tell the receptionist it's critical. Without even knowing what's wrong she says not to fret, which is sweet. Flying on goodwill and falsehood I get through to the Registrar's office. "I need help."

The man sounds wary.

"We gave notice of our wedding a month ago. But I just now realised I didn't book the venue." I snivel a bit. "Can you fit us in? Any day's good."

"You posted your section 27 form here?"

"Your Town Hall's beautiful." A phrase I don't think I've said before. "I can give you all the particulars."

"Can I take your name?"

"Felicity Jean Hepburn."

Computer keys and heavy breath. "I'm not seeing you on the system."

I give a cry not wholly synthetic. "I got it, though. The notice. I can email it you."

"It's a notice for here?"

How thick does he think I am? "Yes, it says Islington. Islington. I need you to help me."

"We have a slot on Thursday. One of the small rooms. It's the standard package. You can't customise the ceremony and there's no time to make an entrance."

"What sort of entrance?"

"You are the bride, I take it."

I park what being 'the bride' actually means. Then there's the credit card.

"It's in your name?"

"No."

I'd stick a bullet in that silence he leaves. "Whose name is the card in?"

"Carolina Delamarre. With a 'a'. Carolina. Delamarre. D-e-l-a-m-a-double-r-e. She's my cousin. She's so good." Four-figure good.

"That's booked," he says, inertly. "You will send through the notice. It's very strange I can't see it on the system."

"Soon as I get home, I'll send it."

"Alright. And, er, good luck with the wedding."

Get the Tube to Elephant, through the enticing City. Moorgate and Bank, those moody ruins of what, once, was high class employment.

London Bridge, where the country cousins lived, before they got minted. I've lost track of my relations and that's a cause for regret.

The Elephant is nasty, as it should be. Tarting it up is wrong. Stop the traffic to cross the road, flashing acres of thigh. Some shout shit, but most are mesmerised.

Message Roc: 'Thursday. Islington.' Hope Thursday's alright. I hate asking her to lose money.

Lunchtime when I swish into the London College of Communication. It's easy to find the Design School. The signs are so well done.

Despite all the hoo-ha, it's still pleasingly simple to get in places with a big smile and tight action. No one stops me. Collar some pretty young bod to ask where's the graphics. He inhales, actually breathes me in.

The studio is screens on high-shine desks. Scanners and printers and words round the walls. Someone riffed a rainbow from the words of Paula Scher: 'It's through mistakes that you actually can grow. You have to get bad in order to get good'. Hard lesson. Each time I get shot I learn, though it's expensive in skin.

Naturally, one needs credentials. I try a dozen terminals before I find the delightfully forgetful student who left themselves logged in. Haul up onto the chrome stool with gratuitous knicker-flashing and get to work. It's an OCR package, sharp enough for designers. Software that can analyse and replicate. I investigate the scanner, miffed at security lunacy that requires a swipe to use it. I pick on a kid pecking away at branding for low-fat milkshakes. I'm appalled at that notion, but pleasantly say, "Can I borrow your swipe? I'm always forgetting."

I presume he's adult or good as. But it's like he's never seen a woman. I have to jimmy the ID from his petrified fingers. While he slowly gets back to his branding principles—consistency, clarity, continuity, visibility, authenticity—I run the birth certificates and marriage notice through the scanner. They're common fonts, the software matches them easy. I add the names I didn't want Spike to know and sort the marriage notice with venue and that. Then the hard bit. With the design software, I remove everything from the scans except the text I put in. For the birth certificates, I delete the words and logos and make the layout transparent, so all that's left is names floating in white space. Same with the marriage notice. Take out what's there, hide the grid, leave names and venue. It's fine, laborious work. My armpits are clammy.

Get the kid's swipe again. Print dummies, to check position against the certificates. Feel something like anxiety as I load the marriage notice into the printer. It looks okay. The fonts match. The details in the boxes. The certificates are tricky. They're an odd size and I'm adding to strings of words. I could kiss every shave-head girl in the place when the certs roll out okay. Two women, their identities adjusted. Scan the new versions and email from a throwaway to the bloke at the Registry office. A gushy, unhinged message, blessing him for his help. A promise to bring the originals on the day. This performance takes two hours.

She messages: 'Thursday yes! Ivory white? I'll get the rings.' This charms me. Roc's no millionaire. That she's been saving for this pricks my eyes. Her trust is her power over me.

A message from Mr. Miller's office. Agnieszka's been arrested driving a stolen car.

When I get to Holland Park, solemnity stalks Mr. Miller's witless boys. I knew Tony Hazell only as a scruffy sod. But to these darlings he was papa bear. They want to exact on who killed him. They may think it was me.

Mr. Miller is tidy and accurate. His quiet voice holds fathomless regret at a loss that—I realise now—cuts deep. These are serious moments and I know why I wear black. Before I even thought to come here, that nicety I inherited from Mum moved my bones. I'm the product of strong, knowing women and calm, violent men.

Mr. Miller, bless his heart, is deeply affected. "Thank you." He gestures at my dress.

The clammy serenity of his windowless office riles my blood. But I force myself to sit, poised and attentive.

"One doesn't realise," he starts a distant way, as though talking of days long gone, "how much one relies on people, until they're taken. Tony came to me as a young man. He never had much aptitude for the action. You understand what I mean. But his charm and good instincts drove massive progress for the business. When I think of the future—oh, you know I do, Felicity—I had wondered if he might lead the firm going forward. The others have talents. But he was so effective with clients and suppliers. Suave and forceful."

I sense he might cry. I don't want that. "Tony was killed by the security services. I have that from a senior officer."

"Thank you. The young men want blood, naturally. I'll speak with my contacts." Surprisingly sincere, he says, "Please don't put yourself in additional danger."

Glad to cut loose from gravity, I pat his leg. "I couldn't be in more danger."

"You must be counting the days till you see your fiancé. I do hope you can get away from all this."

"I've already bought swimwear."

He's not listening. "It was furtive when I started. Toilets and bars. All about sex. Oh, there were couples, old pooves you know. But mostly young men and sex. One never thought of seeing someone again, much less get married. Married! The very idea. We loathed all that straight stuff. And business was lively, no time for distractions. I've no regrets, naturally not. But I think, perhaps, I missed something."

He's so much older than I can imagine being. "You want a hug?"

"That's kind, Felicity. But you are so much a woman. Forgive me, that was old-fashioned."

I need to get this to business, before I'm in bits. "This interference in your work…"

"That Polish girl's been arrested. I suppose we should get her out."

"The Arabs are in this. An arms dealer called Jazin. You know Freddie Dexter's still in the game?"

"I haven't seen Freddie in days."

"One of the Cheltenham set told me about Tony. Those gentlemen want Jazin removed with no spatter stuck to themselves. They think I want to suck them on that."

He shakes his wise old head. "You'll be a corpse otherwise. How many have you seen dead?"

"After the first hundred I stopped counting."

"I've seen plentiful death. Ordered a few. Put some under myself. Not in a while, you understand. It's unseemly at my age. I would like to say each was for a sound business reason. I recall, years ago now, having a drink with your father."

I don't want this. I don't like people's memories of him.

"You know how he was. Strategic, meticulous, concerned. He could have done far more business, but he liked things compact. This was years ago, Felicity. You were first making your name."

"You make me sound ancient." An uneasy joke.

"You are remarkably youthful. Your mother always looked

marvellous, rest her soul. I remember saying to your father how he must be proud of you. I'll never forget what he said. 'Death can't be given away. It starts and ends with us. I fear she won't learn that.' Now I'm old. I share the fears of old men. I see no way to this that doesn't end with your death."

I grip his knee. Bone hard but fragile. "You know I'm Houdini."

But he's away in the old men's world. In a long-gone bar, sipping drinks from a glass long-since crushed to dust, at a table long-rotted in landfill. "I was desperately sorry about your parents. We did all we could. It starts and ends with us."

I'm better among cool machinery in the surveillance room. Agnieszka's a fair technician. This kit is nicely installed. A few blips from Europe and the East Coast, where it's lunchtime. All quiet on the Arabian front. They're a couple of hours ahead down there, a bit of workday left before dinner. People get surprised I like those parts. It's not a message that plays back home, where a lot of nuts still think of the Moors as conquerors. There's a whole fashion scene of hijabs and abayas. It's fabric, pattern, stitching. Beautiful stitching. And when a man unwraps you, their care takes your breath away.

From Dexter's event logs, the traffic of these last few days presumably maps to Jazin's preparations to travel. Proles like me just slip around. But a mighty swell like Sayidi Rashad needs logistics. The super-rich aren't equipped to do anything simply. It's life as performance. And now Sayidi Rashad is here. Landed at Northolt while I was getting these fine certificates. Time for a little recce around his house. After tonight's amusement.

Quiet, just the ticking machines. Draughty, with the aircon. Mr. Miller runs a significant business. Import export. Recreation. Killing to order. He's probably shipped a few tarts in crates. I don't judge. Misery pays the bills. But why would an ace like Jazin punch holes in Mr. Miller's logistics? Unless to trial solutions on unwilling lab rats. These suppositions don't please me. I message Roc. Explain, without explaining, a three-day job that can only be delivered by her exquisite body. That she's needed right after the wedding feels too complex for plain text.

By now, Jazin has kept Asr. Afternoon prayer. Four obligatory and four recommended rakat. I'm a great respecter of piety. I wouldn't mock someone for craving structure in their relations with the universe. Who doesn't want to feel it means something.

Ringing round, I find they took Agnieszka to Agar Street, with the anti-terrorist blowhards. That she's in the game will be quickly established. That she's insufferable, they'll soon find out.

An hour dissolves, watching blips onscreen. Packets of data, sent and received, neutrally sequenced by time. All Mr. Miller's business, while he drinks sherry and mourns. I snoop the chat. Most people—even with clandestine employment—rarely think they're overheard. Everything eavesdrops, from phones to fridges. Yet people are loose with words. I hear who got the goods, who made the drop. What someone thinks of somebody. What they're doing with somebody's boyfriend. That's us. We're a showy, cocky world. I'm sure Mr. Miller remembers Dad ran a tight firm. Dad worked with the same blokes for years. Cardigan-wearing, allotment-tending, reticent men. They rarely blew up and never seemed pleased. They had equanimity. Over decades, those blokes lifted millions. Calm, methodical, applying violence as a doctor prescribes medicine. My children will learn these things. I owe them the best.

Message Chloe Bell to keep Thursday to Saturday free. Nearly add juicy teasers but I'm not an animal. I call Lee. Lee manages property. Works both sides of the blanket. One of that population of fixers, who tend the grounds for our games.

He's a boy, is Lee. A white collar pain. I like that. "Princess!" he bellows, no doubt in a pub, showing off. "What good deed have I done to get you in my earhole?"

When I was a kid, blokes like Lee came round selling on the knock. Sharp collars, thin ties, old patter. They'd call Mum 'Princess' and she'd get silly. They'd say to her, 'Hello, young woman, is your mummy home?' When Dad asked why she bought so much crap she'd say, 'Leave it. They're having a go'.

"Hello, handsome. Long time no see."

"Tell me, treacle. Must be three years."

Glasses clink. A till beeps. There's music and laughter. There's a tall, skinny blonde next to him. It's a voicecall but I hear her blondeness. "We should meet up." Automatic, what he says to every woman. He'll explain me to the blonde as an old school friend or something. Lee's endearingly transparent.

"I got business."

I feel he sits a bit straighter. These things we share. Call us two, three in the morning, we're doing business.

"I need a flat. Thursday to Saturday. Fourth floor and up, nothing low. Vintage, done nice."

What I value about blokes like Lee, they never say 'I'll think about it'. They give you a price. "So happens," he says, "I got a nice block in Kensington. Mansion block. Feature windows. Lovely this time of year. All mod cons. I'll dress it nice. 'Course," he gets confidential, "this is Thursday we're talking about. I need the lob upfront. To galvanise people."

The cost surprises even me. It's a huge wedge. At some point, bills will be tallied and reckonings made. It's not the rent or furnishings. It's not even his commission. Anonymity is a rare metal. "I need the place stocked. Wine, gin, vodka. Food, good stuff, vegan, three days' worth. My associates won't be popping to the shop."

"I'll sort it, sweetheart. I got another call. Ciao for now." The blonde must be chewing his sleeve.

Onscreen, things move. A convergence of information. All useful. All deadly. By now, who's in that scrap of desert knows their intrusions are blocked. They know we got their signature. They know it's me. A second ago that thought wasn't there. Now it's credible theory. Hypothesis: persons connected with glamorous billionaire boot-boy Rashad Jazin are working to diversify their lethal offer. Plausibility: weapons dealers have every interest in new weapons. Beta test: deep-set disruption to networks owned by people in no hurry to bring in the cops. But who might bring in me. Checksum: people are trying to kill me.

Mr. Miller is a stranger to this room. Buffeted by aircon. Gently bemused by humming drives.

"Dexter left trackers. I flushed them."

Mr. Miller looks polite.

"Bugs to call back to Cheltenham. I stamped them."

"Thank you, Felicity." He wipes invisible lint from his suit. "I did harbour doubts. But he seemed so authentically ruined."

"He was using your kit to further their aims."

"And when you came along, his work was done?"

I feel how he feels, cold and confused. "I'm sorry about the bitch. I used her to strongarm Toby Archer. I thought she was some crackpot colonel's daughter."

He's delightful, so judicious. "It's not that it's done well but that it's done at all." His old eyes follow data strings, pulsing from Rome to Berlin. "Is my business safe, Felicity? It's all I have."

Oft-times, mean-spirited people call me selfish. Obsessed with pleasure. Simplistic and indifferent. I'm not a deep thinker. I don't fake compassion well. I act affectionate to get what I want. But my whole life is giving. When a man pounds me beyond the point I can't think anymore, it's not me that matters. When Miquel fucks me for hours, the alloy of my surrender makes his conquest pure. While I pinball around settling scores, Mr. Miller needs to know he won't be poor, now age has embraced him. It's easy to be brave with firm skin. "The intrusions are quarantined. They know we're onto them."

"Will there be trouble?"

"My involvement means less trouble for you."

"Go home." He strokes my leg like a familiar, uninterested cat. "Leave this to those with nothing planned."

Before I got broody, I never considered how Dad managed work with being a dad. He never did much round the house. Mum said she didn't want him under her feet. But he had time for me and Roc. Took us places. Showed us things. If other kids bothered us, he'd have a word with their dads, and those blokes knew they'd been spoken to. He never seemed to put business ahead of us, though he must have done often. Those nights the firm came round and Mum would tell them to wipe their feet and they'd call her 'Mrs. Hepburn' in mild, indoor voices. When the fairy princess raised her wand, when I wished her to make me a girl, Dad told me: always, I'd be a Hepburn. All he achieved, and he was our dad. And Mum's warmth around us. In our tidy-bright little bedrooms. In the best house in town.

With three hours till my date, I go shopping for a wedding dress. Once, girls married so they could have sex and the spinster dames of the stockroom laid judgement on them, even as they carved dresses from tulle and lace. Now, a schoolboy in hairy Moss Bros prinks at me like a dainty spaniel, the eagerness of his wet eyes trite and discordant. "Are you looking for something traditional?"

"Christ no."

He seems at a loss.

"I want fitted. Short. Ivory white. I'll decide today."

He tries his spiel. "Your wedding day isn't the time for a wardrobe malfunction."

"What?"

The floor gleams between us. "Typically, our clients welcome three fittings. To sculpt the gown to the body."

"I'm getting married on Thursday."

Brides-to-be stroll around, arms like driftwood on a blazing sea.

"It's a major decision," he whines.

"Do I look like I don't understand clothes? I want fitted. Short. Ivory white. Lead on."

His mid-range cologne is malignant fog as we walk the aisles of what he calls, "Contemporary looks." Many of these dresses are poorly designed, make ineffective use of material and lack essence. When I get married in Barcelona, I'll wear a vast, antique affair, woven from snow, with a towering headdress pinned by combs. Naturally. Miquel's family deserve respect. But these London nuptials are mine.

These pieces are straight up and down. A second or even third wedding, all illusion rightly pruned back. Some are for brides up the duff. While he gibbers about 'classic elegance' I dig through average stitching and unexceptional lines, to unearth a serviceable length of satin. High neck, bit of ruching, not too much. Hook and eye fittings round back. I wouldn't as a rule, but it's unfussy and I do like this collar. It's a Mischka, so at least it's been near a designer. "I'll try this."

"Clients like to try between four and seven pieces. And of course the adjustments…"

"Fitting room this way, yeah?"

In England fitting rooms never get painted. These scuffed walls from clumsy brides, I've not seen that in Paris. You get coffee and a cheeky lad trying to cop a feel. I had the quickest shag ever in a fitting room in Rome. He had me up the wall and done before the curtain settled.

I talk with clothes. I know what loves me. This dress is a bit standoffish. Reluctant to hug or admire. But it's the dress for a woman bound to be married. Slippy satin tingles my skin. That hint of metallic sheen. And I can't upstage Roc. I want everyone wet for her beauty.

Neglectfully, the young man isn't lurking by the door. He's showing puffy creations to a woman who looks splendid in a Harajuku jacket and could get married in that for all I care. Because I don't hang about, I cough rather crudely. She backs off like a copper from salad. "This'll do. It wants changes."

For a young bloke he's miserably light on gumption. "It is a significant purchase…"

"Only wearing it once, aren't I? Look, this bodice. All this needs taking in. And let the arms out, I got muscles. The waist needs tightening. And it's too long. I need twenty centimetres off that skirt. My bride wants legs, not fabric."

"Your bride?"

"Well, obviously. And I'm getting married Thursday. So I need it tomorrow."

"That might be a problem…"

"Look, son. A problem is a compound of circumstance. No matter how tight bound that compound, it remains soluble. Money is a reagent. Add money to problems, they dissolve. Let's settle up."

The cost of this job is exceeding the take. Even with Mr. Miller's decent generosity, I need to get something for Jazin, to make cream off this caper. The puzzle of who's going to pay me to do what everyone wants—but no one admits to wanting—absorbs me on the walk to Hyde Park.

I drop by a Knightsbridge wine bar to warm up on Penedès. Cap de Trons, grown in the Alt Penedès near Vilafranca. Nice spot for the reception. As per tradition the bride's family is paying, which means I'm paying. Though food and drink comes at a discount, thanks to Miquel's uncles. And the bridesmaids can sort their own dresses. Every Catholic girl's got a white dress. It's a tasty idea, driving up the hills for a vineyard reception. To live in such country; to speak the language; to belong. To have the love of a strong man and the blessing of his mother. What fool would throw that away. I'll marry Miquel, we'll live life together. And Roc: I'll find a way where she's not second best. She'd do well in Barcelona. Discreet, of course, with the family. But things can be managed. The joy of love carries me like a warm tide. Penedès is a fine wine.

The stars shine over Knightsbridge. I'll tell my babies about these days. When we sit in the Catalan night, counting these same stars.

Check my phone. In the usual slab of notifications, a missed call from a strange number. I'm cold. I call back.

"Why don't you ever pick up?"

Instinct jolts me into a doorway. "This isn't your number."

Roc's moving, her breath interrupted. A door slams. "This is a burner."

My spine is ice. "You okay? What happened?"

"I'm working. I don't have long. A man was here. Bought me for an hour. Waited, with other girls available. When he paid, he left his wallet on the side. So I get him to lick me out. I'm pushing him down. With my other hand, I open his wallet."

"You fucking what?"

"Listen. He had ID. No names. But the pattern. The lines on the card."

The mark of courage is selflessness. "You okay?"

"Well, I'm talking to you. He comes up for air. We fuck. I ask what line he's in. You know how slack men get. He tells me he keeps everyone safe from a virus. 'You'll be hearing from us,' he says."

"What about…"

"I'm busy. I'm booked for a gangbang. He obviously knew who I am. You need to get out."

"Not before Thursday."

"Yes, I can't wait to marry a corpse."

"You remember I need a favour?"

"Felicity, I'm late."

It comes without finesse. "I need you to keep a filth out the way. Thursday to Saturday. I got you a flat. Female filth. It's pure guava."

"Guava?" That growl curls her throat. "You want me to take three days off work? And I'm meant to be grateful?"

I so want to hold her. Lose myself in her pictures. "If it's…"

"I have to pay my shift. I pay thirty percent to work here. If I don't pay, they take me off the rota. I don't want to look for a new place."

"I'll pay your shift."

"I don't want you to pay my shift. I'm an adult. I don't want a penny off you."

"Darling…"

"I love you. I'm not on your payroll."

When I call back, the phone's been trashed.

Fulfilment

Diana's granite memorial is not an object I think she'd like. Form and line were her guiding star. Whatever she wore amplified her. She could wear Dior, that's not easy. She knew how to dress for revenge.

The stream bed varies from three to six metres wide. A hundred litres of water per second is pumped uphill from the plant room at the Serpentine. It forms, apparently, a reflective basin. It cost a bomb and still looks cheap.

These arseholes think they're funny, trying to scare Roc. They'll go where she lives, turn over the doorman. I need her in Barcelona. To protect her. Because it's easier to hate them, isn't it.

Hyde Park is a black well, fringed by the orange city. Water bubbles beside me as I sit on these cold stones. One side is smooth, the other stepped. This, apparently, shows her joy and betrayal. I would hate to be remembered like this. Feral noise strokes my skin. Somewhere a fox is prowling. I'm a target. Let them try. I'll show them Hell by morning.

Young and keen, he waits his time. Punctuality is a turn on. For someone who wants a career of nocturnal shenanigans, he's not adept at moving through dark. I see him cleanly. Easy to track a dark moving shape against a dark static background. And he's careless. Grass makes noise. The young have so much to learn.

In wayward seconds, I imagine this for a life. Seeing each other by night. Having each other on lawns and meadows all over the world. In warm summer air and stone frost.

His kiss nearly topples us into the water. His tongue behind my teeth. Already I'm shaking, his power over me astounding.

"Got this." From his puffy jacket he pulls a riding crop. Classic type: leather strap, rubber grip, leather flapper. He strips me with pleasing confidence. Sniffs my dress. "You always wear new clothes?"

"I'm costly to keep."

"I wouldn't have you in clothes."

He tries the crop on my buttocks. A searing stripe that launches me down. My dick jumps to life.

"Naughty bitch."

I crawl away. He follows, smearing pain across my legs. When he whips my balls, I squeal.

"Noisy slut." He gives me one on each tit.

"Please."

"Shut up."

Bite my lip as he lays his anxiety in stinging ribbons along my flanks. Shaking and twisting, he catches the tip of my cock. I leap and break free. Run naked across the black lawn.

Not wanting to smack down full face, I tighten when he collides with me, grab his arm and heel him over in a stunt fall. Hit the ground, winded and splayed.

His cock's in. Full length. He clamps my neck and drills me. Taste grass, earth, succulent life. He fucks and fucks. He grinds till my body ruts the dirt. I don't want this to stop. My dick scrapes the ground and I cum, spunk puddling my stomach. Swimming, I grab his legs. "Not yet. Please not yet."

Frenzy takes him. I'm nothing. A hole. Convenient meat. He slams me so hard my chin drives a wedge through sweet, damp turf. The orgasm takes me. I wail and squeal. A hot jet shoots to my guts. He drags me up and I piss everywhere. "I love you, I love you, I love you."

Hennessy tucked in his coat. Sweet coffee taste on a wet night. Wrapped in his arms, I tell him, "Brandy, from the Dutch 'burnt wine'. Best in the world is Mascaró from Catalunya. Brandy is alchemy."

He laughs. "You like to explain things."

"I'm a bitch with time on her hands." I'm warm and he smells divine. "Fuck me again."

"I like how you ask."

"Always."

Quick, but it's what I need. Young men know. They don't cramp or have work in the morning. When time's short, they lie with proficiency. If someone's waiting at home, they fuck them too. Men falter. They settle to errors as comfortably as a frayed shirt. I love young men. They know what I'm for.

He rubs my dick, twisting and hooding the skin. Picking words cautiously, he says, "Before you, I never touched another cock."

"It's a dolly. A sissy dolly."

"A sissy dolly."

Under relentless fingers I spunk the soft earth. He finger-fucks me. Makes me lick his hand. That salty, gamey taste. But nothing lasts.

"Tomorrow…"

Grip his arm. "Someone there."

He's fly. His voice a whisper. "See?"

"A bloke. Two hundred metres that way. Another on the bridge."

"Fuck…"

"Shush."

"You got a gun?" His voice jagged, excited.

"Pest control. Sit casual."

"I'm no pussy."

"It's me they want." Dress in a heartbeat. The rush kicks in. Swish to the bushes.

The one on the Carriage Drive comes forward. The one on the bridge stays put. A flame floats above the grass. My hero's smoking.

No sound but my heart and rippling water. More than anything, I want to redo my eyes. Sparks from his joint flare and stutter. Must be a joint, to burn that way. Ducks creak restlessly under the lip of the path. I trust my eyes, my hands, my gun. Nothing else.

Grass makes noise. The ground betrays them. These men are small to me. By the statue of Serenity, run my fingers over cool, forgiving bronze. I always expect to die. I calculate death's proximity. In the side of my eye that flame swoops over the grass. Unrest strips my spine. Stop breathing. My lungs constrict. I can hold my breath two minutes. Not bad for a smoker. Step onto the lawn.

Like an idiot rifleman he puts a laser on me. When the bullet leaves his gun, he's already dead.

Run to my man. Hit up on the joint. It stands me back on my heels.

"You fix him?"

"Yeah."

Wonder unsettles his smooth face.

"There's another one. Come on."

We move as the shot comes over the fountain. I jolt with my lover's weight.

Fury takes me. I fire at the bridge. Run and shoot till bullets stop coming. Put one in his head as he bleeds on the ground. The end of a nameless man. Run back to the fountain. On my knees I work the young man's chest. But his sweetness is gone. Kiss his dead mouth. Lick his blood. It's warm, deluded with life. These bastards destroy everything. It's their fulfilment.

Cradle him, till the ambulance wakes the Carriage Drive, slinging blue light through wet granite. I want to ride with him. See him treated right. But I'm too selfish to die. As I leave, it's the worst betrayal.

I meet the cab driver's worry with sweet lies. A domestic, I tell him. One of those things. He asks if I'll be alright. "Pretty girl like you should be treated proper."

The night manager watches Asian satellite in his office. A talk show. He sees me on the monitors. Straightens his tie as he walks to the desk. Black hair, very close, very neat beard. He bathes my face, to take off tears and dirt. He waits while I redo my eyes, watching me watch TV. I understand, without knowing, they're talking about Afghanistan.

Scan my room. No bugs. They're listening, somehow. Gun-runner chat on the dark web is full of Jazin. There's been a shoot-out in Hyde Park. Kept off mainstream, it's already a conspiracy.

Wake still dressed, surprised I put the AK together. It lays wanton on the rug. Four and half kilos. Huge in my dainty hands. I could open the window and put hundreds in mourning. Even that doesn't cheer me.

Don't often have baths, but I'm stiff and wretched. Sunday nights I bathe Miquel. I get on my knees and attend his every part. He loves those macho things. I cry for my young man. Some bloke picking litter will find the riding crop. He won't see my blood on the leather. He'll think a rider strayed from the ring to hack to the fountain. Carelessly lost a new whip. "These people," he'll say. "More money than sense." The earth will settle. The grass will grow. We're all erased.

I can't wear this dress again. This dress will remember his hands. Today I'm a whisper of 24 Faubourg. A plain white shirt, herringbone mini, knee high Guccis. Polyester not leather. No death on my body.

Lee messages the address. Cryptic. A code I enjoy breaking. Call Agar Street cop shop. They won't confirm or deny Agnieszka's there. Which means she's not.

Get a cab up Beaufort Street. Tell the driver to go the long way by the cemetery, to Cromwell Road. Time was, I lived for the game. With Miquel, I found the simple life. Food and wine. Music and friends. Books—I read like a bastard. One big score is all I need. Then my life's mine.

Spring sunshine gets busy with girls in culottes. Blokes doss about, shirts wide. In shorts, showing inked, furry calves. All opportunity I'm missing.

Bail at the Natural History Museum. Can't recall my last time here. Probably with Roc, on one of our tourist days we used to do. When we seemed to have more time. Dodging kids and clowns up Exhibition Road I'm wary at a beep from Agnieszka. "Didn't think you do phones."

"Is necessary. I find interesting things."

"You know, I've been looking for you. Have you been away?"

"Where are you?"

"If you were smart, you'd know."

Even that doesn't upend her. "I am with Mr. Miller."

"Already?"

"It is not early. He tells me you say his system is compromised between these agents of yours and Jazin."

"That's a lot for the public airwaves."

"There is not time."

"These 'agents' are more your business than mine. There is a large…" Check proximity. Especially the clowns. "Large issue playing out. What you doing there?"

"I make sure you have not done damage."

Of course. The Polski crew. She's their project.

"Are you here soon?"

"Are you trying to keep me talking?"

"You think I am foolish? I find interesting things."

I remember her spit in my face. That instant, unmediated heat. "We must do lunch. We've so much to catch up on."

The end of Lee's amuse-gueule is a steep, fantastical eyesore. Ten redbrick floors above ground, arched windows, iron balconies, turrets. White woodwork scrubbed clean. Built for the toffs of the Great Exhibition. Hundreds of flats, so well-ordered even the bins are platooned. Hard to believe, back then, these parts were alive with frauds and brasses. A regular rookery. Till the poor got cleared out. First for the toffs, then for the likes of George Walker. What a gent he was.

When I shoulder the door, the young man in the lobby snaps to attention. Pure Pavlov. In these threads, with this scent, I could be an agent or landlord's posh totty. He palms me the keys and insists on pressing the lift button, so I don't have to grubby my finger. I make a simpering noise with an upper crust twist. One of life's great gifts is the reliability of men's responses. It's not just they see a woman. My pheromones tell them they're in with a chance. My friendly confidence puts them at ease. I'm a social service.

These hallways are ridiculous. Plush red carpet to soak the noise. Bulbous chandeliers. A charmingly inaccurate grandmother clock. The flat is sublime. I couldn't live here. Three hundred square metres, I guess. A bright corridor—wood floor, stained blue—three bedrooms, a hammerhead sweep of space: the dining and sitting rooms. The sitting room is a conscious prod at the forms of yesteryear: high-spec gadgets among tie-back drapes. Sofas too fat to sit on. There's flowers, sideboards, polished tat. A piano, tuned too bright. Grisly English landscapes in gilt frames. Brass lights and a big TV. The dining chairs are upholstered. The kitchen is modern and vile. No table—only servants eat in the kitchen. When I think of our snug kitchen at home, its mazed sink and Moorish tiles, the beechwood table where me and Miquel eat salad and talk for hours, I can't imagine how people live this way. The bathroom's marble. A vast oval tub and lights like bollocks. All three bedrooms are furnished. What I presume is the master is notably swish: polished stone floor, black pillowcases, dark wenge units, recessed lights. That he's had a disco ball put in is madly charming. Roc will destroy it all with her ceaseless emissions.

From the dining room I gaze at the rump of the Albert Hall. Mostly I cry in silence, but I surprise myself with sobs I can't contain. This sound is curious to me. A lost noise like a bell at sea. He gave up everything for a night of me. Today his mum is wondering who took him. Those bastards tell fairy stories. They stole his body. Took him somewhere else for a different death. They're low, these people. Scum. They'll do anything not to look stupid.

There are tissues in black octagons. Wipe my eyes but can't stop crying. He died because some halfwit payroll-gunman couldn't land me with a laser. Fucking eight inches off—what do they teach them? They did it for spite. That beautiful boy. It's their way of flirting.

Fix my face in the overdone bathroom. Hard water, so strict on the skin. Foundation, eyes, lips. Today my lips are Hanoi red. This is the endgame.

Ritual

They done what they can with the dress. They could have done better. Lucky I never travel without pins and thread. Pin a new seam on the bodice, sew close as I can with these dainty hands. Iron it through a wet pillowcase, not to scorch. Let the arms out a bit. I'm proud of my muscles but don't want to look like Popeye's sister. At least they got the length well-short of the knee. Order up a pair of four-inch white stilettos.

This artful measuring, sewing and making good soothes me. I'm okay with a focus. Assemble the AK again. Strip it again. Every cap in this clip will be wisely spent teaching those who don't love me.

Chat up the night manager to hire a car. That way the bill comes to the management company, not Ms. Delamarre. I feel his concern I'm going out late. "Don't worry, I'm not fighting a war."

"Perhaps not tonight."

I must drive. I'm too easily tracked. Each tap of my phone lights a flare. For reasons of discretion, it's nothing more sordid than an Audi S8, which barely does two-fifty. A black job, with sports wheels, and the bloke who delivers it says we should go for a spin. I'm low key in a Jigsaw shirt dress, linen and swishy. Tonight means physical effort of a less-welcome kind.

Soon as I get to World's End, I disable the satnav and sweep for bugs. Kings Road cuts like glass. One side it's food banks and kids fetching pills. Other side they got gold on the mirrors. Crime here is painfully small. Weed and knives. Crime over there is contract. But it's these kids that get banged up. I hate people who say it's natural. It's never natural.

The car and me get attention. Young lads bop over: they're bored, it's distraction. One asks if I want a zip of kush and I buy a couple for cash. He fingers the car and I peel back his hand, till he laughs to cover the pain.

"We thought you was Russian," he says, stretching his wrist.

"Do I sound Russian, bruv? Here." Give him the knife from that racist shit. Its serrated edge gobbles the light. "Stash that till I get back."

They vanish in the rearview, entrepreneurs with all the talent there is.

Head north up Drayson Mews. I don't touch Holland Park or Hyde

Park. They mean death to me now. Closed, shuttered-in flats: garage downstairs and two rooms above. Stables once, for the fine families round St. Mary Abbots. Anonymous space, where a body might sink.

Stop for a smoke. The pub on the corner spills laughing civilians. Work in the morning, drink at night, bit of a lie-in on weekends. Sometimes I feel I'm a different species.

Where Jazin is. Where all the trash are. These grand houses of the Outer Circle. Not actually here. Not right now. This is where money rests, in bas reliefs and moulded ceilings. Drug money, aid money, old-fashioned honest dirt. Sunk in the loosest, most understanding property market on Earth. When it gets a bit hot back home, there's always London. Stash a trillion in your belt and come here. And hire me, to solve your problems.

This lot was put up by John Nash. It's typical of him. Arches and columns. Greek stylings. Plaster depicting some no doubt uplifting story. Statues on the roof, that's plain vulgar. Nash got cucked by George IV but was helpless, the king owned him. And his inability to control building costs made him a risky hire. He had to end his days on the Isle of Wight and, when he croaked, his widow sold the Turners to pay his debts. Leave the Audi on a double yellow and take a recce.

Light slips between trees, alive on the evening wind. Cameras wonder at me. I stroll along, swing my Saint Laurent. Beneath the trees, half a dozen black cars—practical, not flash. In his house every window's lit, for opulence and control. If he's working, he'll be upstairs at the back, unseen, with an escape route.

Give my phone a fake call. An alibi to fuss around. Walk back to Hanover Gate. Check where these houses divide from the flats on Park Road. Wander into the yard of an apartment block. High walls, lit from kliegs over the grass. Walls that need kit to climb.

The dome of the mosque burns bronze. Sayidi Rashad will make an appearance once, maybe twice, a day for good order. But not the night prayer. Security won't want him out at night.

Regent's Park is cold, wild seeming. In scant light, trees clutch the clouds. Kneel in bushes, quiet and still. Nothing moves. I have extraordinary patience. No one knows. No one sees me at work. After two hours, their arrival breaks my trance. They fan out to the gates, relaxed but watchful. They smoke, make calls. I'm up and through the bushes. Cross the road. Giggle into my phone. A lone woman at night is a magnet. I step on the gravel driveway, slip, and sit hard on my arse.

These are gentlemen. They rush with chivalrous gestures. Watchful, I'm sure, for a trap. Tell them I hurt my leg. When they try standing me up, I grizzle with pain. One says, "Get her inside." Doubt signals between them. "It's too much here." So they hobble me into the hallway. Glimpse marble and chandeliers, as I'm delivered to this functional space.

The top dog folds back my dress to get a grip. Quite a fall, he tells me. Nice bruise coming. He tells the others, in Arabic, to get back outside. They drift off moody.

I gasp as his fingers gauge the inflammation.

"Hush. You are brave, surely. You have a name?"

"Araminta."

"I am Salah."

"Like Salah Ragab?" The least contentious I can think of.

He looks puzzled. "You know Cairo jazz?" Digging in, he massages the bruise. "Hush. This will ease the cramp." A cheeky finger tracks my femur.

"Is this your house?"

"I look after things here."

"You have the hands of a magician."

"You have the legs of a dancer."

"I do dance a bit. Shows."

He cups my knee. "Shows?"

"Entertainment. That's so important, don't you think?"

A man at the door gives a potent look. Says something to Salah in Arabic I'm not sharp enough to get.

Salah spreads his palms. "Always something needs my attention. You should be okay."

"Thank you." I hold out limp fingers. "I feel I should repay you."

He thumbs my knuckles. "On Saturday we have a party. You could greet people. Make them welcome."

"That would be so delightful!"

"Eight o'clock. Saturday."

Drive back through the West End. No one cracks a gaff that easy. No doubt they matched my face. But we work the odds we're given.

My night manager is gone. This spoon-face girl took his place. Tell her a hire car needs collecting. "Ask your colleague. Tall lad. Beard. Off-duty, is he?"

"I'm not sure who you mean."

Lay down but can't sleep, not even with long masturbation. In a few hours I'm wed. Whatever else, I'll do that right.

Savage excitement moves the morning. Wash my hair. Slick it behind my ears. Watch myself in the heated mirror. Not bad, still. Few notches and lines. Still a few years before I go under the knife. Slim. I've always been slim. With muscles and hips. I can break a man's wrist with bare pressure. Dad said I could have been a fair thief. Mum said I should marry rich. But the gun laid its sights on me. My destiny. All my days.

Blow dry, moisturise, makeup. My face today is the perfect face. Smooth foundation. Red lips. Mauve shadow. The thickest mascara. Glossy, deadly tendrils. Eyes are key.

A sea-blue Yaya shirtdress, simple and elegant, with my old Vagabonds. My Saint Laurent, with its useful cargo. My Chanel, this old black jacket, this design's not been made in years. A few seamy threads. The pockets are grimy. But cleaning would tear out its heart. There's a hole I patched, beneath the left arm, where someone got lucky. They didn't have long to enjoy it. The right pocket lining is worn, from this gun and the one before and the one before. These miraculous devices. So simple and prodigious. Clip goes in. Bullet comes out. If I had the leisure, the skill and good fortune, I'd make this world a paradise, one bullet at a time.

The mirror holds me. My last time here as a single woman. Ever after, when I look in the mirror, when I fix my eyes and load my gun, I'll be entwined with someone. Our lives clasped and cognate. My identity, that I say is inviolable, I'll readily change. I'm fluid, where I was stone.

Pack dress and shoes in a day bag. Pack my luggage. Book a flight for early Sunday. Economy to Sevilla. Then the slow train to Barcelona. In a Sunday dress with scarf and shades. I'll have to speak Spanish. But I'm going home.

Breakfast in the King's Road. Porridge and honey. On my second cappuccino a young man catches my eye. Scruffy tyke. Seventies rockstar curls. Lazy beard. Silk shirt and hairy chest—don't see that on young men these days. Loose moves, like we have, before life stiffens us. He's drawn on my tractable gaze.

"Is anyone sitting here?"

"Looks like you are."

"Can I be honest?" he says, straight off. A practiced, easy manoeuvre.

"As long as I don't have to be."

That smile is pure delight. "I'm a bit embarrassed just now. Delays getting paid. And they do a fabulous breakfast."

This is what young men do. Mix deference and assurance. Hesitancy and command. The charmed years. Before work and war. I lean close to sniff his patchouli. "So you come in here and scout a woman for buckshee breakfast? And that works?"

That inexpressible shrug. "About sixty percent."

"I'll start you a tab. But you do something for me."

He spreads his hands. Their elegance enthrals me.

"I'm getting married in two hours. You're my last unmarried fuck. Can you do that?"

With gentleness that stirs my heart, he lifts my hand to kiss each knuckle. "It's the right and responsible thing to do."

Tell the waitress this lad can have all he wants when he gets back. "Breakfast after." I donk his nose with the coffee spoon. "I'm in a rush."

He's not broke or he wouldn't live here. What Dad would call 'illiquid'. Plenty of money, just not actual money. His flat's in a nice little terrace by St. Luke's. Dormer windows and slanty ceilings. Cramped and padded with cushions, movie posters, guitars and dodgy old books. He's reading Anthony Burgess, 'The End of the World News'. A Tory, old Burgess. Liked to tell tall tales about himself. He once said, 'Liking involves no discipline; love does'. I feel that every second.

This young prince, who has to stoop in the bevelled corners of his domain, puts Debussy on the soundbox, 'Prélude à l'après-midi d'un faune' as I say in my passable accent.

"You like Debussy?"

"Reminds me of a good seeing-to I had in Paris." Up the Louvre, I got curated by a presentable young treasure. Soft hands. Soft manners. His apartment building had this grisly concierge. One of the old girls, whose hair hasn't been out of a twist in thirty years. She called me a prostitute, quite loud, as he led me upstairs. So I give it a pearl earring turn of the head and told her, 'Je ne fais même pas ça pour de l'argent, madam.' Her fucking face. With his neat ways he did a civilised job. And as I laid in our wet, he told me his dreams. A sculptor. Sculptors are nuts. All weight and equipment. He had maquettes. Silky, lengthened figures, girls riding dolphins, sweet stuff. Maybe it was the clay. The smell of clay I find soothing and sad. This was years ago. We sloshed cheap claret, he told me the shows he'd make, the galleries he'd fill. While he had a piss, I checked a postcard on his wall to get his name. I don't want to know their names, but he was so hopeful I felt sorry for him. Now and then I check sculpture sites. Never see him. We make fools of ourselves, filling the world with dreams.

Hear the clock ticking. I arrange myself on a heap of cushions and this tender music lover flops down next to me. He smiles, like what he found is what he expected.

There's grace to him that's deliciously weary. It drives his fingers in delicate loops of my bones. He goes impossibly slow. Five minutes just kissing. I wriggle beneath him. His hands liven my skin. No hesitation when he strips my panties. He already knew.

We roll together, as the faun's afternoon drifts into 'La Mer'. I don't tell him this music is so physical I shudder. A splendour lost on me. Miquel plays jazz. Things I can get my arms around. But this endless ocean betrays my intentions. Where I'm exposed is never in bed, never in the discourse of violence. It's when this ache opens and I lose grip of the words.

To resist lethargy, I scramble onto his stomach. His cock is inquisitive, stringent. I slip down onto him, relishing delight in his face. Slide up and down as his hips move to meet me, smooth and mechanical. He grabs my shoulders as I buck and rear. Arch my back, flip his cock half out, then crash back on. His nails scrape my arms, his scream in my throat. He scrubs my erection till I squeal. Hard and fast we cum together, him in me, me over his chest. "I love you, I love you, I love you."

To my delight he sets me on all fours, dog rutting as 'La Mer' becomes 'Deux arabesques'. With quick finesse he brings me off, screeching and shaking.

His curls caress my back. "Your husband's a lucky man."

The cab drops me at Islington Green. A sunny morning. Heat coming through. Buoyant, I flirt with some schoolboys. My final pinball minutes, before I set to a new groove.

It's a savage ritual, to say, 'This person and no other'. Even if what we mean has more colour than that. A wedding is distinct. Its participants aren't people. They're symbols of an idea. In Mediterranean lands we have many rituals, popular and religious. So many ways to mark time. A feast of this. An assumption of that. A saint, observed in this village only. The English think they're all for tradition. But we misunderstand its use. It's not a selling point. It's defence against getting sold.

Get changed in the Town Hall bogs. My Yaya is stained with spunk. I have extraordinary expertise for getting the spunk out of men. I coax and encourage. Praise and admire. They can be certain I'll take their spunk. I'll love them for it. It's easy for me and nice for them. Washing stains is the thing I'll never give up.

Take a look at myself. All I can, in this tiny mirror. The dress hangs nice. The colour's sweet to my skin. The hips ride smooth. It's proper short. Slip on the white stilettos. Pack my jacket in my day bag. Brush my hair. Freshen my lips and eyes.

Some weird thing in my chest. Butterfly strange. Curious at this rare frailty, I hold my breath, check my pulse—my heart's in orbit. I feel at a disadvantage. It's exciting.

The door opens and there's Roc.

She's perfect. Her lilac hair clipped in a smooth ponytail, to show the five silver rings in each ear. She's wearing no makeup, her pale skin slightly sallow, bruised under the eyes. Her cheekbones rise like icebergs. A black suit, Jones I think, the trousers tight and tailored. A white cotton tee with 'Lesbian' over her chest. Six-inch white stilettos. She carries a day bag.

Like the shy virgin I never was, I wrap my arms over my body. "You can't see me before the wedding."

Her smile is a clean shot of spring. "This is the wedding, sweetheart."

We kiss and embrace. Her taste takes me back to so many occasions. Days and nights, growing up, living apart. Making our way, always headed for this. I feel her up and she nips my nose. "You got to make an honest woman of me first."

Mimicking her posh voice I say, "You won't let it change you, will you darling?"

Mimicking my common voice she says, "I was born a scrubber. I'll die a scrubber." She takes a box from her jacket pocket. "Don't say I never do anything for you."

The rings are simple and lovely. A pair of rose gold bands, ridged with one carat diamonds. My heart falls through my chest. "These cost thousands."

"Hush." Her finger warms my lips. "I paid by instalments."

The ring fits. "You knew."

"Of course."

"I got changed in that cubicle. It's the least stinky."

"You think of everything. That's a lovely dress."

"It's a solemn occasion."

"I love you."

"I love you."

"One thing." Roc holds the fractured dimples of her chin. "Can you be taller than me?"

We swap shoes. The shoes fit.

Roc licks my neck. "24 Faubourg. Composed by Maurice Roucel in 1995."

"You're good." Nuzzle her cheek. "Old Spice. William Lightfoot Schultz. 1937."

"Let's get married."

This room is necessarily efficient. Blank ceiling set with strip lights. Framed pictures of old Islington on biscuit-coloured walls. Respectable old Islington. No guttersnipes. Three rows of wooden chairs. Their padded seats don't quite match the red carpet, which is not so much worn as wilted. A nice clump of red carnations in an ugly vase. And a shocking omission.

Dive into the hallway. Bods all around, council types and tourists. I zero on a pair of girls, admiring each other's hair. "Oi, you and you."

They startle.

"Five hundred quid each for fifteen minutes' work."

One stares like she's mindless. The other scrunches her angry face. "What you talking about?"

"I need witnesses for a wedding."

"What wedding?"

Grab a hank of my dress. "This fucking wedding. Five hundred. On your phones."

"How long did you say it'll take?"

Get them settled as the Registrar arrives. She shakes my hand like a job interview.

"You are…" She ripples her papers.

"Felicity Hepburn."

"Oh yes." She checks the paper, then me. "You have the same name."

"I know," I simper. "What are the chances?"

She raises an exquisite eyebrow. "I thought you might be cousins."

"Definitely not."

Attractive in her law clerk suit, the Registrar palms her braided locks and strokes her hoop earrings. That she owns the propriety of this affair is evident. So rarely I engage with bureaucracy, my disquiet is the probing hand of justice, indifferent to me personally, yet prodding me to a personal destiny.

"Is this starting soon?" one of the well-paid girls pipes up. "I'm busy at lunchtime."

There's no fanfare. The walls don't shake. No long-buried fires rekindle. But Roc's arrival is seismic. The Registrar stares. The girls are silent. Finally, I look.

Her dress is linen, sleeveless, tight-waisted. The low-cut bodice is under pressure, half-moons of her chunky white bra rise over the froth. Briar rose and grinning skulls gleam along her bare arms. Skeleton angels drip blood on her breasts. Her hair like paint in its glossy tail. No makeup. She dazzles, a risen goddess. My bride, with luxurious buoyancy, moved by powerful hips in compressed languor.

I don't breathe. "You're fantastic."

Her smile is total command. "I was up all night sewing extra panels in this."

The Registrar swallows hard. "Marriage is a desire by two people to share themselves and their experiences with each other. And a willingness to accept each other for who they are. It calls for honesty, patience, courage and, of course, humour. A partner in marriage is loving, caring and above all a best friend. You are here to witness the joining in marriage of Felicity Jean Hepburn and Rachel Marie Hepburn. If any person present knows of any lawful impediment why these two people may not be joined in marriage, they should declare it now."

Who would dare?

When I say, "I give you this ring as a symbol of our marriage and as a token of my love, trust and commitment. I promise to care for you above all others," when I say that, heat releases from her. Its energy thrills my blood.

When she says, "I give you this ring as a symbol of our marriage and as a token of my love, trust and commitment. I promise to care for you above all others," when she says that, I'm drawn by irresistible force.

We sign the register and one of the girls pings pictures to Roc's new burner. We get the certificate, and the Registrar's best wishes, and go to the bogs for a fuck.

In the real world, we'd be on honeymoon. Months of white sand and sheltering forests. Her driving the local girls mad. Me having their brothers. But in this pantomime, we eat roast vegetable pizza, crowded by arty wannabes. To toast our nuptials, the only wine in the place is Chianti, an intriguing blend of strawberries and cold tea.

We're quiet, dwarfed by what we've done. It was inevitable, but the fact makes us shy around each other. As we stab and slice the sloppy dough, these rings are too much dress-up. "I might take mine off for work," she says. "I use my hands a lot."

"Yeah, same." With Miquel's engagement ring it will sit in my bag of hidden treasures. "I'm sorry we can't go away. Not with business."

"Yes." Her blue eyes are cooler than mine, harder to read. "What time are we meeting your friend?"

An anguish I deserve. It's shit for Roc, doing this on her wedding day. Having to pay her shift at Fitzroy Square and getting banged up with Chloe Bell. "We will have a honeymoon, promise."

Her grip is persuasive as mine. "No promises, Flick. Show me when we get there."

It's not just sex. It's all we've shared. Telepathy, synchronicity of our different minds. It's looking at someone and seeing myself, improved. I want to tell her in clear, healthy words. But all I say is what I always say. "I love you."

She swirls a mess of tomatoes and artichoke leaves. "Remember when we realised we had feelings for each other? How scared and excited we were. The scariest secret. Dangerous, even for us. Like a comet grazes the sun, it loses itself to what it can't resist." She twists the still-loose ring. "I wish we could get away from the noise. It's the noise, more than the danger."

"That bastard shouldn't have come to see you. I'll sort him."

"Oh stop. Please stop, sweetheart." She catches my wrist. "Get a place, you and Miquel, far in the country. Stay quiet, till they forget you. We have this." The gold catches fire. "I'm yours and always will be. I need you to care for me. To raise our children. I don't want you killed because you can't leave well alone."

We hug and I bury my face in her warm, sweet hair. Then a bloke says something coarse and I punch him into the wall. He smashes a table as he goes down, blooding punters in salsa. Roc's outside, grey-faced in the sun.

We don't talk in the cab to Kensington. The driver goes on how it's all gone to shit. A comforting, London sound. My wife has more than a wedding dress in her day bag. There's jeans and tees, dildos and straps, the collar and chain I bought for her thirtieth birthday. She packs and repacks. We don't talk.

Glaring from the window, bound with words I can't say, I spot the Ford Mustang in Ennismore Gardens. Tell the driver to stop.

We walk around Kensington Gore. "One of them flats." I point like a tourist.

She sidles me into a dead-end street, where parked vans look bland and suspect. She lifts my hand. The ring glints in the sun. "Do you want me to look after this? So you don't lose it."

The ring comes off, weightless. Feels wrong without it.

"Do we argue?" She runs her arms around my neck.

"Not serious."

Eyes, nose, mouth—we're a mirror. "I married you for the rest of my life. I'm proud of you. Please make this the last time I have to be scared someone will get you. Think of Miquel, me, our children. Stop, will you, sweetheart?"

"Saturday," I tell her.

Roc goes up to the flat. I wait for Chloe Bell.

"I've been in the park." She talks across my shoulder. "Incident, the other night."

She's no right to intrude. "I should think there's incidents. In a park."

"Your favourite people. Another scheme gone haywire. Lucky no outrage was done to the Princess's fountain." She gazes at the block like counting bricks. "I thought we were meeting someone."

"My sister."

"And this gets me out the way. While you make a fool of yourself with Jazin."

"Got to make a fool of myself somewhere."

She's brought a case on wheels, like an actual holiday. The lift carries our stiff silence. Don't know if it's her on the spectrum, or me because everything's awkward these days.

She shivers. "I prefer the flats in Hoxton."

"How is Mr. Nolan?"

She gives a curious smirk. "Don't you know? He's dead."

I didn't know. That riles me. "The Fenian brethren?"

"Electrocuted in the bath."

"He took baths?"

"A small television fell into the water."

Whoever livened Nolan's stinking juice doesn't know the favour they've done me. "I'm sorry if you got the impression I'm not keen on Sweden. Maybe autumn?"

"That voucher expired."

In the stifling sitting room, Roc poses for inspection. She brushed out her hair. It licks her bare shoulders. She's got her business face on: smooth foundation, mauve blusher, purple lips. Dark fronds of mascara. A panelled, slave-girl basque, mesh panties, sheer stockings. No shoes. Never be taller than the client. Her tattoos sing in the vacant air.

She pushes forward a sun-drenched smile. "Roccola. I'm a sex professional. I'm so pleased to be working with you." That voice is exactly right for this place. Clear, assured, commanding. Exquisite Roc, she clasps her hands in hope and beatitude. "I'm sure Felicity has shared my credentials. I work with men, as that's the market just now. However, my sexuality is lesbian and I'm an authentic submissive, so this will be a relaxed and intimate interlude. I have been told I provide an exceptional sexual experience."

"Her reviews are stunning." My voice is foggy and torpid.

Chloe Bell stands motionless, tensed.

"Oh," Roc giggles. "You're looking at these." Magician hands weave her chest. "Fully organic and delightfully versatile, as you'll find out. Felicity," she beams, "are you staying for a drink?"

I've fucked up. This is our wedding night. I should be worshipping her. But I put the job first and she won't forget it.

I leave them to get acquainted and go to the V&A to sulk. Unzip my bag. Pull out a corner of satin. The vivid sheen of a bride-to-be already cast aside. Eight weeks from now, we'll gather in Santa Maria. Aunties and bridesmaids tweaking my dress, presenting me to my man. No one will leave me alone. I'll be la núvia. La princesa. Nothing will move without me. And my maid of honour's sky-blue eyes, reminding me I failed her. I want to kill. Nothing else brings peace.

Agnieszka calls. "I thought we were to meet yesterday?"

"Have you been to the V&A caff? Victoria and Albert. Albert. They got incredible lights. Like galaxies burning."

"The Museum of Warsaw is more instructive. Also the Antonina Leśniewska Museum of Pharmacy. Antonina Leśniewska was very famous chemist."

The dark Baltic stretches north. Sunset clouds, whipped to lava on a harsh wind. A night boat to Kaliningrad. Cold mischief. "Do you ever crave to kill?"

"Frequently. I find interesting things. You should meet me."

"A little trap, sweetheart?"

"Why care? You are so brave."

A Polish café in Wells Street. Interestingly near Archer's place.

She looks placidly over her czarna kawa. "What is in the bag?"

"A wedding dress."

"Of course it is."

Look around. Eyes look away. "Stealing cars, tut tut."

"I did not steal it."

"Jesus." Skull-cracking coffee sears my throat.

"That will clean your tongue."

Robust, self-satisfied cow. "You sure it's alright here?"

"These are Poles and friends of Poles."

"You always this patriotic?"

"Oh." That innocent look. "Then it is not you that fights for rebels, in a country that is not your own?"

"I'm buying beatification. What do you want?"

She surveys the café—a chiselled cat. "Being with police is good to find things out. Once the misunderstanding was resolved, everyone was most helpful. I spoke with people who know this man that fascinates you. He has many meetings today and tomorrow. The men you disrupted in Hyde Park are part of the effort to ensure those meetings are not disturbed. He will host an event on Saturday."

"I know."

"But that is all you know, from your crude intrusion last night. What? Of course you were seen. Many people watch the film of you falling."

I signal the waitress. "I'll take another of these bowel cleansers and a muzzle for my companion." Fuck knows what she writes down.

"So we understand you will be at this event."

"Who's 'we' dollykins?"

She slaps the table. Not hard. Decisive. "You think this is to entertain you. You were supposed to assist Mr. Miller…"

"Supposed to?"

"Of course. It was coincidence only. Until you got restless."

The waitress brings the coffee, fussing with the spoons.

"Leave it."

Agnieszka says something. The girl nods.

"What did you say?"

She grabs my wrist. Her fingers bite. "You never stop. You never think what damage you do. It is like leading a bear. Not an intelligent bear. You are fine to kill. At strategy, you are lost."

"Let go of my hand."

"If you hold your tongue."

Push her away. "But you're intelligent, aren't you?"

"And still you do not know who I mean by 'we'." She gives a plump little sigh. "This temper and noise achieves nothing. Do you not think this business could be resolved now?"

"I don't think. You made that clear." This coffee annoys me. I hate Chloe Bell and this bitch and all of them.

"You are offered chances you do not take. You are offered help and still you complain."

"Is this good for me somehow?"

"I doubt it." She leans forward, confidential. "Naturally, it was no accident I worked for Toby Archer. You did not question why I was there."

"I should have recognised you?"

"You think you are prepared, yet took me at face value. Archer was glad to be involved. It is good for his credit to be an insider. For me was frustration, having to learn what I already knew of Miller's challenges. But satisfaction, also, to fix a problem I helped cause."

My bag lays against my leg, a dazed, wilted dog. I got married today. Filled with excitement, I said words I believed were true. Too late I realised giving back the ring was a test. Why did I need Chloe Bell out the way? I could have just shot her. "It's them, innit? Your friends the Russians."

"You should go to the party on Saturday." A cramped eagerness shapes her. "Find this person of interest. Deliver your message. The people I speak with are comfortable with that. You will not come here again."

I hit the cup with the spoon. Just a small noise, but people turn, hungry for action. "You want me to front for the Russians."

She radiates indulgence. "Some find you charming, I'm sure."

"I don't come to London again? How the fuck you make that happen?"

"Anything can be made happen." When she drinks, a pert pinky fucks the air. "I speak with people. They ask me to give you this message. For this you are useful. Your usefulness ends midnight Saturday. Cinderella."

I'm not having that for a last word. "It's only a two-hour flight."

"So bright and so dull. Our colleagues in Spain—Spain, that is the country—will arrange a move to some pleasing location. You will be comfortable in the hills. Much landscape to admire. You may take up painting. I understand English ladies often do, in later life."

Daubing watercolour. In a peasant frock. Beneath the chestnut trees.

Intermezzo

Many nights I dream. A big house and I chase a man whose laughter rings through the halls. Always out of range. I wake, in flight or pursuit. My hand a gun. At home I go days, weeks, with no hate. I'm loved in the market, the shops. La bella dama sense pictat. The old men defer to me. The old crows cross their sunken chests. When I meet the priest in the Carrer de la Riereta he holds my hand as though it might burn and instruct him. The young black boys in the Carrer de Sant Rafael hustle to carry my bags. 'L'anglesa,' they shout. 'L'anglesa,' their startling young noise.

What is fear? Long black hair. Cobalt eyes, winged in black. Fine skin. Still a few years before I go under the knife. Keen to learn. Quick to forgive. Just a girl.

Disappointed, in the damp warmth of sleeping pursuit. Reassemble my AK. Break it down and build it over. Serbian: the sights are iron. An older piece, but better than none. I can name every part of this instrument. Describe what it does precisely. I've improvised parts, for quick repairs. Guns are agreeable. They work even in a fractured state. It doesn't take much to kill someone. Not compared to difficult things.

Message Roc. She sends back emojis. These jolly, bouncing characters dislocate me. Preening like bodysnatchers. My wife. Forsaking all others. I'm not good with emojis. I'm not good with games. I yearn to be warm and yielding. But life makes me relentless.

Shower, blow dry, makeup—the touchstones of life. Back in the white shirt and herringbone mini. I've got no laundry done. Might not even take these things back. I can buy more. When I'm paid by the last man standing. Wear these white spikes Roc gave me. In the mirror a poised secretary, bright enough and willing, blows a kiss.

Go to that caff, but my lovely Debussy fan's not there. He already found his free breakfast. The news overflows with Jazin's successful partnerships, his love for London, his keenness to invest. Tunes to dance to. Leftie whingers harp on that his business is death. But everyone's business is death.

Spring's coming. The days getting baggy. We always think: 'This summer will be different'. Longer, more vivid, more provocative somehow. But it rains and the seaside's cold and the picnic's full of ants. Want to message Roc. Don't want to look fretty. More and more I regret this. A late honeymoon is too late. Wrapped in thoughts of my beautiful wife, I blank the patrol car. The old sweats are most civil. They ask how I'm doing. They suggest a ride to the Yard.

Superintendent Terence Rotheray makes turbulence with each move. His hands describe baffling directions. "They haven't lost this many since the Russians were at the Novichok."

"Remind me who gave them the recipe."

He grips the desk to restrain himself. "Do you expect to get out of this?"

"I'm not wasting a plane ticket. Think of the carbon."

He cannons into his chair, its futile protest a strangled cat. "I hear you got a party tomorrow."

"You really can see into the present. A certain trillionaire arms dealer wants me to grace his mansion. I didn't realise I had to run my social life through the Met."

This man's a sharp-eyed copper. His manor, the heady space between crime and intelligence. Moonlight operations of no glory. He's never generous but lies with civility. Right now, he's between me and some bony old queer of a judge directed by spite and a spastic bowel. "I got an invitation to this shindig. Perks, for all we've thrown round him."

"And you a superintendent."

"It's the Assistant Commissioner's invitation. She didn't think it was a good look."

"It's always nice to see you, Terence. But why did your woodentops pull me in?"

When he taps his laptop, it's like those experiments where someone mental dances the hokey-cokey. "This pratting about of yours. It's broke the camel's bollocks. I got this message. The Tribunal has called an investigation into use of lethal force."

When operatives get killed, it's sponged up in the smothering bosom of national security. Grunts don't expect to retire. But the Tribunal can do wicked things. They can have senior people taken for walks. There's no detox for spies.

"The Tribunal is iffy with freelance. In their opinion, the service gets enough dosh to make its own mess. They're especially uneasy at your apparent immunity."

"Let me see that."

"Don't be daft." He cuffs me away. "Me telling you is a breach."

"What do these cocks not understand?" When I slap his desk, I don't like the sweat stain I leave. "It's distance. I give them distance."

"You kill. You cause people to be killed when you're not even there. Declan Nolan."

"He stiffed the provos, remember? The same paddies your lot gave forgiveness and cribs in Miami. Did no one tell the Tribunal it's their boys trying to kill me?"

He watches his fingers like engineering. "I don't think they're concerned about that. You've been mayhem since you got here."

I'm not scared of violence. It's confinement. Penned on a chain. I'm scared of ugly clothes and unflattering light. I'm scared all I've worked for is wasted. Stupid people say fear can't hurt them. They're first in the coffins. "Arrest me, Terence. Twelve counts of murder. Seven-figure fraud. Multiple car theft. Indecent exposure. Throw in sex with an underage man. He was rising sixteen. They killed him, Terence. Shot like a fox in the rubbish. For national security. I killed no one that didn't deserve it. I'm glad they're dead."

"Midnight." He wrestles his fingers, puzzled at their tenacity. "Midnight tomorrow, I read that back. With a reminder you don't have to say anything, but it might harm your defence if you don't mention something you later rely on."

"Can't you do the old 'anything you say will be taken down' and I say 'knickers'?"

"I'd like to, but we have to be modern."

Where I had veins, sexy with blood, now are strands of ice. "Midnight, to kill Jazin?"

"Kill Jazin, you get a terrorist trial. Somewhere quiet. No pictures. Maybe a bit of give on the sentence. Our friends in the desert will get righteous. But not all of them and not much. Jazin's useful. Being useful is not a rare talent. There'll be fighting out there. Few thousand civilians killed. Prize-winning footage of little girls clutching dollies in bombed-out houses. The people who matter will see it as beneficial. The people who don't matter will be dead."

Drop me off from this boys' own adventure. "I don't care about any of that. I care about me. You know the Polish headcase? Called the

Kremlin, didn't she? I'm killing Jazin for tovarich as well. And they're giving me a chestnut farm."

Something bothers him with his hands. He watches them, wary. "If anyone asked me what you are, I would never say stupid. That's not in the first hundred things I'd say. You know the Russians don't keep promises. And how do you know this Polish sort even asked them? We been trying to trace her background. It's like nailing fog. We can't even find how she knows Archer. And he's gone AWOL."

"Archer's dead."

His heavy breath shakes the desk. "That a confession, Felicity?"

"Everyone ends up dead." Again it's late afternoon. Again the sky's dirty. When summer comes and days are long, the boys swarm the pubs of Soho. Crowd the bars of Les Rambles. Never 'Las Ramblas'. That's pig Spanish. Young, smiling, lovely boys. Uncomplex lives. Unhurried needs. I walk in. That's all I do. I share and multiply my love, to you young man, to you and you. Never tiring, never jealous, never wanting to change anyone. The most powerful aphrodisiac is to be loved as we are. What men see in me is pure acceptance. A classical virtue. "Look at that sky."

A collision of noise—Rotheray's chair, his bones, his breath. He squints at clouds. "Might rain later."

"If I go down, you better know I'm Houdini. I can't live without buying clothes. Stealing cars. I can't live without seeing the sky. Sunday morning I'm on that plane. You won't see me in London. I won't be back."

A volcano, he grows and subsides, builds steam, fractures on explosion. "One, that makes me look clumsy. Two, Rashad Jazin's death will be an outrage. An outrage must be countered. Having you downstairs is the least those cocksuckers want. I'm concerned for the clout of the Metropolitan Police and, by implication, British law. I hope that doesn't sound selfish."

"What if I flit tonight?"

"The Red Notice has gone to Interpol. You're on the wall with Russian daddies and Serbian fascists. As for going home, Madrid aren't keen on domestic terrorism. They don't want you in Spain."

"I don't live in Spain."

"Proves the point, doesn't it?"

As he leans forward, I smell him. Not sweat. Effort. The machinery of policing in the marshy welts of his clothes.

"You were wrong to come here. You can't be surprised."

There's lightness to the air. Smiles along the Embankment. Everyone loves a white shirt and herringbone mini. The river flows brisk and indifferent. Waves ride the braided water. Party boats, too soon in the evening, shift their chains as they dream of the sea. Stroppy tugs haul platforms stacked with containers: trash and treasure, a body or two. I could swing under Westminster Bridge, jump a tug, and off. Park it in Essex. Nick a speedboat over to Holland. Tart my way back down south. There's no limit to what I can do.

The Temple, those lawyers with their 'stratagems and ruses', like lovely Ian said. I'm not that sort. I get my teeth round life's balls and bite. The Central Criminal Court. In popular parlance: the Old Bailey. Built on the ruins of vile Newgate Prison, where James Pratt and John Smith were murdered for love. I'll not stand in these stale courtrooms, beneath seamy friezes of justice. The copper's hard words. The flustered brief. The livid old nonce on the throne. A woman of style and passion is spared such things.

Along Holborn I go in a gym. Its tang of keen muscles and sweaty bollocks warmly wistful. I buy nauseous athleisure. Black tracky bottoms with gross red piping. Black hoodie, too snug for the weather. Pearly-pink trainers. Soon as the Gore-Tex hits my body, I feel gross, defeminised. Get a plastic tote for my real clothes. The type all the shave heads wear.

In the boxing room blokes curl fists into fifty kilo bags. They get my scent. Their gloves whisper. Pump my arse through the hormone haze. Punch the Everlast bare knuckle, left then right. The bag springs back on its mount. The men whistle.

Get the tube at Tottenham Court Road. Sit with my hood pulled down. Watch myself in the window, a thin dark shape. Like a kid unsure what she wants, I'm breathless and resentful. I don't have my own will anymore. Whatever I do, I'm directed.

Camden Town is too famous, too knowing. Its kids, too clean, too connected. Their sincerity blurs what they're serious about. Shove through, elbowing flyer merchants, burning eyes deep in this hood.

Carol Street makes a neat little shunt of plaster houses, roller shutters and skeletal trees. Quiet. Just the cameras. A narrow front door slits a blank wall. Window arches bricked over. A moment's resistance.

She looks how she looks, all the years I remember. A smoker's skinniness. A nervy, predatory edge. Short, tight blonde hair gelled to blades. A thin, gold mesh top, identical to the one before and the one before that. A cropped denim mini, bruised legs and barefoot. Her toenails red, fresh painted. Her smell is smoky nights and cold mornings. Her voice is London. "What d'you want?"

I tilt the hood.

"My fucking good god. Who followed you?"

"Who would?"

"Fucking get in."

The house is thin, sparse, neat. Aunt Denise isn't one for clutter. Angry, she blows smoke at the yellow ceiling. "You fucking little…"

The room has no excess. Two armchairs, coffee table, sideboard and telly. No pictures, no ornaments, no clues who she is. Smoke hangs a comfortable blanket on everything. Dog ends mount the swan ashtray her Aunt Sadie nicked from Marc Bolan's house. Those smooth, battered legs clench like veined marble.

"You fucking little… Is this a joke?"

How gross I must look in these clothes. "You heard I'm in town?"

"'Course I heard. Something like you don't stay secret." She ravages her cigarette, drawing fire along its length. "I knew you couldn't keep away."

"You're looking well."

"Don't give me that fucking mince. You blown my cover."

"Dressed like this?"

Grudging candour shifts her shoulders. "You look a proper abortion. What you want? I got work in a bit."

"You still at the club?"

"I'm what they come for."

I can't run at things cold. "Seen the family?"

She chains the next cigarette. "They ain't singing your name if that's what you want. Saw Rachel the other day. She's pissed about you."

Roc didn't say. But I don't give her chance to say anything.

Denise rubs her bruises a light, careless way. "She's scared you get killed. In dreams, she sees it. You know how she broods. That girl needs an old-fashioned butch to take her in hand."

She talks like I stop Roc from doing things.

"What shit you in?"

Aunt Denise is Mum's youngest sister. Always made her own way. Never married. Never relied on no one. I can throw my fist. But Denise is proper hard. No one gets under her skin. I wave smoke at her bruises. "You take that to work?"

"Fuck off. Use concealer, don't I? I'm on my knees all night. You know young blokes. Straight down. Straight in."

"Still busy then?"

That stare chills the blood. Reassuring, she never changes. "Listen, Tinker Bell. I'm sixty-two and still getting fucked every night. Come back in a bit, tell me how you're doing." Sharp and rigid, she crouches at the sideboard. Her slim, flared buttocks stress her mini as she sorts bottles. "Vodka." She pirouettes on hard toes. "I'm not meant to go in stinking."

The vodka is warm. The glass is frosted with lipstick. The taste of stale hours.

"So," she throws herself down in the chair, flashing black panties. "What shit you in?"

"Filth. Spies. Arabs. Poles."

"Rachel said you ain't made friends." Smoke sinks her cheeks. Her bones are daggers. "How the fuck you piss the Poles? No one pisses the Poles."

"Misunderstanding."

"Don't dolly shit me." She tops the glasses. "Go on then, brainache. Who was Pierre Smirnoff?"

"Pyotr Smirnov. Pioneer of charcoal filtered spirits. Gave bribes to priests so they wouldn't preach against drink. His son Vladimir pissed off to Poland to dodge the Bolshies. Turned the family name French, for business reasons."

"You here for a favour?"

Hairs on my neck ride a cold breeze. "What faces you seen?"

She pops another smoke. "I was working this job, getting fucked on a yacht. Girls off their heads on chop. These two pricks were running the show. Sons of a third-rate billionaire. They got lairy, throwing this yacht all over. Swimmers getting hurt and resentful. Behind the boat, all I saw was people floundering in the water. Few slicks of blood. Pretty funny. Know what I mean, Felicity? We turned our backs on it all. Then we hit a rock. One little tart gets thrown off the front. Crushed between the rock and the boat. She was still alive in the water, but what you gonna do? I went over the side and swam to shore. You know I'm a strong swimmer. Hauled up on the beach as the police boat came screaming out. I never told what faces I seen." She empties the glass. "There's one at the club. Quiet lad."

"Don't describe him."

"I wouldn't. He likes a drink, a dance. He likes my arse."

"See him tonight?"

"My name's not Petulengro."

"Is he in the game?"

"He's the sort who would be."

Pile on another Ducados. I'm sharp and light-headed. Denise was the sparkle. The aunt who travelled. The aunt with stories. "If you get him tonight, say I'm at Jazin's party. He'll know what that means."

When she leans to fill my glass, her small breasts lay contours through the gold mesh. "What you up to?"

Don't want her regretting this. "Work. Middle East business."

"Is it just me you can't lie to, or have you lost your touch completely?"

My Aunt Denise looks exactly her age. She'd die before taking the knife. She's lines and canyons, eye bags, lagoons of brown skin where freckles have fused. Scars from lovers and other occasions. Thirty years back she started dressing like this and hardly wears anything else. I can't imagine the strength it takes to be her. "It's me, Den. They're closing me down. I didn't think it'd be this. Not without cause."

She skims the empty cigarette pack at the bin. It goes down with a sigh, nestled by layers. "You give 'em cause. Rachel's dying inside. I ain't seen her so worried. Why now? Why do it?" She twists apart a fresh pack.

So rare I wear trousers when I fall to my knees, I miss the burn. Haul up on the side of her chair. She turns with sharp eyes, flammable breath. I French her, sealing her splintered, truculent lips. My fingers on her slick thigh, drawn by her heat.

A muscular arm grabs mine. We tussle, but I've no advantage. "No," she scolds. "That's for big men. I'll give you handjob. That's far as it goes."

An eager child, I scrub the clumsy track pants from my body.

"You are tiny, aren't you, sweetheart? I wouldn't feel that." Strong hands. Soothing. "Always had a thing for me haven't you?" Professional seduction. A lifetime of bolstering men, so they cash cheques. "For all your cock and teabagging."

"You're beautiful, Den."

"I'm the only one left." Her fingers know just when.

Feel the charge. The tangible instant. "I love you, I love you, I love you."

"Little squirter, intcha? You can clean that up."

I do as I'm told.

"Got to get my face on. I'll tell this bloke what you said. But you should clear out."

Stay on the floor. It's comfortable. I kiss her leg.

Hard, clever fingers scrag my hair. "I mean it. Clear out."

"After this job."

"Who's paying?"

"Spooks."

"That why they're trying to kill you?"

"There's moving parts." I grip her legs. She tenses but lets me. "People want Jazin settled. It's friction. Shaking things up." She lets me work her knees apart, taut denim across her thighs. Not a hair on her legs. Not one stray pokes through her panties. "You're beautiful."

Though her hands are thin, their strength is immense. "This is sixty-two years of life. You live a long time for beauty. You're just starting. Round your eyes, your beauty is just beginning. You work hard at yourself. You're clever. Don't jack it because you're impatient."

Wasted and drab, these Camden streets. Locked in ghosts who, once, came here for something. People say London ain't what it was. Nothing's what it was. We think we remember the grand days when our optimism burst like gassed-up cider. Life is the intermezzo. The masquerade. The laughter dying to awkward silence, as the audience understands there's nothing left.

Forever

One dull morning I got punched in the face. At a London beach, that hungry mud that slinks to light at low tide. The job was some bloke on a boat. But he jumped me from under the canvas. I been shot and stabbed but never so righteous as when he punched my face. He presumed his sopping fist in my china doll features. I let him get up the ladder before I shot him. Seeing him broken in a mud angel was sweet.

Slow runs the Thames below Chelsea. Rising or spent, the river rolls on. This city is always my home. This is the last day I'm here. Tonight everyone will adore me. But for now, I'll show quiet lights. Une petite sérieuse, a little demure, jolie, una noia amb estil. Una bonica petita catalana. I could throw in Arabic. Russian, a little. A pinch of rotten Italian. Some shoddy Turkish. Comes easy, languages. Words stick to my brain. I like people to understand I'm grave and potent. When I was a young girl, starting out, people thought I'd be easy to sidestep. But they learned all about me. One bullet at a time.

A plain grey A-line skirt. Black shirt. Low heels. Smart and understated. I clean this old XD 9 mil. Strip and build this AK-47. A weight to carry but it makes me a better person. Amateurs shoot and think it's no more than shooting. They're the ones that go down. What matters is the silence within each shot.

Miquel loves me too much. He studies the ground where I walk. He collects my shadow. That boy in the park, greedy and young. They killed him. No reason. The frenzy of the game where some must fall. The only response is the game.

Hire a car. Repack my bags. I've done no laundry. My luggage is musky. Temptation says: change the flight, leave now. But this princess goes to the ball.

Breakfast with Saturday women. This ordinariness, drinking coffee. Sly looks from kids who think what's now is forever.

A message, number unknown: 'You there?' I know who it's from and whatever's took place needs my craft and proficiency. Soon as I message back, those words 'Be here' consume the whole day. Cab it to Kensington. The air in the block so still, the corridors so plush, a pearl of sweat licks my spine.

When Roc calls out, "Who is it?" her voice echoes off hard space.

She's barefoot. I pick up the click of her smooth toes on blue woodblock. The worst is over. She's alive and moving freely. Whatever happened is small, beside her survival.

She opens the door, her face slashed with sunlight. Angry fear in her cold blue eyes. She barely gives room to get through. Want to hold her, restore our affection. But she walks away. In jeans and sleeveless tee, her patterned skin vibrant against tedious luxury.

Before sense compels me, I tell her, "I was stupid to take off your ring."

She shows her wedding finger, one ring stacked on the other. The ring she gives me cups tight to my skin.

"I won't leave this again."

Roc shakes her head. The words seem alien to her.

Now I remember someone else should be here.

Chloe Bell hangs from the chandelier, its ornate bolts capable of her weight. She used a restraint. The type that hooks over the shoulders, binds the body and up through the crotch. In BDSM it's for denial. Chloe Bell tied the restraint to the chandelier stem and looped its cunning hawsers round her throat. This performance took ingenuity and, likely, some time. Left over leather wilts across her dead torso. The chair she stood on is from the upholstered dining set. She kicked it an impressive distance when she swung.

Roc's voice weakens. "I'm not afraid of hard work. She didn't seem receptive. She was okay to watch, to play with me. But I struggled to move her. A lot of the time she wanted to talk. Police talk. The job seemed to absorb her. She found it hard to take control. I explained I'm a sub, I need certain things. But she was unwilling. She didn't cum, not properly. That upset me because I worked hard."

"You're a phenomenal fuck."

"Maybe I've got used to thinking that." She stares at the reproving shadow, blonde hair parted around its stunned face. "We had a big meal. We drank wine. She drank all the vodka. I'm used to people with robust habits, but I did think she drank a lot. I slept because I knew she wouldn't wake me." Moisture kicks from her lashes. "You know that idiot Lee put a disco ball in the bedroom? It makes this clacking." She shakes her head. "I thought she'd gone out. Or left. I thought she might do that. It was ages till I found her. Isn't that funny? I mean, here, in this flat. But I was in bed, thinking how to please her. I really liked that strap."

I fuss her hair, stroke her breasts, bite her neck. Her sadness soaks my shirt.

"I'm sorry Flick."

Wash her with kisses. "It's not your fault."

"If I'd done better, she might have stayed."

How the dead insist on themselves. "You okay to help get her down?" I want no commotion from sensitive neighbours. A falling body, stiff with rigor, spills bones.

"She wasn't unkind to me."

"Me neither."

We stand on the furry dining chairs. Roc grips Chloe's waist while I tease knots from the leather. "These are tight."

"Cut it. I won't use it again."

Fetch a big knife from the kitchen. A slick carver for jointing murdered animals. It chews the strap, spitting fibres. "You can get veggie ones." Can't help myself, just say it. "Polyurethane."

The body swings with the arc of the knife. Poised on a chair, Roc moves with it. "The business wants leather. Clients expect it."

No claw marks at the throat. She didn't change her mind and try to get free. Her tongue is out but not severed. Most likely relaxed by alcohol. Foam round the mouth. Busted capillaries, indicative of asphyxiation and vodka. Her hands are clenched: that happens at brain death. To my inexpert touch, her neck is not broken. She went slow. Uncomplaining. She's not shat herself.

A body, dropped deadweight, resounds. There's delight to watching Roc brace for the catch: a misplaced pleasure, yet necessary and instructive. We're the heirs of strong women. Competence invigorates us.

I cut the last sinew of leather. We dance Chloe down, easing her stiffened limbs. She lays in an attitude of hanging, as though upright and it's us hurtling in space. I check her pockets. Roc does her bag. Her overcoming of fear enchants me.

Unsurprising, there's not much. Her gun, ID. Her cards are maxed, my scanner says. Her clothes are charity rummage. Nothing signifies Chloe Bell.

Roc brushes Chloe's hair. It picks up a sly gleam. "She wanted me. But she couldn't begin. Like she was breaking a promise."

"She would have gone on the same till they dumped her." I get a couple of pillows. Pack them around Chloe's head. Put a bullet through her brain. To spare her the humiliation of being a suicide. Roc understands. She doesn't flinch. The crushed bullet feathered and bloody.

Roc goes to shower. I call Lee.

"Princess!" All night gravel to his voice. "To what do I owe this unfiltered pleasure?"

"Spillage, love. Need a clean-up."

His voice doesn't change but his mind runs ahead, pricing arrangements. "Serious?"

"A careless guest."

"Sorry to hear that. I'll have someone take a look. 'Bout an hour, okay?"

"Sweet. My other guest… I don't want 'em disturbed."

"Totally. With tact and care."

More money I don't have leaves an account that's not mine. A reckoning will come. The back of the Albert Hall lays pocked with dirty weather. The mansions of Kensington Gore are stained and cracked. Cement leaks from walls. Rooftops of dead birds and yesterday's favours. Small tragedies, unnoticed, die away.

Roc's naked. Hair rains through her pictures. "You doing this thing tonight?"

"It's the score." The words have no meaning.

She trails a hand across her vagina. "I don't fuck for free."

"I'm paid."

"By who?"

"Everyone wants this guy dead." Don't need to see her beautiful face to know I sound absurd. "The cops, the spooks."

"The spooks trying to kill you? The Russians and Arabs and everyone?" The stiff blue shape that was Chloe Bell waits between us. In Roc's gaze, shrewdness and love are one. "Do you know how much I earn a year?" She says a good, respectable number. "Do you know how hard I have to work for that? I don't have time to get sick or sore. All this," her tatts, "hides the bruises. But I still want to fuck. I add my body to other lives. I please people. But you spread heartbreak. Wherever you go death follows. I don't want to live in fear of the chaos you cause." She raises her hand. The ring catches light. "Three years I don't see you. Then we're married. Think what we've done. You kick that poor woman's body and tell me tonight's 'the score'. While maniacs hunt you down." Her hands slide through ships and skulls. "And I'm stupid enough to love you."

Her unmasked smell draws me like a shadow on the horizon. "What do you want from me?"

"You tell me."

Roc goes to make money. I leave before Lee's clean-up boys arrive. I've disregarded my wife. Disrespected her wishes. We used to have sex and milkshakes, released by love for each other. I owe Roc more than I can repay. But these fuckers shit on my shadow.

Pick up the hire car. Beige, electric, forgettable. Dowdy to drive. A woman, bland to the point of not caring.

Bags packed and guns clean, I take another shower. My DNA in everything, from hair down the drain to cum in the sheets. I'm not attracted to incognito. This last dress I haven't worn. My party dress. Valentino red. No frills. No flounce. Straight on the collar. Tight on the waist. The red of a blazing sun through sacrificed blood. With long black hair and long legs it's the succulence of body parts in motion. A woman to be unpeeled. On the second of December 1971, Marie-Hélène de Rothschild did a costume ball at Château de Ferrières to celebrate Marcel Proust, of all people. Aunt Audrey was there in an ivory Valentino sheath like chainmail. Audrey could wear anything. Would have been good to meet her. We could have played dress up.

The past persists. Today erodes too fast. Soon as I step in the corridor, a message is sent, idle hands activated. Wheel my bags down the hall. Get the lift to the basement. When the doors open on cold tarmac, no one's there.

Drive south, to cause friction. Skim where Chloe Bell lived. That weird flat, patiently waiting for her. Getting grimy and stiff, till uniforms come knocking. Who gets her death-in-service pay? Some elderly parent. A failed love. No one. Suspicion falls on Jazin. It was his accounts she was dissecting. Bell vanishes. Jazin gets killed. He will get killed.

Turn north, then east along the Embankment. The Tower looks sly. It knows where the bodies are buried. Shoreditch, so different to what it was. Kingsland Basin, in late afternoon light. Who killed Declan Nolan? Someone wanting to teach me a lesson. Not realising I don't learn.

Left at Dalston Junction. West on the Balls Pond Road. John Ball owned a pub, mid-eighteenth century. It had a pond, Ball's Pond, though the road wasn't called that till a hundred years later. Once very Jewish round here, before they went up Stamford Hill. And Jack the Hat got ended just round the corner. Jack got paid to do a job. A job Jack did not do. But he kept the money. Not clever.

Highbury Corner. Holloway Road. Sleeping bags in doorways. Cracked windows. Worn clothes. Stains of past fires. Old boys on benches in Mary Magdalen yard, hurt behind their eyes. But young people take long strides. Their spines are their credentials. I'm middle-aged, I'm not the future. That girl or that girl, they're the next gun. South along Camden Road. At dusk, Regent's Park.

Hook the car to charge. Its dial beams optimistically through the haze. I want my kids to have fresh air and clean water. Good food, the best of everything. Maybe one of these houses, glinting against the rising night. I want my kids to know their mothers did our best, with what we could hold in our hands.

Boss man Salah is busy with party arrangements. His boys don't get what I want.

"I'm invited," I say. "To meet and greet. Araminta."

One points at the holdall. "What is there?"

"My costume. For dancing." Try to make the AK light as chiffon. "It's so important to create a mood."

In Arabic, the hired man says they should check the bag. He grips at it.

"Please," I say. "Don't spoil the surprise."

In Arabic, the man on the step says he'll watch me.

I grin with appealing bemusement. Men are lovely.

With tight smiles, I get filtered to the action. This house was built for players. John Nash didn't work for the council. But even tall windows and rose ceilings are cramped for today's opulence. There's girls in sheaths with ridiculous tits, trapped off by blow-dried geezers in suits and no ties. There's jewels and gold. Doesn't mean jack shit. Because the reason a rich man throws a party is business. You spend money, gain face, advance your interests. Parties are for the beautiful and connected. So I'm okay.

Now obviously, there's a certain decorum. These prominent glass bowls to deposit zakat. Compelling the rich to give to the poor is one of the most admirable aspects of Islam and the bowls are already weighty with notes, necklaces, watches and promises. Unseen, piety is wasted.

I grab a pomegranate juice and a mücver. Gentleman Salah finds me. "It's wonderful," I gush. "So elegant. Shall I stand here to greet your guests?"

My dress is not modest, but naturally Salah's concern is old wounds. "I see your bruises are improved."

"Dab of concealer. Don't want to look frightful."

"You do not look frightful. Shall I take your bag?"

He's on a tip from the boys outside. "I'll keep it if you don't mind. The costume belongs to a friend."

"It's an honour to be trusted with valuable things."

For an hour I make myself charming. Where waiters set drinks and nibbles, I grab the hands of unsuspecting guests and guide them to things on sticks. Tell the gents where to hang their hats and the girls where to fix their faces. I get quite a rhythm, sending maids scurrying to the cloakroom and earnestly asking strapping young men if they're okay with wheat. No one knows who I am, but curiosity is so vulgar. I'm assumed to be something and that's enough.

It's a shocking let-down when Terence Rotheray shambles in, his old coat a husky affront. "What are you? The cigarette girl?"

"I'm not old enough to understand that. You want this garment quarantined?"

"No, ta, I'm superstitious. Seen our host?"

"Give it a chance."

With what he thinks is menace, he says, "Midnight, Felicity. And I'd rather collar you without fuss."

"You're a gent, Terrance."

"No, I'm the filth. I'll miss those legs." Remarkably, the crowd receives him. His wise, heavy head looms around a suave young bunny—so handsome he must be a jewel thief. Cops and robbers. Filth and slags. We're composites of each other.

The room gets busy. Interesting outfits, slight conversation—what else is there? The unbelievers are mostly drunk. Shrewd, long-limbed girls tell yacht war stories. It's like nothing happened since 1966.

Salah's strong hand snugs my waist. I respond with a little grunt. "Mr. Jazin wishes to greet his guests. He welcomes your opinion on the mood of the room."

"I don't have an opinion."

"Mr. Jazin thinks you do." As he traffics me into the chessboard hallway, Cheltenham man circles with other spooks. Heavy eye-bags jut in my direction. Gratifying and alarming Salah gives them the freeze.

I get squired to a corner, where a lift is artfully concealed by a statue of a lion with big bollocks. Clinical mirrors, sharp lights, no surprises. My eyes are pristine, dark and unforgiving. My lips blood red. My slender face framed with thick black hair. My skin's not flawless but busy with life. I know the challenge of femininity, and that contempt reserved for me. Always, I'm a woman.

So unsurprising, Salah stops the lift, persuasive hands on my shoulders. He nudges my hair aside with his chin. His beard shivers me. He kisses my neck a long, slow time. Then I'm released to a hallway. I accept his cruelty. It's what I deserve.

Rashad Jazin works old-school. Oak desk. Glass lamps. Tasteful paintings of dunes and distant cities. A framed photo of Mecca, the holy Kaaba majestic on a sea of devout bodies. His look dismisses Salah, who retires, wordless, closing the door with exaggerated delicacy. Jazin stands. Handsome, of course. Power and money do that. His dark suit flawless, expensive. The dagger motif of his tie echoed in silver cufflinks. Clutching my bag, I'm a traveller, arrived in a place where I hold no currency.

"Reports of your beauty are understatements." He speaks with that care for language shipped from English private schools. "You are exceptional."

I simper, lost in a heat haze.

"Audacity is not your least feature." Then, in Arabic, he says I've done well to get this far.

I reply, in Arabic, it's a pleasure to meet such a distinguished man.

With a tidy laugh, he switches to English. "Your accent is North African. And you flatter me, Ms. Hepburn. Coffee?" The order goes down to the kitchen. "Please, sit."

Fold myself into buttoned leather. This dress leaves no slack. "Nice place you have."

"It's convenient. The weather doesn't suit me. You are English, of course. You speak of the weather."

"I prefer warm climates."

"Barcelona is beautiful. I share your antipathy toward the Spanish. Old wounds run deep." His reaction to the knock at the door is instructive. Relaxed and controlled, yet tension shapes his fingers. The maid hurries in, presenting the tray as offering. His brisk, "Thank you," bowls her out the room. More gossip for below stairs.

The silver pot and china bowls could be the same I saw at that place in Surrey. Each detail builds from the last.

"Please, have some fruit." He sets the plate with admirable precision.

"Arab coffee," I say, needlessly. "I love cardamom."

"Smoke and mint and sweet pines. I become nostalgic. Some are nomads, I respect them. Some of us belong to a place."

The coffee is strong, something animal.

He watches me, his eyes profound. "Life brings provocations. I'm sure you find so. As we seek our way, oppositions assail us. You are not the first who has come to kill me. You will not be the last to fail."

I fidget. I've nothing to tell him.

"It is to your credit you approach directly. A small lie to get in the door is no matter. Not even a lie, I'm sure you're an excellent dancer. You do not have a costume in that bag. Regrettably, I must x-ray my guests. Regrettably, without their knowledge."

"I knew."

"Your wit is worth more than rubies. Not only will you be frustrated in your mission. The plans of your friends downstairs will, likewise, go awry."

That gets a pout. "Not my friends, Mr. Jazin. And if I fail, it will be at the extremity of trying."

The wall is padded with books, their ribbed spines dull with old gold. He picks a red volume that looks to have seen hard use. "You like Keats?"

"I'm a keen student."

"'The weariness, the fever, and the fret / Here, where men sit and hear each other groan'."

"Go on."

"'I cannot see what flowers are at my feet, / Nor what soft incense hangs upon the boughs'."

"Nightingale."

"I'm gratified my assumptions of you are correct. 'And mid-May's eldest child, / The coming musk-rose, full of dewy wine, / The murmurous haunt of flies on summer eves.' Please continue."

"'Darkling I listen; and, for many a time / I have been half in love with easeful Death, / Call'd him soft names in many a mused rhyme, / To take into the air my quiet breath; / Now more than ever seems it rich to die, / To cease upon the midnight with no pain'."

"Are you in love with easeful death, Ms. Hepburn?"

"I'm a great respecter of death. People don't think of it nearly enough."

Easy power inhabits him. His shadow draws towards me. "In my due diligence on you, some said your life should be spared. I had not expected such sentiment. I assume they're not all your lovers."

"Don't be so sure."

"Some believe you add to the world. I find that hard to equate with your malice."

"You're speaking as a charitable arms dealer, I take it?"

That ravishing, artful smile. "Where I come from, everything is a matter of conscience. We walk the same road, say the same prayers, but intricacies undo us. History cannot be escaped. You know the disputes and schisms. For us, what occurred does not stop occurring. The Jews are the same. They fight the old battles and sing the old songs. This world, where I do business, is indifferent to the past. Men talk margin, advantage. The slender fraction that makes it worthwhile to ship thousands of guns past hundreds of eyes, that need to be paid to turn blind. Where I come from there are mad people, no doubt. But here they are worshipped as saviours."

"I like the Middle East."

"You don't find it restrictive?"

"On the contrary. Men are most hospitable."

That smile, warm and disdainful. "The West sees us as awkward. We see ourselves as solutions. Not rapid, but change goes on. This I feel, while I sell guns to your spies and bombs to your discontented. Neither you nor I decide when I die. Only He decides it. And come the Day, I shall be brought from my grave to answer for my deeds. I am not created for death, why should I fear it? I can answer what will be asked of me. I know nothing of your faith, Ms. Hepburn."

He pushed a call button. He must have, that knock at the door so on cue.

Salah doesn't bow to his boss. He's too much the prince in his skin. But there's deference in his ways.

"How are my guests?"

"Praising your hospitality. They wish to see you."

Rashad Jazin doesn't check the mirror. He's always perfect. "We could speak of the poets, Ms. Hepburn. The strategists of old. Our mathematicians you so admire. In some other world, perhaps. You are finished here."

Salah leads me down concrete stairs to a bare space carved from the house. Limewashed walls and earthy boards like the cellar of a Catalan mansió. I do not accept I won't see Catalunya again.

His gun is unmemorable, a cheap Walther. "Ms. Hepburn, I am a soldier. I go where I'm told. Perhaps you deserve better than me. But we do not choose."

"You take duty seriously."

"How would you have me take it?"

No echo in this tight space. The shot blunted as he falls dead. Take a second to realise my jacket's on fire. I pinch it out. The pocket of my old Chanel ragged and accusing. I can patch and stitch, but the scar of this moment shames me. A panicked shot is worse than a miss.

Impact from so close makes a loose and careless entry. He knew I was armed. They all knew. They did nothing about it. That confidence, from making the weather, convinced them they could contain me.

Now I build the AK. With this on my shoulder, I must use it. Virtue without force is laughable. Use my phone to check my eyes. Eyes are key. Refresh, thicken, darken. No one escapes my eyes. Look at Salah, dead on the ground. Paradise is the reward of the righteous. Believe that and grief becomes needless.

Through these corridors, cameras betray me. I don't blend. I don't hide. I can't be different to this. These offices drive Mr. Jazin's enterprises. I poke around but the laptops are locked. There's maps and graphs. I take pictures. Might be useful. There's posters. 'Meetings: a practical alternative to work.' I like that. 'You miss one hundred percent of the shots you don't take.' Wise words. I like to think sloaney girls work here, accessorising and mussing their highlights while shipping death round the world.

In the tick of lights and creak of old wood, a voice is intrusive, obscene. The man in the room beyond speaks Spanish with abrupt efficiency. Whoever's far end of his call is taking instructions. A short man, rounding out. The remains of grey curls slicked to gluey tendrils. Reflected in the dark window a spread nose, bushy brows, the smooth white beard as obligatory as medallions of office. He's talking defence. He wants kit for troops and a blank cheque on crowd control. He wants gas and sponge grenades and blinding lasers. He wants sanitised streets where he can piss on the bodies.

"M'enfrontaràs!"

Those sloped shoulders clench. He turns, stiff and resentful.

"Sóc Felicity Hepburn."

The faraway phone voice curdles.

"Visca Catalunya."

That Kalashnikov kick hangs me on the door. I'll have a bruise tomorrow. Check the stiff's pockets to get his ID. Spanish trade delegation. A spook.

Now I move through rooms and halls. My body and the gun. First lot I meet go down easy. A domestic patrol, not knowing the situation. Laughter and song, whooping indulgence rises like smoke off burnt tarmac. The party's a hit, the men placated, the women pliant. No one expects a maniac. A conga line pulses from the lounge and I drop them like cans off the wall. Still, the music plays.

Muscle wakes up. Boys in suits, Glocks out, drilling the staircase. Not one bullet gets close. I don't need to aim this thing. Its benediction showers peace. Smiles turn to terror. Squeals to screams. The Kalashnikov rams my shoulder like a big man's greeting. Its stain skin deep. Back when, you knew a triggerman by his spade finger. That's what they called it, in the mindless bigotry of the good old days.

The dogs are bunkered, giving it high and over. The civilians are learning that under their skin is fragile bone. Someone goes for my back, and I roll with the instinct, firing over my shoulder. Rotheray's at the door. He gives a pitying look and turns away, beyond caring.

See the dead bodies and smashed up tat. Bloody wreckage of beautiful people. Her neat lime dress, with a stain that won't clean. Life fleeing like some little breeze. And Cheltenham man: I'm surprised at him, laying stiff with the rest. His Anderson & Sheppard weeping. Some of his friends got out. Screaming down their phones to Vauxhall. The clean-up squad are on their way. I need to be gone by then.

Jazin flits, two of his best shooting cover to reach the back stairs. No elegance now. Pure poetry. Resistance from soldiers whose lives are worth nothing without him. I take a few burns I don't feel. The AK pumps like a dream. I ride its tide. Beneath me, tattered curtains, walls bloody, bodies gaping. Cries from the remains, seeing fabulous lives scroll before them.

Tearing up hallways, I search for Jazin. He can't blame me. His staff could have stopped me anytime. You trust people and they disappoint you.

Soon, a car will pull up outside. Then another. And a van. Serious women and men with calm precision will enter the building. They'll secure the most valuable assets. They'll make sure there's no survivors. Then a fire will start. The headlines are already written, the soundbites recorded. This is how it works, so people have faith in the bastards that protect them.

The corridor ends in illusory space. A mirror wall, enticing the unwary to pass through themselves. That woman in the mirror, a hot gun the length of her body. A classical beauty, tall, dark-eyed, long fall of black hair. Some stains, some wounds, but that's character. Those nights the firm came to our house. Those conscientious, violent men, they'd greet me with such gentility. It's not just about me. It's never just about me.

A creak on the boards. A breath through the statues. Anyone here alive is quiet and hateful. If they haven't run, they're hunting.

Move through rooms of ornate junk, this filler the rich sling around them. For all Jazin's grace, he's no collector. The place is furnished job lot. Some sloane designer dolled up a pastiche of old times. Got a spread in Homes & Gardens. Spent her clean cash with clean hands. Death pays so many ways. There's no economy, no industry, no poetry without it.

The pull of resolution keeps me nimble. More rooms, more gilded air, to the balcony above a marble stairwell. Swirling down, flushed with lamps like flaming torches. Check my phone. Ten to midnight. But Cinderella won't falter. A missed call from Roc, a voice message. Save it for later.

Jazin and his most trusted spill shadows up the stairwell. Lay aside this AK-47. It's no use to me now. My XD 9 mil will be his fall from virtue.

These stairs cling round a column. What I'm thinking: wing a bullet off that column. Use smooth marble to curve the shot into his body. Sixteen-degree angle to the ridge of the groove. Nine-degree angle off that to Jazin. A planned ricochet. A trick shot. And I get him. That hand on the ground is wearing his Rolex. And his two dumb goons shooting the wrong direction. A beautiful kill, worthy of wonder.

A shot from behind. Reflex springs me through a doorway. A sighting shot, for range and attention. Some envious bastard craves my back. Squat by the door, my dress riding my hips. Shoot out the lights. Chandeliers rain on slick marble. Shoot the mirror. Its jagged implosion cascades knives. Silence is electric. Distant light, above and below, throws uncanny attitudes on paintings of lithe gods and astonished heroes.

Put a shot along the landing. That quickness, as someone jerks back. Jazin's boys downstairs are gone in a beat of hard footsteps. It's you and me, triggerman.

Edge forward. He pierces my shadow. Send a shot back. That move again but less startled. One mistake, triggerman. A millimetre and you're done. You had my beautiful Aunt Denise, didn't you? She sent you to be my bitch. You were promised millions to get this done. Tell me it's worth it when you bleed out on the tiles.

Another shot. Close. I like a man with ambition. Keeps giving me his shadow. His profile of a lonely, serious man. We are lonely, aren't we, triggerman? Nothing else is ever enough.

Work the silence. Let him wonder what I'm up to. There he is. Knew he couldn't resist. Denise was right. He's no charmer. A pale-face runt from some shit town. His hair like it's been cut with knives. Catalogue suit. His tie drags the floor as he crawls like a bitch to position.

I just need a fraction. A margin. I reach. Just a little. Slant my aim on his skull. My dress hugs tight as a sure thing.

I move.

He fires.

www.ingramcontent.com/pod-product-compliance
Ingram Content Group UK Ltd.
Pitfield, Milton Keynes, MK11 3LW, UK
UKHW041808110425
457312UK00002B/17